YOU
KILLED
ME
FIRST

ALSO BY JOHN MARRS

PRAISE FOR JOHN MARRS

'Clever, twisted, and dark as mighty hell.'

—Lisa Jewell

'Marrs is brilliant at twists.'

—Peter James

'A proper twisty thriller.'

—Sarah Pinborough

'Whatever you do, don't read this in the dark . . .'

—Cara Hunter

'John's thrillers never fail to keep me furiously turning the pages.'

—Sarah Pearse

'John Marrs is a master of suspense.'

—Jeneva Rose

'This one will leave you with paper cuts.'

—C. J. Tudor

'Tensely plotted and terrifyingly imagined.'

—Harriet Tyce

'A smart, gripping and scarily believable story.'

—T. M. Logan

'What a twisted sinister book that was. Loved it.'

—Peter Swanson

'One of the most exciting, original thriller writers out there. I never miss one of his books.'

—Simon Kernick

YOU KILLED ME FIRST

JOHN MARRS

THOMAS & MERCER

Text copyright © 2025 by John Marrs
All rights reserved.

Published by Thomas & Mercer, Seattle

www.apub.com

Amazon, the Amazon logo, and Thomas & Mercer are trademarks of Amazon.com, Inc., or its affiliates.

ISBN-13: 9781662506499
eISBN: 9781662506505

Cover design by Liron Gilenberg
Cover image: © Miguel Sobreira © Tony Watson / Arcangel; © Lidiia Koval © By atk work © hecke61 © Artiste2d3d / Shutterstock

Printed in the United States of America

For John Russell, the better half of John²

If you burn your neighbour's house down, it doesn't make your house look any better.

Lou Holtz

If you're gonna be two-faced, at least make one of them pretty.

Marilyn Monroe

PROLOGUE

5 NOVEMBER, BONFIRE NIGHT

It's a commotion of crackling, sputtering and popping noises that brings her back to life.

She opens her eyes but it's close to pitch-black in there, and when she tries to focus on anything, it's blurred. Her head is pounding like a pneumatic drill trying to penetrate concrete. How much did she have to drink last night, she wonders. She can't remember even the most hellish of hangovers being as debilitating as this. Or is it something more sinister? Has she been involved in an accident, injured her head and blacked out? Or did she suffer a stroke in her sleep? Is that why she can barely move or see a thing? Is her brain holding her body prisoner?

A scent of smoke follows. It's vague at first and she can't be sure if it's getting stronger because she's regaining her senses, or if something is actually on fire. Is it the house? The fear of God flashes through her. Her worst nightmare. She tries to sit up in her bed but she barely budges. She can feel her hands, fingers and feet moving but they won't lift up. Something is stopping them, a weight pushing her down, along with the rest of her body.

She's still so woozy, but panic, she learns, can be sobering. She tries to think rationally.

She's suddenly aware it isn't a mattress she's lying on. It's way too firm, icy cold, and her clothes are absorbing something wet.

Her vision is slowly returning, and she knows that wherever she is, she needs to get out of there. She curls her fingers in on themselves and realises there's something binding them together – it feels tight like cling film, but it won't stretch or tear. It's a heavier plastic wrap. She's wedged in more tightly than a tinned sardine. It's no accident she's here. Someone has put her here. Why can't she remember anything?

She is straddling the fine line between confusion and terror.

There's a terrifically loud explosion and she screams – or tries to. Something restricts her mouth from opening as it should. She's been gagged. She feels sick with fear, but knows that if she vomits, she'll likely choke on it. So she twists her head as far as she can from side to side, until she lowers the gag and it rests on her chin.

'Help me!' she yells as best she can, but even she knows how pathetic it sounds. However, the self-preservation instinct that's been both her downfall and her salvation all these years drives her on until another deafening explosion drowns out her whimpers.

She begins to cough. The smoke has grown slowly thicker. She wriggles and squirms to breathe in unpolluted air and it's only when her ear touches the ground that she feels something lodged inside it. Before she can figure out what it is, there are more thunderous outbursts, and through gaps in her prison, she spots the flickering of bright multicoloured lights.

Only then does it hit her with the force of a wrecking ball. She knows exactly where she is and why she can't escape.

It's November the fifth and the explosions are fireworks.

She is trapped in the middle of a burning bonfire.

She shrieks as she tosses back and forth, contorting her body. But the wrap she's cocooned inside limits her movements.

Suddenly, there's a vibrating in her pocket, like a phone, followed by a resounding ringing in her ears, and she realises what's lodged inside one of them – some kind of open-ear headphone device attached by a hook over the top. The ringing continues but she is powerless to answer it. Then she remembers it'll likely have a touch-sensitive tab that, once pressed, allows you to answer the call. If she can explain to whoever is trying to contact her what's happening, maybe they can help?

She rubs her ear upon the ground beneath her and nothing happens. She lifts her head up as far as she can and slams it down on the ground. It hurts her and it hasn't worked. She tries it again, and again, over and over, her ear throbbing with each collision. Meanwhile, all around her there are more and more explosions as the heat intensifies.

And then it happens. A voice manifests through the headphones.

'You're conscious then.'

'Please help me,' she cries, barely able to get her words out. 'Someone is trying to kill me and I need you to . . .'

Her voice trails off as the words sink in. *You're conscious then.* Whoever it is knows where she is.

'Please get me out of here,' she says.

'Do you think I'd go to all this trouble just to free you now?'

'I'll do anything,' she pleads in desperation.

This earns a laugh. And only then does she recognise her caller.

'I don't know what you think I did, but I'm sorry,' she sobs. 'I'm begging you, I'll do anything. Just help me.'

'I'm sorry, but I can't. You are going to burn alive in a bonfire of your own making.'

'What? Why? What did I do to you?'

The laugh is short and cuts like a blade.

'I'll tell you what you did. You killed me first.'

PART ONE

DECEMBER

ELEVEN MONTHS BEFORE BONFIRE NIGHT

CHAPTER 1

MARGOT

It's the sound of a beep-beep-beeping and a heavy engine that stirs me from my sleep.

I peek between the window shutter slats in my bedroom and spot a large removals truck parking outside number twenty-three, the house opposite. A second vehicle further up the street is blocking the junction, much to the irritation of parents on the school run. It hasn't affected me though, as my two make their own way there. Tommy and Frankie are self-sufficient, thanks largely to me ensuring they have limited expectations of what I'm willing to do for them. At the ages of eleven and twelve, they wash their own clothes, iron their uniforms, make their own breakfasts and lunches, and pack their schoolbags. That leaves me time to remain snuggled under my Bavarian goose-down duvet for longer than your average parent.

The front door is to the right of the new neighbours' property and under a wooden pitched roof porch, but I've yet to see so much as an elbow belonging to anyone aside from the removals men. However, there's a lot you can learn about a person you've never met by what they surround themselves with. Firstly, they definitely have children. At least two, as I've caught a glimpse of two bikes being carried into the rear garden along with two scooters.

I've googled the Land Rover Defender that's been parked on the driveway since I awoke and learned that model's worth at least £85,000. It could however be leased. I don't see any mud on the tyres so I assume that, like most Land Rover owners, it's more a demonstration of status than for practical use.

It's hard to get a good look at their furniture as so much of it is covered in thick bubble wrap. But there are a couple of pieces I'm sure I recognise – a dark wooden sideboard from Rockett St George that I've had on my online wish list forever, and a mahogany chest of drawers from Made. Neither come cheap. I side-eye the Ikea Billy bookcase in the corner of my lounge that Nicu insists doesn't need replacing. I have a feeling its shelves might 'accidentally' break very, very soon.

Another thirty minutes pass and, to my frustration, I still haven't caught a glimpse of who's moving in. The house once belonged to Sue and Pete Cooper, and what she knew about interior design you could fit on the back of a Dunelm's receipt. I don't mean to humblebrag – but I will: I have a knack for knowing what goes where and why. My instinct is so on point, I could give Philippe Starck a run for his money. So when Sue asked me to help her, of course I said yes. I considered it charity work. Then, just as we'd finished, she announced she'd been offered a job at Microsoft in Texas, and within a month, they were on a flight and out of sight. Some people only think of themselves.

The house has been a rental property for the last couple of years. Three families have come and gone but there's no point in befriending renters because they're transitory. Apart from Anna, who seems to be hanging around for longer than most in the house next door to the one I'm watching. And when the last lot of occupants went on their merry way, Nicu scared the hell out of me by suggesting their replacements could be asylum seekers. I mean, I'm not entirely unsympathetic to their cause – war, poverty, displacement, yada yada yada – and I know they must live somewhere. But why here, of all places? I emailed the chairman of the parish council with my concerns and he all but suggested I was being racist, which is ridiculous. I'd swap a kidney for a date with Idris Elba.

To my relief, an estate agent's 'Sold' sign appeared in the front garden soon after. Months of noise, rubbish skips and tradesmen's vans followed as the place was gutted. The new owners replaced everything, installing a new Shaker kitchen and four bathrooms and en-suites. I took a photo of the empty boxes in the skip and looked up brands I hadn't even heard of. They aren't scrimping on the finishes. I hate show-offs.

Curiosity finally gets the better of me and I decide to head over there and introduce myself. On my way to the bathroom, I pass the Christmas tree I arranged in front of the picture window on the landing for the neighbours to admire. It is simply gorgeous. The kids have their own, covered in tacky, gaudy baubles with no uniform design or colour scheme, which remains hidden in the dining room. I shower, slip into a pencil skirt and casual T-shirt, apply a little make-up then run a wet wipe over my Pandora bracelet and the diamonds in my Tiffany wedding ring. It gives them an extra sparkle. After carefully selecting an expensive bottle from the wine cupboard complete with presentation box, I'm ready to impress.

I'm halfway across the road when Anna's front door opens.

'Hi,' she says cheerily and raises a hand. 'You're up and about early. I don't think I've ever seen you before midday.'

Had it come from anyone else, I might have rubbed a little Savlon on that burn. But everything about Anna is harmless, unthreatening and enthusiastic. She's the kind of woman who'd lead a round of applause when the pilot lands her plane. However, we all know that too much sweetness can make you diabetic.

'I thought I'd pop in and meet our new neighbours.'

'Ditto,' I reply, although I'm a little rankled. As an original resident of the cul-de-sac, I think it's only fair I lead the welcoming committee.

'Moving house two weeks before Christmas wouldn't leave me feeling festive,' I say.

'That's why I've brought these,' she replies, and holds up a Tupperware box, gently shaking the mince pies inside.

I hold back my scowl. 'Did you bake them yourself?'

'Of course,' she says, as if it would never cross her mind to drive to an artisan patisserie in town, choose a handful of theirs and pass them off as her own.

'That's very Bree Van de Kamp of you.'

Her blank response suggests the *Desperate Housewives* analogy is lost on her. Sometimes she makes me feel much older than my almost forty years. I hold up my own welcome gift.

'Great minds think alike.' Anna smiles.

No, they don't. Because if they did, she wouldn't be punishing her body in that supermarket own-brand outfit.

We make our way up the brick cobbled driveway and towards the house. It's the largest one in this cul-de-sac, although not in the village. With six bedrooms – that's two more than Nicu and I have – plus a swimming pool, I've quietly envied anyone who's lived here.

The two oak front doors are open so I peer into the porch and hallway. The removals team are milling about unpacking furniture. Anna knocks with the impact of a squirrel tapping a walnut on a lawn, so I clasp hold of the black knocker and bang four times.

No one pays us any attention, and I'm about to do it again when a voice from behind us sends me leaping out of my skin.

CHAPTER 2

ANNA

We turn our heads and I think I might have just found my first girl crush. She's beautiful. Her skin is fresh and lightly tanned, her nose perfectly symmetrical, her cheekbones razor-sharp, and when she smiles, she draws you in. Her blonde honeyed ponytail hangs from the back of a baseball cap, and she has a figure I'd kill for. She's dressed from head to toe in white, wearing trainers, skintight joggers and a sports T-shirt. Nike might have created its tick logo in appreciation of her. I know in an instant Margot is going to *hate* her.

I open my mouth to speak but Margot beats me to it.

'Hello,' she says. 'You must be our new neighbour?'

'Yes, I must be,' the woman replies cheerfully.

'I'm Margot, I live opposite.'

'I'm Anna,' I add. 'I'm on your right.'

Margot is eyeing the woman up and down, desperately searching for something to critique. She has her work cut out for her.

'Oh, I was wondering who lived there,' the woman continues, looking at Margot's place. 'The sun shines directly into your bedroom at this time of the morning and I kept seeing a figure moving about behind the shutters.'

Margot blushes, a rarity for her.

'I'd have done the same,' she assures Margot, sensing her embarrassment. 'It's human nature to be curious, isn't it?'

'A house-warming present,' Margot says, holding out her gift.

'Oh that's so sweet of you,' she replies, reading the presentation box, which is labelled 'I love chocolates'.

'It's wine,' Margot corrects. 'Châteauneuf-du-Pape, 1976. I always say you should never scrimp where wine is concerned.'

'Such a shame, as it gives me terrible migraines,' the woman says apologetically, but accepts it regardless. 'My husband, Brandon, enjoys a glass of anything, so thank you. It's very thoughtful.'

I sense this is not the reaction Margot hoped for. Meanwhile I feel ashamed of my humble offering. Someone who can fit into the clothes she's wearing is unlikely to touch pastries with a bargepole. As I move to hide them behind my back, she offers a theatrical gasp.

'Mince pies?' she asks.

'Yes,' I reply, almost apologetically. 'They're vegan. No sugar, but you'd never know.'

'Christmas really has come early.' She grins. 'Oh, where are my manners? Come in, I'll make us a coffee and we can treat ourselves. I'm Liv,' she adds as she leads the way along the hallway.

It's the first time I've been inside this house, and it's stunning. Everything in the kitchen is decorated in grey and white tones except for the dark brown herringbone flooring. I assume she's yet to unpack her electricals or crockery until she slides back a concertina false wall to reveal them. Margot and I perch on two of ten stools that fit comfortably around an island larger than most sheds.

Behind us, bifold doors have been opened to let in fresh air from an unusually mild December day. They overlook a generous garden and the fields that surround most of the houses in this cul-de-sac. Outside is another seating area, a huge barbecue and a tall brick chimney. Next to the swimming pool is a summer house.

'Tea or coffee?' she asks as she plates up our mince pies.

'Tea, please,' I reply.

'Espresso, if it's not too much trouble,' says Margot, knowing it likely will be. She's eyeing up a coffee machine the size of a suitcase on the worktop. 'Is that a Sage Oracle?'

'I wouldn't know.' Liv shrugs. 'I don't drink the stuff, so all coffee machines look the same to me.'

'So what brings you to Lower Ignis?' I ask.

'Village life,' Liv says. 'After a decade working in private banking in London, our priorities changed when we had the kids.'

'How many do you have?'

'Four-year-old twins, a boy and a girl. Oh, and the cat. It was during my maternity leave that Brandon and I started planning our great escape.'

'So you'll commute each day?' asks Margot.

'Oh, no. The city and I, how did Gwyneth Paltrow once put it? Ahh, "consciously uncoupled".'

I have no idea what she means. 'So what'll you do now you're here?'

'A lot of yoga and Pilates, if all goes according to plan.'

'Well, the village community centre holds weekly sessions if you don't mind sharing a room with OAPs,' Margot informs her. 'I went once myself but it smelled of cabbage.'

'Sorry, I didn't explain myself.' Liv smiles. 'I'll be opening my own wellness studio in the new year.'

'Oh,' says Margot. 'Well . . . good for you.'

Her smile is as fake as her nails.

'How about you girls?' Liv asks. 'What do you do?'

'Nothing as interesting as opening your own studio,' I say. 'I make jewellery from home and sell it online and to independent stores. And my husband, Drew, is a delivery driver.'

'Oh, I love jewellery that's not mass-produced,' says Liv. 'Handcrafted pieces are always so much more personal, aren't they?'

I spot Margot slowly covering her Pandora charm bracelet with the palm of her hand.

'I'd love to see some of your designs,' Liv goes on. 'I have some fashion influencer friends who love championing fresh designers.'

Imposter syndrome strikes and my face reddens. 'They're probably not that good.'

'I'm sure with a little more practice you'll get better,' says Margot.

'And how about you, Maggie?' asks Liv. 'What do you do?'

'It's Margot.'

'I am *so* sorry,' Liv replies.

I'm not entirely convinced Liv didn't say that on purpose. And if I'm right, I think I like her already.

CHAPTER 3

LIV

Of course I know her name is Margot. But even after a few minutes in her company, I recognise her type. I've met a thousand versions of her in my time. Their narrowed eyes bore holes into you, searching for a flaw to help them feel better about themselves. I could be doing her a disservice. We'll see.

'So *Margot*,' I continue. 'What do you do?'

'Like you, I used to be London-based, but now I'm a full-time homemaker.'

Again, I might be misreading her, but she utters the word 'homemaker' with barely disguised contempt.

'How old are your kids?' I ask.

'My eldest turns thirteen in a few months and her brother is eleven.'

'Tricky ages. They must keep you busy.'

Her smile is tight. 'I'm very hands-on, so I barely have a minute to myself.'

I catch Anna raising an eyebrow ever so slightly, suggesting Margot isn't quite as she'd like me to believe. I'm not saying to be an involved parent you must neglect yourself, but she is turned out almost too well. Nails perfectly manicured, no visible grey roots in that thick, shoulder-length head of auburn hair, and a wrinkle-free face. There are hints of freckles under her make-up that start at her pronounced cheekbones and spread under eyes that are so green, I'm not entirely convinced she's not wearing coloured lenses.

'You must have help with the kids if you're planning to launch your own business too?' Margot asks.

'Actually, Brandon's taking a career break to be a full-time dad. It made financial sense.'

'Must have been a little emasculating for him,' she says – a presumption, not a question.

'Not at all, it was his idea. What did you do before you became a homemaker?'

'Oh, that's a long story,' she replies, but I'm left with the impression she'd like me to ask more.

'Who wants another mince pie?' I say instead, then I answer my phone when it rings. 'How goes it, babe?' Brandon grins via FaceTime. The kids are behind him, strapped into their car seats and waving vigorously. I left London at the crack of dawn, long before my family stirred.

'All good here. Whereabouts are you?'

'Junction two of the M1. We'd only just reached it when Imogen needed a wee.'

'We have guests,' I say, and angle the camera towards Anna and Margot, who smile stiffly at a man they've never met. 'Brandon, meet our new neighbours Anna and Maggie – sorry, *Margot*. Guess what Anna brought with her? Homemade mince pies.'

'Well, you two are going to be BFFs then,' he says.

I don't think Margot realises I can see the reflection of her rolling her eyes in the screen.

I wander into the hallway and explain what's left to bring in from the lorries. It's as I'm returning that I hear Margot talking to Anna.

'Should you really be eating a second?' she's saying, pointing to the mince pie in her hand. 'Salad can taste nice too, you know.'

An embarrassed Anna moves the pastry from her mouth and back to her plate.

I enter and Margot rises to her feet, patting out the creases from her skirt. Anna follows and I wonder what the dynamic is between them.

'We should leave you to get on with it,' Anna says.

'Brandon and I were thinking of having a small get-together on New Year's Eve,' I say as I lead them towards the front door. 'It's short notice and you probably already have plans, but it's our way of apologising to the neighbours for all the noise the remodelling must've brought.'

'It has been quite loud at times,' Margot says.

'Why don't you come over if you're free?'

'I'd love to,' says Anna.

'Nicu and I already have a few offers,' Margot replies, 'but if we can make time, we'll drop by.'

'Oh, yes, well you're more than welcome to come too,' I add, unable to resist a final opportunity to tease. Her face turns the colour of the wine she gave me.

Of course Margot will come. She won't be able to resist. I press the AirDrop symbol on my phone, select both their mobiles and send them my telephone number.

'I'll text you with times,' I add. 'Thanks again for coming over with the mince pies. Oh, and the wine.'

I give them a wave and close the door behind them. Then I remove the cork from Margot's bottle and pour myself a very full glass.

CHAPTER 4

ANNA

Liv's and my definition of a 'small get-together' are worlds apart.

She made it sound like she was asking a few friends for a late New Year's Eve supper. Then her text said there'd be a theme to it, 'Summer In Winter', that it was starting at 2 p.m., and there'd be a barbecue. But as Drew and I leave our house and spot cars parked back-to-back, and laminated signs attached to lamp posts reading 'This Way To The Party!', it's evident that Liv had something much grander in mind.

Drew takes a puff from his asthma inhaler as we make our way into Liv's back garden. I'm immediately struck by the number of people already here. There must be at least a hundred, some I recognise from the village and others I don't. I'm suddenly aware of how overdressed I am in my coat, tights and winter boots. There are gas heaters everywhere which are creating their own balmy microclimate. Some men wear shorts, and most of the women are in floaty maxi dresses and flip-flops. They look as if they've just stepped out of the fashion pages of *Grazia* while I look as if I've fallen out of the winter edition of budget catalogue *Damart*.

Lighting rigs shine down upon a DJ whose headphones barely reach her ears over her copper-coloured Afro. Some guests are dancing while others laugh at a joke under a tile-roofed pergola. At the end of the garden are a dozen or so kids shrieking and jumping into the heated swimming pool. A white mist rises from its surface.

The aroma of cooked meats directs my attention to the barbecue. A ginormous grill is being manned by two chefs dressed in full whites. Chicken, salmon, burgers, coleslaw, salads, breads, cheeses, prawns and ribs are all on the menu.

'Wow,' I say as I turn to Drew, but I only catch the back of him. I wish he hadn't, but he's spotted the free bar and he's not going to waste any more time with me.

A burning firepit catches my attention. If I don't move, I know it'll be the only thing I focus on all afternoon. I turn sharply so it's not even in my peripheral vision.

I spy Margot waving at me as she and her husband, Nicu, arrive through the gate with Frankie and Tommy. I'm quietly relieved when their kids hurry in the direction of a group of young people they recognise. I've tried and it's not their fault, but I will never feel comfortable around them.

Margot is as well presented as ever and slips an unnecessary pair of sunglasses down her nose to take in the party with those piercing green eyes of hers.

'Well, this isn't what I expected at all,' she begins. 'It's quite . . .'

'Lavish?' I suggest.

'I was going to say *desperate*.'

'Why?'

'Well, it's a bit "look at me", isn't it? "Hey everybody, come to my party and be my friend." Don't tell me you weren't thinking the same thing.'

Nicu shakes his head wearily. 'My wife has a unique way of putting a negative spin on just about anything.'

Liv appears from inside the house and makes her way towards us.

'This party is a-maz-ing,' Margot says before I have the chance to say hello.

'I'm so glad you could make it!' Liv replies and air-kisses all three of us.

I take in her figure-hugging lace dress and matching white Birkenstock sandals. She's flawless from her styled hair down to her perfectly pedicured feet. I curl my callused toes in my knock-off UGGs.

'I love that necklace,' Liv says, reaching out her thumb and forefinger to gently bring my gold chain closer to her. 'Is it one of your designs?'

I tell her yes and she examines the gemstones more closely. The design is of two flames shaped from orange carnelian and amber.

'I meant it when I said I'd love to see what else you do,' she adds. 'I'll text you to see when's best.' She looks down at our hands. 'You don't have drinks!' She makes eye contact with a waitress and politely beckons her over to take our order. I ask for a lemonade, Nicu a San Miguel and Margot a vodka and cranberry juice.

'Brandon,' Liv says, her voice raised, as a tall man with thick, wavy blond hair approaches.

He's dressed in a floral short-sleeved shirt unbuttoned midway down to reveal clippered chest hair, and shorts that cling to his muscular thighs. Does this woman have *everything*?

'This is my husband,' she announces, beaming.

If I was her, that smile would never leave my face.

I'm about to shake his hand when he comes in for a hug. 'You must be Anna,' he says, and holds me so close to his chest that even through my coat, his pecs make my nipples hard. A perk of being a wallflower is that no one notices.

'And I'm Margot,' she says, introducing herself. 'So lovely to meet you. This is my husband Nicu.'

The two men shake hands and, for a moment, I imagine them wrestling in just their shorts. Good Lord, what is wrong with me today?

'And your husband,' Brandon says to me, 'is he here?'

'You'll probably find him at the bar,' Margot chips in. She squints ahead of her. 'Yep, there he is, settling himself in for the afternoon.'

I shift from foot to foot.

'Daddy!'

Two small children run up to Brandon and tug at his arm. 'Can we go swimming now?'

'Good to meet you all,' he says to us, 'but duty calls.'

But before he is dragged away by two pairs of small hands, his attention lingers on Margot for a fraction of a second longer than the rest of us. She reciprocates.

'He's so hands-on,' Liv coos.

'I bet he is,' Margot replies, with a subtle smirk. 'This is quite some bash,' she continues.

'You think it's completely over the top, don't you?' Liv says apprehensively.

'No, not at all,' lies Margot. 'Who cares if you make friends or buy them?'

'Margot!' I chastise.

'Oh Anna, I'm joking. Sometimes you're much too woke for your own good. Who are all these people?'

'Some are your neighbours,' Liv explains, 'others are friends from London. And a few are potential clients and investors in the wellness studio.'

'Have you chosen a location for it?' Nicu asks.

'A redevelopment close to the railway station in town, as I'm targeting pre- and post-work commuters. The refurbishment started a few weeks ago and we hope to finish by early June. I also want to attract new mums who want to exercise under the same roof as their babies, so we're installing a crèche and a café. Are any of you yoga fans?'

'Margot and I went to a couple of classes last year but I wasn't very good,' I admit. 'I'm not very flexible.'

'It was like watching Geppetto operating Pinocchio,' says Margot.

'And you, Margot?' Liv asks.

'I'm a little rusty. I don't have as much free time as I used to.'

'Self-love is so important, you should definitely make some time for yourself.' Liv shoots a glance at me with a twinkle in her eye, then says to Margot, 'It might have been a while since you had your kids, but I bet we can still get your pre-baby body back in no time.'

I cover my smile with my hand. Margot's kids are her stepchildren.

CHAPTER 5

MARGOT

Has she just called me fat? Do I look bloated? My hand slips to my waist where I allow it to rest on my stomach.

Nicu keeps his head down but I hear him emit one of those snort-laughs that he tries to disguise by clearing his throat. He can be so rude sometimes. I put it down to him being Romanian. They're much more direct than the British. They'll just stand up and leave mid-conversation if they're bored, while we're in it for the duration and wait until later to be snarky about it.

The fact is yes, I should keep more active than I do. Motherhood doesn't keep me as busy as I'd like people to think. And when God was handing out maternal instinct, I was probably too distracted by *The Kardashians* to stand in line. But I try my best. We all make mistakes and I like to think I learn from mine. Sometimes. It's my family who are in the wrong anyway, so there's not actually that much to learn.

'If you excuse me, ladies,' says Nicu, and wanders off in the direction of an egg-shaped man who has stuffed himself into a pair of ill-fitting chinos.

'So, have you finished everything you're doing to this place?' I ask Liv.

'Most of it, but we're hoping to start work on an orangery at the back of the house in the summer.'

Why she can't call it a conservatory is beyond me. As is why she needs another room in an already oversized house. My guess is it's more for bragging rights than usable space.

'Would you like to have a look around?' Liv asks.

'Oh yes please,' says Anna a little too eagerly.

But quietly, so would I.

We follow her and step through a second set of bifold doors and into the dining room. A cat brushes against my legs, a plump off-white thing with so much fur, it looks like it's wearing an over-sized Afghan coat. Perhaps sensing I'm not an animal person, Liv shoos it away.

'Sorry,' she says. 'Cat Face doesn't believe in personal space.'

'Cat Face?' I repeat.

'It's what happens when you let your kids name the family pet.'

She stops like she's a guide at an art gallery expecting us to admire a painting.

'It used to be so bright and floral in here,' Liv continues. 'Like Orla Kiely walked into the room and exploded. Not the aesthetic we wanted.'

'Margot,' chirps Anna, 'didn't you help decorate this place for the last owners?'

I silently curse her.

'Oh, sorry,' Liv says. 'I hope I didn't offend.'

'Not at all,' I reply. 'I showed them a couple of Pinterest boards, that's all.'

The main lounge follows, and then we are upstairs, where Liv and Brandon's room reminds me of an over-styled boutique hotel room, with its panelled walls, low-level lighting, carpets so deep you can't see your toes, and floor-to-ceiling shelves crammed with books. No one could possibly read this number of novels in their lifetime. I'd swap another kidney for some of the outfits in her walk-in wardrobe. I'll never give her the satisfaction of admitting it aloud, but her sense of style is impeccable.

'And the best part of this room?' Grinning, she opens the wardrobe and inside is a minibar. Now we're talking. She removes a chilled bottle of Veuve Clicquot from a fridge and, before asking if we want a glass, a cork flies through the air and disappears into the carpet.

'Sit, sit,' she encourages, and Anna and I sink into a chaise longue under the window while she plonks herself on a bed that could fit a football team.

I can't help but wonder why she's holed up in this room with two relative strangers while her old friends and potential investors are outside making the most of her hospitality.

Tears fill her eyes. This, I was not expecting. Anna and I look to one another.

'Liv, are you okay?' Anna asks and moves towards her, putting a hand on hers.

'I'm sorry,' Liv says as she takes a handful of tissues from a chrome box on a nightstand. As she stretches, her dress reveals the outline of what looks like a belly bar in her navel. Newsflash, Liv: this isn't 1996, and you're not a Spice Girl.

'I think it's only just hit me this barbecue is sort of a farewell party,' she continues. 'Only, most of the people I've spent my adult life being around don't know it yet. That version of me, she feels like a stranger. I want to start the new year living a normal life amongst normal people.'

Normal? Isn't that another way of saying boring? So first I'm fat and now I'm dull.

'I never truly fitted in down there,' she moans. 'I was always playing a part. But here, I want to be myself. And only today has it registered that it's no longer a pipedream. It's actually happening.'

Quite the oversharer, isn't she? When tears spill again, I beat Anna to the punch, slide on to Liv's bed and wrap my arm around her. Christ, she's skinny. It's like comforting a chopstick. Her head tilts towards my shoulder, and before I can stop it, a blob of wet mascara drops on to my pink top. The thanks I get for being a nice person.

'I'm sorry,' she says. 'Let me get a cloth. It should be okay, polyester doesn't usually stain.'

'It's silk,' I reply.

'You girls really are too kind,' she says to us both.

'You're one of us now,' says Anna.

Liv's face crinkles and her smile returns.

'If you make her cry mascara tears again, you're paying for this to be dry-cleaned,' I warn Anna.

They laugh as if I'm joking.

CHAPTER 6

LIV

Oh God, I think I've made a fool of myself in front of Anna and Margot, two people who barely know me. Hardly a great start. I'm grateful they don't appear fazed by my tears. But I want to start as I mean to go on, and that'll only happen if I'm being myself. Not the version I have been, because I'm not that Liv anymore. Margot and Anna don't need to know who I was or what I'm capable of doing to get what I want.

'How did you deal with leaving London, Margot?' I ask. 'You mentioned before you once lived there.'

She rises to her feet and makes her way back from the bed and on to the chaise longue.

'Oh that's all such a long time ago now, I barely remember,' she says dismissively.

'I remember you well,' Anna says to her. 'You were everywhere when I was a teenager.'

'What am I missing?' I ask, genuinely confused. I have no idea who Margot is or was.

'I used to be in a pop group,' Margot says. 'But like you, that version of me feels like light years away.'

I sense a contradiction here. Part of her clearly wants to tell me about it, but there's another part that's reticent. Regardless, this time, I bite. 'Oh really? Which group?'

'The Party Hard Posse,' Anna pipes up. 'You must remember "Never Stop (Yeah Yeah)" and "Get Up On The Dancefloor"?'

I look at her blankly.

'Four boys, three girls?' she adds. 'Margot, sing something.'

'No!' Margot replies, aghast.

'Then I will,' says Anna and launches into the chorus of a song I vaguely recall. Margot looks as if she's fighting to swallow down bile.

'Yes,' I say, 'I think I know that one.'

'They toured with Britney Spears, Enrique Iglesias and Will Young,' Anna continues as if she's written their Wikipedia entry.

I'm slowly beginning to decipher their dynamic. I think Anna enjoys having someone to look up to and Margot delights in the applause.

'Why did you give it up?' I ask.

'It ran its course. Singer-songwriters fell into favour and there wasn't any room in the charts for bands like us.'

'But if they ever got back together, you'd rejoin, wouldn't you?' Anna asks.

'If the right offer came along, maybe,' she concedes. 'It might be fun to be back on stage.'

There's more to her story than meets the eye and I make a mental note to look her up online later. There's nowhere to hide on the internet. Unless, like me, you hide behind a paywall.

'I suppose I should venture downstairs and start playing hostess again,' I say as I top up their glasses with the rest of the Veuve. I raise mine up. 'But first, here's to new friendships.'

We clink glasses. Margot knocks hers back so quickly it barely touches the sides.

We're re-entering the garden when Anastasia, one of my soon-to-be-former London friends, appears, tinsel draped around her neck and a piece of mistletoe wedged under a hairband. Going by the way she sways as she stands, she's making the most of the bar.

'Margot Ward!' she cries at the sight of her, eyes ablaze.

'Not for a decade,' Margot tells her. 'It's Rosetti now.'

'My little brother used to have the biggest crush on you. He used to say that when he grew up he was going to marry you. He's gay now.'

None of us are sure how the two are linked.

'So did you stay with that dancer?' Anastasia asks.

Margot's face hardens. 'Yes, we're still together.'

Something tells me I should be steering Anastasia away from this conversation, yet I can't help but want her to drive towards it. So I say nothing.

'You two were always on the covers of the celeb mags, weren't you?' Anastasia persists. 'What did they call you? "The Homewrecker"?'

Anastasia momentarily loses her footing. I grab her arm to stop her from falling. The distraction provides Margot with an excuse to remove herself from the situation.

'It was lovely to have met you,' she says, 'but I need to check on my kids.'

And with that, she slips her sunglasses back on, throws her head back and walks away, every inch the star she apparently used to be.

CHAPTER 7

'Why do you think you're here?' he begins.

His voice is soft and calming and at odds with the spikiness I feel.

'I'm not mad, I know why I'm here,' I reply. 'Read your notes.'

I look towards a brown manila folder lying on the wooden table that separates us. A few sheets of white A4 paper poke from the side, but I can't make out what's been written. I can hazard a guess though.

'I read them this morning,' he says. 'But I'd prefer to hear it from you, in your own words.'

I look around the room. It's white and sterile, much like the rest of the building. Everything here is colourless: the people, the bedroom I'm forced to share, the lounge where the only voices are those coming from a television no one watches, the dining room where we eat in silence.

He and I are both sitting in leather armchairs opposite one another. There are two framed photographs hanging from the wall, both generic Ikea images. One is of a pier leading out into a blueish lake and the other is of grey pebbles on a calm shore.

'What is it with psychiatrists and water?' I ask.

'You've seen a psychiatrist before?'

'You haven't answered my question.'

'If I answer yours, will you answer mine?'

I nod.

'Well, some of us believe being near water can induce calm and make people feel at ease. It promotes a sense of relaxation, especially for those experiencing mental health concerns.'

'Like me.'

'Is that what you believe you're experiencing?'

I raise an eyebrow to suggest it's a rhetorical question and he moves on.

'What do you think when you look at those pictures?'

I study the one featuring the pier. 'I think,' I reply, 'how far would I need to swim before I could drown myself.'

He doesn't react.

'Kidding,' I add.

'Are you still experiencing an urge to end your life?'

'No. Not anymore.'

'Could I ask what's changed? You were brought to this facility because you were found by Beachy Head – historically, a popular cliff edge used by people planning to end their lives.'

'Planning to end your life and actually doing it are two very different things.'

'Your medical notes suggest a history of depression. You spent time in a facility similar to this one, eighteen months ago.'

'Why did you ask if I've seen a psychiatrist before when you already know the answer?'

He doesn't answer.

'Okay, so yes, I did go to Beachy Head to kill myself, is that what you want to hear? But I didn't go ahead with it, did I?'

'Why?'

I think back to three days ago, and to the storm. To the rain lashing my face, the soaking wet clothes clinging to my body, and to looking out over the silver sea and its beckoning waves. Finally, down to the jagged rocks below. And I remember how, just as I was about to relinquish control of my body to the wind and let it carry me over the edge, I heard her voice. She spoke to me, quite gently but with absolute clarity. I decide not to answer his question but ask one of my own.

'Does everyone have a voice in the back of their head?'

'Most people have an internal monologue, yes.'

'What if it's not your voice? What's that called?'

I have all of his attention now. 'It can be one of many things, such as dissociative identity disorder. People can feel as if they can have several personalities inside them, that can control their behaviour at different times and in different ways. These identities can have their own histories and traits.' He gazes at me for one long moment. 'Is that what's happening to you? Did a voice belonging to someone else suggest you end your life?'

I don't tell him it actually saved it.

'No,' I say. 'I just changed my mind.'

'And what's to stop you changing your mind again and going ahead with it when you leave here?'

'I won't,' I reply confidently.

It's true. Because she won't let me. And now I know she's here, I don't want to. She has my best interests at heart. She has shown me a way forward. A way for me to live.

She's made me understand that it's not myself I need to kill.

JANUARY

TEN MONTHS BEFORE BONFIRE NIGHT

CHAPTER 8

MARGOT

'You are not wearing those bloody awful things to school,' I object as Frankie reaches the bottom of the stairs.

'What's wrong with them?' she asks, defiantly folding her arms.

'You know perfectly well. They're not part of the school uniform.'

'But they're black.'

'They're Crocs, Frankie.' I'm always willing to put myself in someone else's shoes. But not if they're wearing rubber crimes against couture. 'The letter your head of year sent you home with last time says school shoes only.'

'And did you always do what you were told when you were at school?'

'Of course,' I lie.

As it happens, I had my eyebrow and nose pierced and was sent home every time I refused to take them out. But once again, the truth will not serve.

'They're unflattering and make you look like a boy,' I continue.

'So what?' she snorts. 'You still don't get me, do you, Margot?'

She stopped calling me 'Mum' on her sixth birthday. Nicu was more concerned by it than me.

'Fine,' I say. 'Wear what you want. But if they say you have to come home and take them off, don't think you'll be lounging around here all day.'

I leave her so I can finish unboxing my new Sage Oracle coffee maker that was delivered yesterday. It's a more up-to-date version of Liv's antiquated 2024 model. I haven't told Nicu we have it, as I know he won't approve of me spending so much money on something that makes a drink he doesn't even appreciate. If it was up to him, we'd be spooning our coffee from a glass jar.

Earlier this morning, as I watched him leave the house, I couldn't deny there's still an attraction there. He's as handsome as he was when we first met in that rehearsal room. His twenty-something leanness has transformed into thirty-something muscle, and those salt-and-pepper streaks at his temples only add to his appeal.

We've been together eleven years now, married for ten. Would we still be together if I didn't have this ring on my finger? The one I paid for myself? I can't be sure. I'm also uncertain if either of us really wanted to get married in the first place. But back in that dark, dark period, that was what we were 'strongly urged' to do by the damage limitation experts we paid a small fortune to for advice.

Before I read the coffee machine instructions, I swallow a couple of painkillers for the headache that's been stalking me like a charity worker rattling a can in the high street. Then I hear the schlepping of the crime-against-fashion footwear behind me.

'Why don't you respect me?' Frankie asks, relatively calmly.

'I don't really know why we must go through this again,' I groan. 'You don't identify as a girl, I get it.'

'No, you don't get it, because if you did get it, you'd know I don't identify as either a girl *or* a boy. Why's that so hard for you to understand?'

I sink into the chair next to the kitchen table and rub my cheeks with my palms. 'Because it doesn't make sense to me. Biologically, you're born one way or the other, and if you feel nature's made a mistake and put you in the wrong body, then you fix it when you're old enough.'

'So if you accept trans people, why can't you accept non-binary people who don't identify either way?'

'Because you have to be . . . *something*.'

'Says who?'

'Says the world!'

'But I'm part of the world and I'm telling you what I am. You won't listen. You don't have to understand something to accept it. You don't know how a rocket flies into space, but you accept that it does.'

All right, that's a new one. I can hardly argue that point. But I can move on: 'Can't you just be a lesbian or bisexual and have done with it? That's where this is heading, right?'

'Jesus, Margot! I'm no more a lesbian than you are.'

'You know that I wouldn't care if you were gay. Your dad and I have been surrounded by LGBTQ blah blah blah people for our whole careers.'

'He still has a career. You don't.'

She can be such a bitch sometimes.

'And whose fault is that?' I say pointedly.

She knows who I'm referring to. Immediately, I know I shouldn't have said it.

'Look, you're not even thirteen yet,' I push on. 'When you cut that beautiful blonde hair short, I didn't say anything. When you stopped wearing anything other than greys, blacks and blues,

I let it pass. But this is too important for me to just go along with because it's the trendy thing to do. You're too young to change your identity.'

She opens her mouth to argue and I know what she's about to say next. 'And before you ask, I am most certainly not going to ask your school to use non-binary pronouns,' I add.

For an uninvited moment, I return to who I was at her age, and my skin prickles. My desperation to fit in and to surround myself with people who understood me came close to ruining my life. Frankie is the opposite, and perhaps I resent her for thinking she knows who she is when I didn't. Regardless, I can't backtrack now. Frankie is a girl and it's as simple as that. I'm not budging. And she needs to be reminded who the parent is here.

I turn my back on her. I've lost interest in trying to fathom how the coffee machine works. I search for some capsules instead with the strongest possible blend, to use in the old one. They're not in the cupboard where I left them yesterday. I open a few more doors before giving up my search and finishing the half-empty glass of warm white wine by the sink instead.

Frankie drives me mad sometimes. I never wanted children, and then suddenly, I was lumbered with a one- and a two-year-old. I knew immediately that nothing was going to be the same again that night Nicu brought them home. But to be his wife, I had to be their stepmother too.

By the time I return to the hall, Frankie's Crocs are lying in the middle of the floor. She's left them for me to put away. So I do as she wants, opening the back door and putting them away, only in the recycling bin. Now they've been put away. It's collection day tomorrow. Let's see if she finds them in time.

The clattering of the letterbox distracts me. A brown padded envelope lands on the doormat. It's addressed to me, and a chill runs through me when I recognise the printed label. I tear it open in the kitchen and remove the box inside. It's a doll effigy of me, one I haven't seen in years. They were mass-produced when I was in the Party Hard Posse. It's only when I take it out of the box that I realise its head has been severed.

I throw it in the cupboard under the stairs alongside the rest of the similarly anonymous gifts, and slam the door shut.

CHAPTER 9

LIV

I nudge Brandon in the ribs with just enough elbow force to make him roll on to his side and stop snoring. His deviated septum, a hangover from a rugby injury, makes it difficult for him to breathe through his nose when he's lying on his back.

I'm struggling to tune him out tonight. Though I can't solely blame his impression of a steam train pulling into a station for keeping me awake. There's too much whirring around in my head for me to switch off completely. I think the shift in our lives over the last six weeks is catching up with me, alongside our plans for the studio.

I admit defeat and quietly leave the bedroom. Downstairs, in the kitchen, I turn on the under-cabinet lights then make myself a hot chocolate. I glance at the space that surrounds me and compare it to our London flat. We could never have bought this place unless I'd thrown away just about every principle I ever had.

I think back, and for as long as I can remember, I've wanted better for myself. For three years running, the north-west England town where I was born and raised won the undesirable title Most Deprived Town in Great Britain. Government neglect and soaring unemployment had crippled Sandlehope – or Abandon-All-Hope, as locals nicknamed it. As a child I was often moved about from one squalid bedsit to another, until something more permanent appeared. I vowed to do better for my own children.

The gold-paved streets of London felt like somewhere I ought to be, but for years I was treading water in dead-end cashier and cleaning jobs, and during a particularly low point, hosing down the bloodied floors of an abattoir. Eventually I scraped enough money together to put myself through secretarial college.

'Why bother?' the friends I'd grown up with asked. 'Find a bloke, settle down, get married and let him worry about work.'

That attitude was ingrained in them. It was what our mothers had done and their mothers before them. But I deserved more than a life that was dependent on, determined and financed by men.

So I made a plan to escape. I listened to hours of lessons on the Get Rid of Your Accent app and followed Instagram pages offering tutorials on the right clothes to wear for the right situations. I completed more than a hundred and fifty online application forms and attended a dozen interviews before an employer took a chance on me. Harrison, Murray & Kline, a private London-based bank, offered me a junior role in a secretarial pool at their Mayfair Place offices. I accepted before they'd even revealed the wage.

The only accommodation I could afford was a box room in a flat-share south of the river with three other young women. I lived hand to mouth for the first year, my wages swallowed up by rent, food and commuting. I could go out at night maybe once or twice a fortnight, and I shopped in supermarkets after 6 p.m., when the unsold fresh food was price-reduced.

It was Kelly, a medical student who'd just moved into the bedroom next to mine, who offered me a way to live in the city, rather than simply existing in it.

'I make specialist videos to sell to my website subscribers' was how she put it to me after treating me to a yoga class one evening. 'It's given me a life beyond the hospital.'

'What do you mean by "specialist"?' I replied with a raised eyebrow.

'Not what you're thinking.' She laughed. 'Fetish stuff. I have nice feet apparently. I never show my face, just my legs and feet, wiggle them around for the camera, maybe play with them a little bit, paint or trim my nails, slip on a few pairs of shoes, whatever the client wants.'

'And that's it? Nothing sexual?'

'No. Some ask, even beg, for more. But I'm not risking my career over a side hustle.'

'Does it pay well?'

She nudged me in the ribs. 'Why, are you interested?'

'Just curious.'

'Between about £50 and £75 for each private video, and there can be five or six of those a week. I earn more in a month from subscribers alone than I do on my junior doctor's wage. By the time I'm qualified, I'll have paid off most of my student loans.'

'Wow,' I replied, a little lost for words.

'You know one thing I get a lot of requests for? Verbally abusive behaviour. Me telling men they're worthless and useless, criticising their appearances.'

'So, Twitter, basically.'

'I've tried it a couple of times, but it doesn't work for me,' she continued. 'But you could give it a go. Create a persona for yourself, wear a mask so no one will ever recognise you, and just hurl abuse at paying customers.'

I wasn't sure what it was about me that gave off a 'you'd be a natural at intimidating men' vibe. However, I couldn't deny its appeal.

'But one of the reasons I moved away from home was to build a life for myself that didn't involve being reliant on men,' I argued. 'If I'm taking their money to do things that turn them on, how am I being an independent woman?'

'Because, Beyoncé, they'll be playing by the rules *you* set. This is your game, not theirs.'

What did I have to lose? Kelly attached a link on her website to a separate page she'd built for me. Then we made a handful of videos where I lay seductively on my bed, dressed head to toe in a latex outfit and mask I'd bought second-hand from eBay, and told viewers how worthless they were. There were instantly takers, believe me. It felt ridiculous until I separated myself from the character I was playing.

As the weeks progressed, my follower numbers and requests continued to increase. And soon, I was no longer turning down invitations for nights out because I couldn't afford it. My long-delayed London social life had begun.

It was through work colleagues that I ended up spending much of my time on the Kensington and Chelsea scene. Most of those I rubbed shoulders with were born into money, and when asked, I was vague about my underprivileged background. And I admit to losing myself by trying to be someone I wasn't. I dated men based on their net worth instead of their worth as human beings. I became accustomed to being bought clothes and jewellery, taken to fancy restaurants or away for weekends, without ever having to put a manicured hand in my pocket. By the time Brandon and my worlds collided, I barely recognised myself.

He was someone's plus-one when he sat next to me at a Knightsbridge restaurant at the leaving dinner of a mutual work friend. And aside from the fact he was so bloody good-looking, I noticed he was the only one around the table clocking the exorbitant menu prices before giving the waiter his order. I felt for him because I'd been him. No, I was still him, just in designer heels paid for by someone else. I surprised myself with a sudden urge to show him who I really was.

'They're not exactly Nando's prices, are they?' I whispered in his ear.

At first he was unsure if I was mocking him. When he realised I wasn't, he smiled.

'Is tap water an acceptable starter?' he asked.

I said nothing about my extra-curricular money-making ventures, but there was something refreshingly honest about him. I learned that like me, he wanted to better himself, and had relocated to London following a failed business venture with a friend. Now he was a personal trainer in an upmarket gym. He also sold subscriptions to personal-training videos on the website OnlyFans. In a short space of time, the site had become a one-stop shop for musicians, chefs, authors, artists and adult entertainers to release original work to paying subscribers.

I waited all that night for a red flag or a hint of toxic masculinity, but there was none. So we made arrangements to meet the following week for dinner, at the much more credit-card-friendly noodle restaurant Wagamama. And after that second night, we barely left each other's side.

The weeks progressed as quickly as our growing closeness. But it gnawed at my conscience that this man I was falling for was oblivious as to how I was funding my life. He deserved transparency. So I slid my iPad towards him one evening and played a video I'd made for a client who'd wanted me to be critical of naked images of his genitals. Five minutes of work had earned me £120. Then, as I fixed my attention on Brandon's expression, I braced myself.

He closed the screen and turned his head towards me.

'To be fair, you're right.' He smiled. 'That guy really does have an ugly cock.'

With that, I knew Brandon and I were going to be just fine. In the years that followed, we bought our first place together. It didn't bother me that I'd put down most of the deposit. In fact I preferred it that way. We were happy.

And then a spanner hit the works. More accurately, two twelve-week-old spanners, the size of plums and with heartbeats, which were growing inside me.

And here we are now.

This morning, I finish my hot chocolate, leave the cup in the sink and check the time. The kids will be up in an hour, so there's little point in going back to bed. Through the window, the interior light of a car catches my eye. It illuminates Anna's husband Drew. I briefly wonder what my new neighbours really think of me. Do they see me as the woman I'm trying to project myself as? And will their opinions change if they ever discover how I actually found investment in my new studio?

Because it took a lot more than just making a few sexy videos.

CHAPTER 10

MARGOT

My knees are bent and my feet are tucked firmly under my bum as I sit on the sofa watching *This Morning* on mute. The persistent prattle of today's conveyor belt of presenters is already getting on my nerves. But now the house is silent. Too silent. Because silence and I aren't great bedfellows. Silence gives me too much time to think. To dwell on the past. To relive the old life I miss more than anyone could know.

Soon after the kids returned to school post-Christmas holidays, Nicu began making regular trips to our neighbouring town of Milton Keynes to rehearse. After this spring, my professional ballroom-dancing husband will begin a four-month countrywide tour performing in a brand-new show. He mentioned the theme, but I wasn't really listening. *Old School Hollywood or some other rehashed cliché*, I think. Every show looks the same to me, full of perma-tanned, glittery bodies wearing the same sequinned, glittery gowns or glittery shirts unbuttoned to their glittery navels performing the same glittery dance routines. And all for a paying audience of sexually frustrated women who fantasise that my husband is about to dance them into bed. I suppose it's not inconceivable.

He danced me flat on my back once upon a time. Then as winter approaches, he'll return to his regular gig on TV's *Strictly Come Dancing*, where he first found fame and I found him.

Today, he's borrowing my car while his is being serviced, which leaves me stuck in the village all day. I glance at the fireplace clock: it's not even 10.15 a.m. It's going to drag, like watching an old person sucking a boiled sweet.

I need a distraction, so I pick up my iPad and visit the favourites section. Then I spend half an hour being pissed off as I re-download apps that have vanished overnight. This bloody gadget keeps erasing them for no reason and it's driving me mad. I know I'm not very tech-savvy, but it's even confused the bloke at the so-called Genius Bar at the Apple store who I went on to harangue about how useless he was. Genius Bar? No. Acne-ridden virgin bar is a more accurate description.

I respond to some of the messages left on an app I've hidden inside a subfolder titled 'Home Decor'. The kids are banned from using my device, but if they were to pick it up, they'd have no reason to look there. It's my little secret. Next, as the YouTube app opens, I choose a 2009 episode of Christmas *Top of the Pops* I've previously favourited. My band the Party Hard Posse is sandwiched between a JLS studio performance and a Sugababes video.

Amidst the cheering of the audience I'm taken back into the studio when the opening synths of our biggest-selling single kick in, and I'm reminded of how young I once was. Twenty-five, all tan, tits and teeth. The latter two, along with my nose, had by then already benefited from a little surgical revision. The following February we were at the Brit Awards in Earl's Court accepting an award for British Single of the Year. Somewhere up in the loft, I think I still have that award, along with some gold and platinum discs. I considered trying to sell them once, as I'm sure the fans would snap them up, but I decided against it. They and YouTube are all I have left of that Margot. Christ, I miss her.

The song comes to an end, and the applause begins before the camera moves away and focuses on the next big thing. A metaphor for the rest of my career, it turned out.

I'm reminded of the turning point for the band a few short months later. The name Glastonbury still sticks in my throat like a particularly well-endowed Brazilian I met backstage during Rock in Rio. It was my idea for us to pitch to perform, and I was overjoyed when they offered us a forty-minute Friday afternoon slot at the festival, following Florence + The Machine.

My fellow band members lacked the vision to see how a successful show could alter the trajectory of our career. They hadn't accepted our time in the spotlight had a shelf life and that somewhere, another group of fame-hungry pop puppets were being groomed to replace us. To quote our own lyrics, 'shaking our booties on the dancefloor' or 'partying with a capital P-A-R-T-Y' weren't going to cut it for much longer.

In hindsight, our management team were right to have warned us against Glastonbury, as it turned out to be an epic fail. We couldn't have counted the number of bottles of wee that were hurled at us when we reached the chorus of the second song. It was like an orchestrated missile attack. But the bottles and the booing didn't stop us. We ploughed on right until the bitter end. Some critics praised us for our 'stoic, if unwise performance', but to everyone else, we were a laughing stock. Potty Hard Pissy became our nickname. Even now, footage from that performance makes regular appearances on those TV list shows, like *The Fifty Most Embarrassing Moments in Music*.

Soon after, management dropped us and the band went their separate ways All these years later, and we still haven't spoken.

I move on to another YouTube clip, this time for my first solo single. It has almost 500,000 views now – about 499,999 more than the number of copies it sold. Try as it might, my new record label couldn't get either the airplay or the press's interest. There were thousands of thumbs-down symbols on YouTube, which stopped the algorithm from suggesting it to other users. Two years after the Party Hard Posse imploded, I was playing the songs I'd fought so hard to distance myself from on cruise ships around the British Isles like a low-rent Susan Boyle.

I'd earned enough money to delay finding a real job for a few years. I'd co-written a handful of songs for a German pop group who were huge in Europe, which paid reasonable royalties until one of their singers was found guilty of getting handsy with underage fans and radio stations ditched them.

But it wasn't only the money I missed from my old life, it was the acclaim. It was the magazine covers, the parties, the fine-dining restaurants, the camera flashes, the awards shows, the other celebs, the free, limitless wardrobes, the hotels, the holidays . . . everything that came with being famous. I knew who I was then.

I wanted it all back. Until I got it. And then fame became infamy.

A passing car draws me out of another of my all-too-frequent wallows in my ruined career. It parks outside Liv's house and Liv herself exits. Why she can't park on a drive with room for at least five vehicles is beyond me. Instead of going inside, she rings Anna's bell instead. Are they meeting without me?

I survey this empty room and the empty hours that I'll need to fill.

'Balls to this,' I mutter to myself.

I grab the cupcakes Tommy made at school yesterday and open the front door. The sudden movement scares a cat taking a shit in our borders. It's that bloody furball of Liv's. It turns to glare at me like I'm the one in the wrong. I clap my hands and it scampers back home.

I'm about to head across the street to see what I might be missing out on when I spot the side of my car. One word has been daubed across it in red paint.

Murderer.

CHAPTER 11

ANNA

'Oh hi,' I begin when I find Margot on my doorstep.

She looks a little like someone trying to disguise they're flustered. I spot red paint on her fingers and catch a whiff of white spirits. The smell makes me want to recoil.

'You've left your garage door open,' she says.

I turn and see it is, indeed, rolled to the top.

'Drew,' I tut. 'He's always forgetting to close it. I keep telling him it's open invitation to be robbed but he never listens.'

She shoves a plastic food box into my chest.

'My calorie-counting app tells me I've had enough trans fats for one day. And as you aren't so bothered by your appearance, I thought I'd share these, if you're not too busy tinkering?'

I hold back from informing her that yes, I do care about my appearance, and no, I'm not 'tinkering' but designing and creating jewellery, which is how I make my living. And then I notice she's not making eye contact with me. She's looking behind me. She's spotted Liv in my kitchen. That's why she's here. She has FOMO.

'Oh look, Liv's here,' Margot says.

I have little choice but to move to one side because she's already crossing the threshold. I thought vampires couldn't enter a house without an invitation.

It's when I turn to go back inside that I spot a white envelope shoved part way through the door. The name it's addressed to catches me unawares, as I haven't used it in years. Then I recognise the blue-stamped postmark. I open it and skim the contents. It's an appointment date nine months from now. It's taken more than two years and three cancellations to get this far. But now a date has been attached to it, I'm not sure how I feel. I'm also unsure if I'll mention this to Drew. He has it in his head that it will solve all my problems. He won't accept it doesn't work like that. I stuff the letter into my pocket.

'Hello Liv,' I hear Margot saying even more chirpily than when she greeted me. 'How are you?'

Liv is hunched over the kitchen island, working her way through an array of necklaces and bracelets I've laid out in front of her on velvet sheets.

'What a lovely surprise.' Liv smiles as they air-kiss one another. 'Anna didn't mention you'd be joining us?'

'I've been meaning to see her latest little creations for ages.'

That's news to me. I've tried to show her my work a couple of times before. Once she broke a clasp, and the second time she told me a pendant reminded her of an orange poo emoji.

'Look at these, aren't they incredible?' Liv enthuses. 'She's so talented.'

'She certainly is,' says Margot, I suspect through gritted teeth. 'They're . . . neat.'

Strange choice of words.

'You made your and Drew's wedding rings, didn't you?' Margot asks me.

'Yes,' I reply. 'Mine is gold and Drew's is silver.'

'Well, perhaps one day he'll earn enough to buy you a proper ring.'

She joins Liv at the island, chooses a necklace at random and picks it up, pretending to give it her full attention.

'Do you mind if I take some photos to send to my influencer friends?' asks Liv. 'Some are stylists, others are buyers, and a couple are Instagrammers.'

'That's really thoughtful,' I say, perhaps a little overzealously.

She must take at least a dozen pictures, and I look over her shoulder as she sends them to a WhatsApp group titled 'Fashion Huns', then adds a carousel of them to her own Instagram page and tags me. She has almost ninety thousand followers. I realise Margot's also watching, and going by her expression, she's equally surprised by that figure.

'Can I try that one on?' asks Margot, pointing to a necklace.

It's one from my recent Inferno range: a brass drawn cable chain holding flame-like loops made from red spinel, rhodonite and citrine.

'It really suits you,' says Liv as she helps Margot affix it. 'Women with slightly thicker necks often struggle to pull off thin chains, but that looks great on you.'

Liv winks at me and I turn my head so a blanching Margot can't see me react.

'I think I'll have this one,' Margot says. It'll be her first-ever purchase from me. 'Invoice me.'

She takes it off and I give it a polish with a fine cloth before slipping it into a box. Liv turns her attention to Margot.

'I feel like I should apologise for my drunken friend Anastasia at our New Year's Eve party,' she says. 'I hope she didn't embarrass you by bringing up the past? She really has no filter.'

'I haven't given it a second thought,' Margot replies. 'Those days are long behind me.'

I suspect they aren't. You're unlikely to forget being called the most reviled woman in Britain in a hurry.

CHAPTER 12

LIV

I'm judging Margot. I wouldn't be if I was only basing my opinion on her past behaviour. People can change. And who she was a decade ago isn't necessarily who she is now.

She's certainly a complex beast. I'd had no idea she used to be famous until Anna told me. When Margot was at the height of her fame, I was more interested in rock than fluffy pop. And I didn't really read newspapers or magazines either, so her rise to fame – and subsequent fall – passed me by.

It was only when I was googling her that I began recalling parts of her story. I hadn't realised just how badly the press savaged her. Some of it was deserved, but for the most part, it was a witch hunt. Nicu got away lightly, all things considered. But men so often do, compared to women. Suggest a historical sexual assault by a male celebrity and the first thing social media wants to know is either 'Why did you wait so long to report it?' or 'How much money are you trying to get from him?' Not, 'I'm sorry that happened to you, how can I show you my support?'

But I'm not judging her for any of that. My view is based on who she is now, and that's someone who constantly demeans

Anna. It doesn't sit comfortably with me. The comments about her appearance, her weight and her husband must all be chipping away at her confidence, which is unfair because, from what I've learned, Anna is a good-natured soul. I've met bullies like Margot before. I've worked with some. And I have this big-sisterly urge to fight back on Anna's behalf when Margot makes her jibes. If I'm given the opportunity and it feels appropriate, I'll ask Anna why she puts up with it. Or maybe she needs someone like me to help her realise how negating Margot's behaviour is.

My phone pings with a message.

'It's my friend Stephanie, the fashion blogger I was telling you about,' I tell Anna. 'She says she'd love to use some of your designs in a shoot early next week. Would you be able to send some? Can she send a courier to pick them up tomorrow?'

Anna's face reddens. 'Yes, of course,' she says in a voice that's too small for her. 'That would be amazing. Thank you so much.'

Another message appears with photos of the items Stephanie wants.

'Do you have any more of the one Margot chose?'

'No, I don't.'

'Please, take this back,' says Margot, a little too quickly, before she slides the box across the worktop to Anna.

'I'll make you another one,' Anna says gratefully.

'No hurry,' Margot assures her. 'Take as much time as you need.'

'I have an idea,' I say suddenly. 'What are you girls doing two Saturdays from now? I have vouchers for a spa weekend which are burning a hole in my handbag. Who fancies keeping me company?'

'Count me in,' says Margot. 'I'm long overdue a pampering.'

'To be honest, I don't know if I can afford it,' says Anna sheepishly.

'Don't worry about that, Anna. We'll split my vouchers. So, how about it?'

CHAPTER 13

NAVYA, THE FIRST

It's a parent's duty to guide their child as best they can. To teach them to love and steer them clear from the path of hate. But there are exceptions to that rule. And this evening will be an example of that. Because I am to show the person I love most in this world how hate can be harnessed and channelled into a force for good. And we will do that together, by killing the one responsible for putting a bullet through my brain and robbing my child of its mother.

That is the plan. My plan, for us, together.

For years, I lay dormant. I fought for so long against allowing anything other than my vague presence to be felt. I remained silent when they whispered to me, begging for guidance, even though it broke my heart to think they believed I wasn't listening. However, I felt every emotion they did. When they experienced happiness, so did I. When they felt love, I felt the same. When they were frightened, I too lived in fear. But more often than not, we shared sadness and pain.

Eventually their need for me became so desperate, I had no choice but to relent. Had I not, neither of us would be here today. They'd have deliberately fallen over that cliff edge and their body would have been swallowed by the waves. No parent can stand idly by when they know there's another way.

And when I allowed my voice to be heard, I grew wings powerful enough to carry us both.

They made a wise decision in keeping me a secret. Family, friends and doctors can never understand. They'd claim I'm being used as an excuse for questionable behaviour. That I'm a fantasy, a comfort blanket. But my child and I know the truth.

The names of the guilty were not hard to find. They had been arrested and questioned soon after that night, and all were later released without charge. An old policeman contact of my late husband's wrote down their names and passed it to my brother-in-law. But he was not strong enough to act as we are about to act tonight. He failed us. I will not allow that mistake to occur a second time. Because I know we will only get the peace we crave when each of them who has hurt us dies.

I have decided Zain will be the first. Soon after his arrest, he fled the country, returning to his Iranian birthplace to live with extended family. Eleven years later and now in his late twenties, his name was easy to find on a business networking site. He's back in the town he ran from.

So we have spent many an hour sitting inside a parked car, watching as he goes about his work alone as manager of a mobile phone repairs shop in a small, prefabricated building. And now, as dusk falls, it is time for us to come face to face not with the monster, but with the man. Monsters cannot be beaten. But fragile men made of flesh and bone can be.

I don't allow myself to become consumed by fear as I lead this man into conversation with my child. He chats amicably while he replaces the screen on a cheap phone deliberately cracked for this moment. Through my child's eyes I scan the room, searching for security cameras. There are none. It's when Zain's head is bent down and he's distracted that we strike. Even when the pocketknife is plunged into his throat *he feels no pain, only confusion. I sense panic in my conduit so I take complete charge, pull the knife out, struggling to keep a grip of the bloody handle, and make short, sharp stabbing motions into his neck until he is too weak and muddled to fight back, and sinks to his knees and then to his side. It's over in less than a minute.*

Then we pick up the phone and I scan the road outside for pedestrians, drivers or any other witnesses. When I'm certain there are none, I guide us three streets away to the car. Blood-soaked clothes are bagged up and left in the boot to dispose of later, along with the knife. Then we continue our journey as if nothing out of the ordinary has happened.

It's in that moment everything shifts.

Quite unexpectedly, I feel myself slipping away. I stretch out my arms across an invisible doorway as gravity drags me inside where a dark abyss awaits.

I don't want to go. I want to remain here forever. But someone is taking the choice away from me. I sense another voice is readying itself to replace me.

To my dismay, I realise it is Zain. His death is the catalyst for my release. He is ready to sully the vessel I was so fortunate to create and, since my own death, to inhabit.

I wish I could stay with my child, whom I love with all my heart. Even though my voice can no longer be heard, my essence will remain buried deep within my blessed child.

If you can still hear me, my love: I promise that I am with you, always.

FEBRUARY

NINE MONTHS BEFORE BONFIRE NIGHT

CHAPTER 14

ANNA

I'm learning never to underestimate Liv. This isn't what I expected when she suggested the three of us spend the weekend together at a spa. I expected a country hotel with a sauna, steam room, swimming pool and a few treatment rooms. But the moment Liv pulls up on the gravel driveway of this country estate and we enter reception, I know I'm out of my depth.

I slip off my sunglasses to take it all in. The arrow-like design of the charcoal-grey floor directs us to a grey and white marble reception desk adorned with two glass vases arranged with dozens of white peony roses. The desk is manned by two women, immaculate in appearance. Dark hair scraped back tightly, they wear identical black dresses and bright red lipstick, as though they've stepped out of that 1980s music video for 'Addicted to Love'.

Above us is a mirrored ceiling and a crystal chandelier with more lightbulbs than I can count. Behind the reception desk is another mirror, one that runs from floor to ceiling. We're constantly being reflected, no matter at what angle we stand. It adds to my self-consciousness.

'Oh,' says Liv, 'isn't this just *gorge*?'

Margot's phone rings to the tune of Madonna's 'Material Girl' – a bit on the nose, I think – and I spot Nicu's face flashing up on the screen. She declines the call and rolls her eyes. Nicu calls back immediately, and this time, she turns her phone off.

'Everything alright?' Liv asks.

'It is now,' she says. 'Nicu and the kids have gastroenteritis, so I don't want to be anywhere near that house.'

Liv and I look at each other. Margot can't help but notice.

'It's okay,' she assures us. 'They'll be fine. And there's nothing I can do there apart from rinse out a few sick bowls. I'm much better off here.'

It hasn't crossed her mind that she too might be contagious.

Soon after, we arrive at our bedrooms – two located next to one another, the other adjacent.

'Sorry,' says Liv, 'but I could only get two deluxe suites and one executive.'

'There's nothing to apologise for,' says Margot. 'Anna, you don't mind, do you?'

I'm about to nod because of course I don't mind. I wouldn't complain if I was told I was sleeping in the janitor's cupboard.

'Actually,' Liv says, 'I was thinking Anna could have one of the deluxe suites, as it's her first time at a spa. What do you think?'

Margot blinks quickly as her demotion registers. 'Of course,' she says, gritting her teeth so hard they might give off sparks.

'Well then,' Liv continues, 'why don't we settle in, freshen up, then reconvene in the relaxation room in say an hour?' We all agree.

Before I'm even inside my suite, I think I can hear the door of Margot's minibar opening. I WhatsApp photos to Drew, but he doesn't reply. I suppose that shouldn't surprise me, as he already made it clear he didn't want me coming here.

'It's not your world,' he argued. 'You're a tourist.'

Only now do I accept his point.

As I slip out of my jeans, I rub my hand over the raised scar on my left thigh. I'm gentle at first, but gradually, I place pressure upon it until eventually I'm kneading it roughly like a fistful of dough, trying to bring my pain receptors to life. Then, once I do, I stop as quickly as I began and take a breath. *No*, I tell myself, *not today*. After slipping on my shorts and a white towelling dressing gown, I make sure to tighten the cord around me so it won't fall open.

Margot is already in the relaxation room when I arrive. It's comfortably warm in here and soothing piano music plays quietly. She's sipping from a pink metal flask. I doubt it contains water.

'Got to stay hydrated, haven't we?' she says with a wink.

'No Liv?' I ask, taking one of two sunbeds Margot has reserved for us with towels.

'Not yet. She's probably having a top-up.'

'Of what?'

She mimes a needle jabbing her forehead and the pushing of a plunger.

'I don't see Liv being a fan of Botox. She's all about healthy living and a healthy lifestyle.'

Margot rolls her eyes. *If they go far enough back*, I think, *they might just find a human version of herself.*

'A few sun salutations, a downward dog and a flaxseed smoothie don't give you a forehead as smooth as a baby's arse.'

'Well, that's her business. It's nice of her to have invited us.'

Margot moves closer to me. I can smell alcohol on her breath.

'Don't you think it's a bit odd that she asked you? She has all those rich, stuck-up *Made in Chelsea* friends she could be hanging out with and instead she asks me and a neighbour she barely knows to join her. No offence, but this is hardly your scene, is it? You'd have been just as happy with an inflatable garden hot tub and a clay face mask?'

'She knows you about as well as she knows me, but you still got an invitation,' I point out, a little heatedly.

'I think she's trying to impress me. She knows you'll be easy to reel in, but she forgets places like this were ten a penny when I was in the band. They were an absolute must after a gruelling tour. You've no idea how stressful it can be.'

'Try telling that to a single parent working for minimum wage.'

'Well I'm hardly likely to know any of them, am I?' she asks. 'My point is, Liv wants us to think she's better than us.'

'Why do you always have to try and find a negative to focus on?' I ask. 'I understand there's been a lot of awful, awful things thrown at you over the years, and I get why it might make you suspicious of people when they try and offer you something nice. But not everyone has a hidden agenda.'

Margot rises from her bed and drops her flask back into her bag.

'You don't have the first clue what it's like to be me,' she snaps, then leaves the room.

CHAPTER 15

LIV

I was supposed to relax this weekend before the madness of the final phase of work begins on the wellness studio. But instead of starting my Sunday morning with a run around the acres of beautiful grounds surrounding this spa, I'm in my room, firefighting. Jamal, the studio's project manager, has called to report a problem with the underfloor heating. He's struggling to find a workaround. And if he can't, it's going to cost me a small fortune to replace.

It's not even 10 a.m. and I've already rubbed topical menthol into my temples and swallowed two herbal belladonna tablets to thwart this creeping headache.

I find Anna in the spa area, lying on a sunbed next to the pool. Her knees are pointed upwards and the book *Big Little Lies* is perched upon them. I've yet to see her make use of the pool, sauna or steam rooms.

'Where's Margot?' I ask as I scan our immediate vicinity.

'Having a treatment,' she says.

'Another one?'

'Yes, to add to her pedicure, manicure, eyebrow tint, deep-tissue back massage, Indian head massage and full-body seaweed wrap.'

'Is there any part of her that hasn't been touched?'

'Aside from her heart?' Anna replies, quite quickly. 'I'm joking.' We both know she isn't.

'I wondered if she might have left early to take care of her family.'

'Our Margot isn't quite the Florence Nightingale type, is she?'

'More like Nurse Ratched,' I quip and Anna laughs.

As we are on our own, I take the opportunity to ask her a question. 'I'm curious as to how you two became such good friends,' I begin. 'You have very different personalities.'

'Margot rubs a lot of people up the wrong way,' she replies. 'It's a defence mechanism. Attack before you're attacked.'

'But you're no threat to her and I've heard some of the things she says to you.'

'Me?' she asks, as if this is news to her.

I tread carefully. 'She can be . . . quite blunt. With you. Sometimes. Don't you think?'

'That's just her way.'

'But it can feel . . . unwarranted.'

She shrugs. 'I haven't noticed.'

'I'd just hate to think you were taking to heart any of the things she says. About, well, you know, your weight, or your appearance.'

'I'm a tough cookie. I can handle myself.'

'Okay,' I reply, and sense a slight shift in the atmosphere between us. Now I'm worried I've said too much. Maybe Anna has spent so much time around Margot that it really is water off a duck's back. Or perhaps she has Stockholm syndrome, where a hostage forms a bond with their kidnapper.

Brandon asked me why I spend so much time with Margot. At the time, I couldn't answer, but now I think it's because I know how to handle the Margots of this world. I know how they think and what motivates them because I once surrounded myself with people like her. On the flip side, I'm at a loss as to how to handle someone as kind and selfless as Anna. She reminds me so much of my sister Amelia, someone I so badly wanted to protect but couldn't – a failure that will forever both haunt and mobilise me.

The alarm on Anna's phone chimes.

She beams. 'Facial time!'

Her robe falls open as she swivels her legs to climb off the sunbed and I spot scarring on her left thigh. It looks like a burn mark, the size of a large hand, and going by its paleness, it doesn't look recent. Below are diagonal scars, a dozen or so, and they're wide. Some are faint, almost white lines, and others red or purplish, suggesting they're more recent. And one has scabbed over. They're too organised and too symmetrical to have been accidental.

Anna realises what's happened and her face reddens as she ties her robe up tightly and looks at me to judge my reaction. I pretend I haven't seen anything, but I'm fooling no one.

CHAPTER 16

MARGOT

I stand naked in front of the bathroom mirror, looking at the phone in my hand. Every inch of my body has been peeled, pummelled, plucked, massaged, manipulated, and coated with something luxurious. I've been scraped, waxed, primed, tanned and glossed, and up until now I've felt there are parts of me that look bloody amazing. I've convinced myself that when I get home, Nicu won't be able to keep his hands off me.

Only the selfie I sent to him a few minutes ago has gone unacknowledged. I can see it's been read, but he hasn't responded with so much as a thumbs-up emoji.

I give him a little longer, but still, nothing. And then I start finding fault with myself. I grab the kangaroo pouch around the centre of my belly, push up my breasts and pull my cheeks towards my ears. Perhaps the ugliness I know that lies inside me has started to seep out beyond the surface for all to see.

'Fuck you, Nicu,' I spit at the phone and throw it on to the bed.

I slip on my clothes, top up my water bottle with the Belvedere vodka miniatures from the minibar, and take the Molton Brown body scrub, shampoo and hair treatments from the complimentary basket in the bathroom. Then I join the others waiting for me at reception.

Liv looks much like she did on her arrival, but a little spit and polish has done Anna the world of good. Her beauty therapist must also be a magician because her normally dull, dry skin is shimmering. That must have been like sanding Artex from a ceiling. She's scowling at her phone, and I assume she's been arguing with Drew again. What she sees in a man with permanently scuffed shoes and frayed laces is beyond me. I'd never let Nicu out of the house looking like that. And don't get me started on the godawful tattoo of a lion on the back of his hand. You're not Justin Bieber, Drew.

'Look at you!' Liv says to me. 'You're positively glowing.'

Glowing? Isn't that what you tell a pregnant woman? Is she telling me I look fat again? I suck in my stomach before I'm reminded of Anna's words yesterday. She's right. Not everyone has a hidden agenda. And I suppose Liv has been generous by spending her vouchers on us.

'Okay girls,' Liv continues, 'are we ready to check out?'

We approach the reception desk and a young man loads our suitcases on to a trolley and takes Liv's car keys. One of the clones working behind the desk moves her skeletal fingers across the screen of a tablet until she finds what she's looking for.

'And the total to pay is £2,270,' she says in a clipped tone.

Liv removes her phone and finds an email with a barcode attached to it.

'I have a voucher,' she says. 'A leaving gift from work.'

She must have been popular to have been gifted an amount that covers this bill.

'It should pay for myself and Anna,' she adds.

Huh? What did she just say?

73

'And how will you be paying, Mrs Rosetti?' the receptionist asks me.

I freeze. What? This was a freebie, wasn't it? Liv's treat? And then I recall the conversation we had in which Liv invited us to join her. To my regret, I can replay it with some confidence. When she said she had vouchers, it was true; she didn't specify she'd be using them to pay for us all. She only said it to Anna.

Everyone is looking at me. There are so many mirrors in this bloody place it makes the glare of this attention even worse.

'Your total comes to £969,' the receptionist informs me.

I pull out my purse, choose a credit card and hand it over. The machine rejects it.

'Can I split it between cards?' I ask, trying not to look at the others while I'm dying inside.

'Of course,' the receptionist replies.

Three credit cards later and we are at last back in Liv's car, and all the knots and stresses the masseuse pummelled out of me have returned, ten-fold.

CHAPTER 17

ANNA

I can smell it in the house the moment I open the back door. A scented citrus aerosol clinging to the curtains and carpets. Drew is trying to disguise something. Alcohol. He's been drinking again.

I turn, lift the recycling bin lid and peer inside. There are no cans or bottles in here, which is evidence in itself. If he had nothing to hide and he wasn't binge-drinking, it'd contain at least a couple of empty lager cans. So he's hidden his empties elsewhere. Last time, I found them in the boot of the car we share, under the false floor next to the tyre jack. The time before that, they were in the box that attaches to the back of the lawnmower and catches the grass.

He's wearing his delivery driver's uniform when he appears: green jacket, white shirt and black trousers. He's been employed by a haulage firm for the best part of a year and I hate to think of the number of hours he must have exceeded the drink-drive limit while behind the wheel. Each time I confront him, he promises that he's never driven while drunk. I've yet to believe him.

'Oh hi,' he says, faking surprise. 'How was the spa?'

'Good,' I say. 'Really good. How are you?'

'I was upstairs putting the washing away,' he adds, holding up the blue wash basket he's carrying.

His eyes are ever so slightly glazed and he's trying hard to focus on mine without allowing them to wander.

'What was it this time?' I ask without emotion.

'Huh?'

'Lager? That's what you normally turn to when things get bad.'

'I don't know what you're talking about.'

'Your breath smells of mints, so I assume you've been sucking the life out of a packet of Polos.'

'I've just cleaned my teeth.'

'At half past four in the afternoon?'

'I didn't get around to doing it earlier.'

'You're struggling to maintain eye contact with me.'

He closes his eyes, then opens them and forces himself to hold my gaze. 'I had a couple of drinks last night,' he concedes. 'There's nothing wrong with that.'

'Where are your empties?'

'In the recycling bin.'

'I looked. They're not.'

He folds his arms and fixes me with a cold gaze.

'You're checking up on me?'

'Don't turn this around on me, Drew. You shouldn't be drinking at all. I let it go at Liv's party but I shouldn't have.'

'Don't start,' he says, and puts the basket away under the worktop in the utility room. I follow him.

'I'm not starting,' I say, when in reality, that's exactly what I'm doing. 'We need to find you help again.'

He shakes his head. 'I'm not going back into that place.'

'I'm not saying you have to. But maybe you could try an AA meeting? They hold them twice a week at a church in town.'

Drew removes his asthma inhaler from his pocket, and I wait until he takes two puffs.

'I can go weeks without a drink,' he argues.

'And when you start again, you make up for lost time by binge-ing. You have an unhealthy relationship with alcohol.'

A darkness descends upon him. I can see it in his eyes. I don't like the version of him that's about to rear its head.

'I'll tell you what, Anna,' he sneers. 'I'll get help for my "unhealthy relationship with alcohol" when you get help to stop your own unhealthy relationships.'

My face heats up.

'I haven't done that in a long time,' I say.

'Really?'

He edges closer to me and I swallow hard. I worry that one day, his verbal aggression will manifest itself as something physical. But I can't abandon him. I love him. I open my mouth to protest again but he beats me to it.

'The bedsheets don't lie,' he says.

Then he opens a cupboard and thrusts a bin bag at me. It's transparent and I see the stains on the bedding and the other objects I threw away.

'Not nice being spied on, is it? I told you I wasn't going to drink again and you told me you weren't going to do that again. Yet this is where we find ourselves.'

He grabs the car keys from a cabinet and slams the back door so hard behind him, the glass vibrates.

I make my way into the lounge and sink into the sofa. I thought I'd been careful. Is he going to tell Liv or Margot? I'd hate for Liv to think any less of me. She might not want to be my friend anymore.

And it only takes worrying about it to make me want to spiral again.

CHAPTER 18

MARGOT

I hold my breath as the front door opens, delaying the inevitable sight and stench that awaits. If the kids and Nicu have spent the weekend vomiting, then the house will need either fumigating or burning down and rebuilding. But as I step inside, it's not as bad as I thought.

My suitcase has barely touched the floor when Nicu appears. Over his shoulder I spot his parents in my lounge, glaring at me with their piggy little eyes. He must have rallied the stormtroopers to assist while he and the kids were under the weather.

'How the hell did you spend so much money in two days?' he demands to know.

I thought I might have a grace period before Nicu noticed I've drained our account. And by then, I might've found a way to pay it back without him noticing. But I forgot he's set up push notifications that flash up on his phone every time a payment has been made. Bloody technology shafts me again.

'It was a misunderstanding,' I say. 'I didn't realise I was going to have to pay for my stay or my treatments.'

'You said the weekend was Liv's treat.'

I lower my voice. 'Can we not do this here?'

I lead him upstairs, leaving him to pick up my suitcase and his parents to imagine our conversation. I bet they've been egging him on because I'll never match up to his ex. Even if she was a mad, vindictive bitch. I thank my lucky stars they stay at a hotel each time they travel to the UK. I don't want to put up with them, let alone put them up.

I try to explain to him the misunderstanding over the vouchers but he can't understand why I didn't ask to split the bill three ways.

I let out a half-laugh, half-snort. 'And have her think I can't pay my way? Have you met me, Nicu? I'm not a charity case.'

'But you *are* someone who can't pay your own way, because you don't work.'

'And whose fault is that?'

'*Iar începem,*' he mutters. He always reverts to his native tongue when he's angry.

'In English,' I say.

'I've moved on and rebuilt my career, and you need to do the same.'

I unzip my suitcase and begin removing my clothes. He shakes his head at the half a dozen moisturisers and oils I also purchased.

'It's easy for you because you're a man,' I huff. 'The public has forgiven you. They don't forgive women. Especially *other* women. There's no work for me out there.'

'*Rahat.*'

I recognise that one, it means 'bullshit'.

'We share a manager, remember?' he says. 'Geri tells me each time she comes to you with a job offer, you turn it down.'

'And does she tell you why I turn them down? Because they're beneath me. Margot Rosetti is better than the shitty little reality programmes Geri keeps trying to talk me into. I am not going to jerk off a pig on a farm to entertain the public. I'm not going to be locked in a coach with a group of TikTok tossers for a holiday from hell in Hungary. Haven't I been humiliated enough for you?'

'You are only as good as your last job, and you don't have a last job.'

I throw my make-up bag on to the bed. 'So you're saying I'm good for nothing? Is that it?'

Nicu knows he's stepped too far over the line and backtracks. 'That's not what I meant. I'm saying you need to go back to work.'

'I find it difficult, you know that. You heard my therapist when she diagnosed me with PTSD.'

'She wasn't a therapist; she was someone you talked to on X.'

'She had a PhD in psychology.'

'Which you only have her word for. And if you do have PTSD, what have you done to try and overcome it? Nothing. You use it as an excuse to sit around doing nothing all day but spending my money.'

'*Once!* I got to pamper myself *once* in Christ knows how long, and now you're punishing me for it.'

'You can pamper yourself every day of the week as far as I care, as long as you're paying for it. Enough is enough, Margot.'

He is too bloody stupid to realise I haven't only done this for myself. I hoped my refresh might make him notice me again. I'm sick of being his blind spot.

'You're not spending another penny until you get a job,' he adds. 'I'm the primary name on our bank accounts. I can have all your credit cards cancelled with one phone call unless you sort yourself out.'

As he leaves the room, I hurl the first thing at him that comes to hand, a bottle of nail polish remover. It hits the door and the bottle bursts, spraying a sharp-smelling liquid across the wallpaper and carpet.

If he thinks I'm cleaning that up, he has another think coming.

CHAPTER 19

LIV

Brandon and the kids are in the snug when I return home. They're huddled under decorative sofa throws and ensconced in a *Hey Duggee* and *Bluey* marathon on BBC iPlayer.

'Mummy!' shouts Rupert, the first to spot me.

He scrambles towards me, hugging my thighs. Ingrid follows and I pretend to fall on to the sofa. God I love these kids. Even Cat Face sidles up to me, burying her face in my neck.

'How are we all?' I ask as they throw themselves back on the sofa and in front of the television.

'We missed you, Mummy,' says Ingrid. 'We're having pizza for tea.'

'Are we now?' I say, raising a playful eyebrow in my husband's direction.

He replies with a 'sorry, not sorry' smile, and I'm reminded of the rule we have that when we're flying solo, anything goes to get through it unscathed.

I lean across the sofa to kiss him. I'll never tire of his lips.

'There's some kale in the steamer to put on your half,' he says.

He knows me too well.

'Well, this house looks a lot better than I thought it might,' I say as I look around me. There's the usual detritus of semi-complete Lego sculptures and half-coloured-in pictures.

'How was the spa?'

'Sooooo relaxing.'

'And Margot and Anna? Have you found yourself a new coven yet?'

My smartwatch vibrates. It's another message from Jamal. I need to read it but I don't want to. Not yet.

'I did something that perhaps I shouldn't,' I begin. 'I didn't use all my vouchers, so Margot had to pay her own way.'

'Why?'

'Nicu and the kids had some sickness bug and she left them to fend for themselves while she came to the spa. She hung up on him every time he called. She was so dismissive of it, it really pissed me off.'

He chuckles. 'And how did she react to footing her own bill?'

'She tried to style it out, but it's hard when you're spreading payments across several credit cards.'

'Sounds like she deserved it.'

My phone vibrates again. 'Look, I'm sorry, but I need to make a few calls.'

'It's Sunday afternoon,' he protests. 'Can't it wait?'

'It won't take long.' I lean over to kiss him again. 'I'll be down by the time the pizza arrives.'

I read Jamal's messages on the way to the office upstairs. He's also left me two voicemails about the underfloor studio heating. It's the worst-case scenario. And now I need to find an extra £20,000. I clench my fists and hold back from screaming at the top of my voice.

I haven't wanted to admit it, but I have totally overstretched us. I've always been in charge of our finances and I thought we could have it all – the home I dreamed of as a child and a job I love. But I've tried to run before I can walk and now I'm in a mess. I shuffle figures from one column to the next in the hope I can make the numbers work. I'm sure Alan Turing took less time to crack the Enigma Code.

Eventually I step away to find a bottle of eyedrops and a packet of herbal headache tablets in the medicine cabinet. But as I emerge from the office, the kids scamper from different directions like a family of excited meerkats, having relayed the message to one another that Mummy has left her office and is fair game. They tug at my sweatshirt and want me to play with jigsaws and dinosaurs. Guilt tears chunks from me with each 'I can't', 'I'm sorry' and 'not at the moment darling'. Nothing spears your heart deeper than the disappointed face of your child.

Then comes a knock at the front door. I answer it to a harassed-looking Anna.

'Sorry to bother you,' she says, 'but have you or Brandon taken in a box for me? It should've been delivered while we were away?'

'No, sorry, we haven't. What's in it?'

'Gemstones. None of the other neighbours have seen it, and as far as the couriers are concerned, it's no longer in transit so it must've been delivered. If it's been stolen from the garage because Drew forgot to close the door again, I'll kill him.'

She leaves soon after and I return to my office. There's only so long I can keep moving money around like a circus juggler spinning plates. Every person under this roof is counting on me to succeed.

I take a deep breath, scroll through my phone and search for a mobile number. The last thing I want to do is go back to *him*, cap in hand, begging for more money. He'll have no choice but to say yes, even though he despises me. And I understand why.

Because if I were him, I'd hate being blackmailed too.

CHAPTER 20

ZAIN, THE SECOND

I don't have any actual memories of the night I was killed that belong to me alone. Only from accessing those of my murderer do I know I was stabbed to death in my shop and left for dead. My murder remains unsolved, the police believing it to have been a botched robbery.

There are things I've wanted to explain to my host since I've been here. About how much I changed since the fateful night that brought us together the first time all those years ago. And all the positive things I did with my life afterwards. But such is the nature of my presence, I am unable to say anything they don't already know. There are bits they pieced together about me after my death, like how I was married and father to a fifteen-month-old daughter. And it was only later, when reflecting on our meeting in the shop, that they closed their eyes and remembered the gold wedding band I wore on my finger, and the photograph of the baby attached to my keyring. Their conscious mind might have conveniently chosen to ignore them at the time, but the subconscious forgets nothing.

Deep down in parts I can't reach, I hope it's understood that I haven't always been a bad person. I don't reckon anyone is born evil. Everyone makes a thousand different choices each day, so it stands to reason some might be poor ones. Did I deserve to die for mine? No, I don't think I did. But someone clearly thought differently.

There was someone else here inside this new home of mine when I arrived all those months ago. We didn't get a chance to meet, but I felt her presence brush past me as I entered. And soon, I will be like my ghostly predecessor, brushing past my replacement, who presently lies in front of us, unconscious and sprawled across the sofa in her lounge. She is sick again and close to death. And I cannot wait for it to happen.

We're sitting in a chair opposite Jenny, listening to the cackles and splutters coming from her throat. She is a familiar face to us both, but for different reasons. And we both want the same thing from her – for her to die. Because the moment I get my wish will be the moment I am set free.

Jenny's final moments are very different to mine. My passing was instantaneous but hers has been drawn out. More care has been taken with it.

Jenny's name, along with mine and two others', was included on the list unearthed in a house when its occupants were packing up their belongings to emigrate. Only there was no current address for Jenny and, despite searching, no social media profile either. But a contact made through work at the Driver and Vehicle Licensing Agency offered Jenny's most recent location, alongside a married surname. Then, bingo! An Instagram profile was found under that name. Like me, she'd only recently returned to the UK after spending years working abroad, but as a holiday rep. No doubt she'd also been running as far as she could from her past.

Jenny liked to post throwback photographs of her carefree days, a much younger version of herself on boating excursions or bar crawls with captions suggesting that while such hedonism was fun, it was also long behind her. They were peppered with inspirational quotes about second chances, along with several references to the Serenity Prayer, often used as a comfort to those now free of addictions. I felt the anger swelling inside my host, learning Jenny was getting her life back together while her victims remained hamstrung by theirs.

She now works for herself as an event planner. At least she did until this morning. A bogus appointment was made to meet at her house to discuss a marketing opportunity for a fake company. Once invited inside, she returned from the kitchen with two cups of tea, only to find a bottle of vodka sitting on her coffee table.

I watched through the eyes of my host as Jenny panicked upon learning who her guest really was. Her face paled as she tried, with a tremulous voice, to end the confrontation. Instead, she was given a choice: she would either watch helplessly as social media was flooded with the truth about her wayward years, or she would drink a bottle of vodka – every drop, there and then.

Desperate to cling to her hard-earned sobriety, she tried to retaliate, suggesting there was no proof as to what she was being accused of. But it was quickly explained to her why it didn't matter, that cancel culture always sides with the accuser above the defendant. Then a question was posed to her: What would upset her new husband more – that she had fallen off the wagon so soon into their marriage, or that she was being publicly accused of murder?

She glared at the bottle, then at her aggressor. And she poured her first half-pint glass.

Jenny's initial sips were tentative, cautious, but the next were confident. It was like reuniting two old friends. She cried as she drank the second glass and said she thought she might vomit with the third. The substantial quantity of ketamine that had been poured into the bottle earlier that day knocked her out before she had a chance to pour the fourth.

An hour later, as she lay sprawled, unconscious, upon her back on her sofa, the first of the convulsions began.

And this is where we find ourselves now, in Jenny's lounge, watching her slowly die. Any vomit that hasn't spilled from her mouth like *lava over the rim of a volcano remains trapped in her mouth and throat. As we await her suffocation, third-party fingerprints are wiped from her glass, and the vodka bottle is also cleaned and swilled out with water to rid it of any traces of ketamine. Her mobile is held to her face until it unlocks, and potentially incriminating telephone numbers and online calendar appointments are deleted.*

Then finally it happens.

Without warning, I'm traveling backwards as if I'm on a moving conveyor belt, watching through someone else's eyes as the world grows smaller and smaller until I'm completely alone. It's then that I hear Jenny's voice and I know for certain I've all but left my host behind, because Jenny is dead.

Inside our murderer, though, she is only just coming to life.

MARCH

EIGHT MONTHS BEFORE BONFIRE NIGHT

CHAPTER 21

MARGOT

I've been guilt-tripped into this. A five-kilometre walk in aid of one of an endless number of breast cancer charities. It's not that I don't believe in the cause; I'm not entirely uncaring. It's that I'd rather donate than actually have to beg for money like a *Big Issue* vendor.

'Wouldn't it be fun if we did the walk together?' Liv asked Anna and me a few weeks earlier after announcing her participation.

No, it would be pretty much anything else aside from fun, I wanted to reply. And when I told her I'd check my diary and get back to her, I meant it. I'd get back to her with an excuse, then sponsor her £50 and think no more about it until she virtue-signalled her way across Instagram after the event. Then her water-works flew like a lawn sprinkler as she explained how she was doing it in memory of a dead sister. And who can say no to a dead sister? Well, me, had it just been her and me in the room. But Anna was there too and she's as malleable as Play-Doh. So of course she said yes, which meant muggins here got roped in.

What's irritated me the most about this whole debacle is that Liv failed to mention it was a midnight walk. Bloody midnight!

In March! Who goes for a walk at midnight in March aside from badgers and sex offenders?

It's just before 11 p.m. when I leave our en-suite bathroom clad in a shapeless pink sweatshirt that I swear Liv deliberately ordered for me in a larger size (she claims it was a slip of the finger), with the name of a dead woman I'll never meet emblazoned across the back. But the pièce de résistance is a headband with a light attached to the front.

'Don't,' I warn Nicu when he clocks me in my full regalia. He's under the bedcovers, smirking. 'Just don't.'

My headband suddenly starts flashing like a strobe light.

'Worst. Rave. Ever,' he says.

I laugh, despite myself. It's not often we amuse each other these days. There was a moment last week in which I thought he might be offering me an olive branch. He asked if I wanted to watch him rehearse at a studio in Milton Keynes, and after a little false protestation, I agreed. It was the first time I'd seen him dance for a long, long time.

Seven years after our last dance together on that awful, awful night, producers asked him if he'd consider returning for a new series of *Strictly Come Dancing* after one of the regulars broke his ankle in rehearsals. The chance to redeem himself in the eyes of the public was worth more to him than the offered wage, so he agreed. The one and only time I asked to come along and support him, they'd saved me a seat right at the very back of the studio. I monitored the cameras shooting the audience's reaction and they didn't once focus on my area. I haven't asked to make a return visit.

As I watched Nicu glide across the dancefloor, I couldn't help but be reminded of how there is something undeniably attractive about watching a handsome, masculine man move with ease and grace. His body floated and swooped as if he was a part of the song, not accompanying it. Almost as if neither would exist without the other.

'Come on, your turn, Margot!' his dance partner Katrina urged, and beckoned me to join my husband.

We hadn't danced together since our last night on the show, not even at our wedding reception. So we began by looking at each other through the eyes of two nervous teenagers at a school prom, before he took charge. He entwined his fingers through mine, slipped his arm around my waist as 'We Found Love' by Rihanna and Calvin Harris blasted from the speakers. I remember when that song was released, and thinking that lyrics had never been more fitting for us as a couple. We had found love in a hopeless place. Then we danced as if we'd never stopped. And as the song came to an end, our moment passed. I left him in the studio, returned to my car and cried. It had been a brief snapshot of who we used to be and who I'm terrified we'll never be again.

'God knows what time I'll be home,' I say now.

Nicu moves towards me as if to kiss me goodbye. But no, he's reaching for the remote control from the top of a chest of drawers.

I make my way across the landing. Tommy is sound asleep – he's always been a boy who loves his bed – while a glimmer of light shines under Frankie's door. I knock, wait, then open it. She's typing into her phone and scowls at me. I expect we'll end the day as we began, in conflict.

'You know the rules,' I begin. 'No phones after nine p.m.'

'I'm talking,' she replies, returning her attention to the gadget.

'To who?'

'You don't know them.'

'That doesn't answer my question – to who?'

'Dana.'

'Who is Dana? A boy or a girl?'

'They're neither. Like me.'

I shake my head. 'I'm not starting this again.'

'I'm not starting anything. You asked and I answered.'

'And how do you know this Dana, because I've never heard of *them*.'

'Through Liv. She's friends with their parents.'

Why is Liv giving my daughter's number to people I don't know, and without my say-so?

'We were talking about how I identify and how you don't support me, and she told me about someone she knew who'd recently come out as non-binary,' Frankie continues. 'She thought it might be useful for me to chat with someone who understands.'

'What? When did this happen? What else did you tell her about me?'

'And there we are,' Frankie sighs, as if she's been awaiting this moment. 'Once again, you turn this around so it becomes about you and how you feel. Not about what I'm going through. I talked, Liv listened. Which is much more than you do.'

I am fuming. What the hell gives Liv the right to talk to my daughter about how she identifies, or about me? And to put her in touch with a stranger without discussing it with me first? I've spent enough of my adult life being criticised, dissected, opinionised and judged by strangers and keyboard warriors without it happening on my own doorstep.

'Turn your phone off and go to sleep,' I snap, and wait until she does as she's told before I shut the door with more force than necessary.

And I'm still angry by the time I reach Anna and Liv at the park.

CHAPTER 22

LIV

There must be at least three hundred women here, all of different ages, races, appearances and backgrounds. And we're all bound together by the C word.

I'm feeling quite emotional as I look among us and think of my sister Amelia and how, in a different life, she'd have been standing shoulder to shoulder with us. I miss her.

She was both my inspiration and my biggest fear. She inspired me to get out of Sandlehope because I was terrified I might end up like her. She was trapped in a coercive relationship with an older man she'd dated since her teens. She wasn't allowed her own phone or social life and rarely saw our family. And her opinion of herself was too low to allow her to escape, despite my frequent encouragement.

Amelia did nothing about a lump she found in her left breast, scared she might add an extra layer of complication to her and her husband's already complex relationship. Thirteen months later and she was gone, dead at thirty-five. I look up to the dark sky above us and the one star I can see. 'This is for you, Amelia,' I whisper.

Anna is already here and limbering up, stretching her arms and hamstrings. I recognise a lot of my sister in her. The people she spends the most time with don't bring positivity to her life. Margot takes cheap pot shots at her as and when she can, and I don't think her marriage to Drew is a happy one. All of which makes me want to protect her. Maybe I can succeed with Anna where I failed with Amelia.

Margot's oversized sleeves flap like windsocks as she strides towards us. She must hate me for ordering something so large. But I couldn't help myself. Sometimes we all need a gentle reminder not to take ourselves too seriously. She makes her way through the crowd to join us.

She's about to say something when a voice through a megaphone expresses the organisers' gratitude to everyone for taking part. Then a klaxon sounds and with our head torches illuminated, we begin the first of three laps around Abington Park. When I turn to Margot, my torch's white light blinds her as if I'm preparing for an interrogation.

'What were you going to say before the walk started?' I ask Margot.

She clears her throat. 'I hear you've had a conversation with my daughter.'

'Frankie,' I say, without misgendering them. I have a feeling I know what's coming next, so I wrongfoot her with praise. 'They're a credit to you and Nicu. A really perceptive, self-aware kid who knows their own mind. I bet they've got that from you.'

'Thank you,' she says. 'I'd like to know what she's . . . what *they've* told you.'

'About what specifically?'

'About them. About our relationship.'

I could tell her the truth. How I pulled the car over in the pouring rain to give Frankie a lift home because their mum had forgotten to pick them up and wasn't answering her phone. How they described Margot as an 'ignorant bitch who never listens' and who doesn't care about them, or how Frankie was in tears for much of our conversation. I could tell her that if Frankie didn't care about Margot, they wouldn't be carrying such strong emotions. And I could add how I hugged them and told them it will be alright in the end because often these things are. How the majority of parents aren't like Margot and are supportive of their kids' decisions. About how young people's brains aren't fully formed yet so they can't yet see the big picture and how they just need to hang in there, because change will come.

However, I decide against it. People like Margot don't respond well to being told what they need to do, even from an objective standpoint. Instead, they retaliate, fighting fire with fire, then complaining when the flames are too high to extinguish. So I take a different approach.

'Well, Frankie told me what self-identification means to them,' I continue. 'And they admitted how, at first, you grappled to understand where they were coming from and how, eventually, they're sure you'll see things their way. And then I put them in touch with Dana, the child of two of my friends, Sylvia and Ian Carmichael. You might've seen Sylvia on TV – she's one of the judges on that *Super Chef* show?'

Margot's eyes widen. The fact it's the child of a celebrity on prime-time television makes a difference.

'She owns that restaurant in the Cotswolds that has a two-year waiting list,' she says.

'Yes, that's her. They've been through the same thing with Dana. And Sylvia says I can pass her number to you if you ever want to talk. I hope you don't think I've overstepped the mark?'

'Um, no, not at all,' Margot says.

'And you know that you can talk to me if ever you want to vent,' I add. 'Parenthood is about rolling with the punches, just hoping you get it right, isn't it?'

'Yes, it is,' she replies.

But I think she'd rather roll away from, than with, the punches.

CHAPTER 23

MARGOT

'It's here again,' I say aloud, banging on the window. Its head turns, but it doesn't stop what it's doing now. I swear to God it's smiling at me.

'Nicu!' I shout.

'What?' he replies as he leaves the en-suite bathroom. He's only wearing a pair of black Calvin Klein fitted briefs and he's drying his wet hair with a towel. Something inside me stirs.

'I said it's here again, taking another shit in our garden.'

'What is?'

'Liv's cat.'

'That's what they do, isn't it? Never on their own doorstep.'

'Why here though? Do you think she's trained it just to come over here, just to wind me up?'

'Yes,' he sighs, 'because Liv has nothing better to do and cats are renowned for how easy they are to get to do as they're told.'

'Well, the next time I go to her house, maybe I'll take a crap in its litter box. See how that thing likes it. And why isn't it doing what it's designed for and catching mice? God knows there's enough of them around here after that warm winter. I heard something scurrying about again in the loft last night.'

'I put poisoned bait up there and again in the garage, so I doubt you'll be hearing that for much longer.'

Finally, after kicking soil with its back legs from the borders and on to the lawn, Cat Face saunters away and out of view.

'I should complain about it to the parish council,' I say.

'You have too much time on your hands.'

'I can think of a way to fill my time,' I say and grab his waistband, pulling him towards me.

'Margot, my parents are downstairs.'

'So what?' I wink.

I slip my hand down the back of his Calvins, cupping a buttock before sliding it around to the front. He must have only just shaved his balls because they feel like two eggs wrapped in cling film.

'There was a time I wouldn't have to ask twice,' I remind him.

'There was a time when you could read the room.'

I remove my hand and the waistband slaps against his skin.

'Fine,' I say sulkily, and quietly ponder the legalities of spiking your husband's tea with Viagra.

Nicu's right, I have too much time on my hands. Everyone's lives feel as if they're moving on while I'm so static, I'm not even treading water. The further I'm left behind, the more embittered I become. And I can't snap myself out of it. Not even double-dosing my antidepressants is helping.

My mood isn't helped by how I'm feeling about my appearance right now. The spa break was a quick fix that improved the exterior. But it's under the bonnet where the real work is required. I need to shift a few pounds – and as exercise is supposed to release happy chemicals in your brain, I press the button to open the garage door and make my way inside to find my old Peloton exercise bike.

Maybe being yelled at through headphones by a pissant instructor half my age can inspire me.

I turn on the light and pass the package that Anna was moaning to me about last night. I've had it for two days, since the delivery driver left it on the wrong doorstep. I've kept hold of it because I'm sick to death of hearing about how Instagram fashionistas who weren't on her radar until five minutes ago are now her best friends. Come back when you're on Anna Wintour's speed dial and maybe then you'll impress me. I might drop it off to her later, or make her wait another day or so.

By the time I've plugged in the bike, a notice pops up on the screen telling me I need to update the software, which will take an hour. Balls to that. You had your chance, Peloton.

Just as the door begins rolling down, I hear a noise. A meowing. I squint at the back of the garage, and perched on a box is Liv's bloody cat. It must have followed me in here.

'Time for a valuable life lesson, Cat Face,' I tell it, and I allow the door to keep rolling until it's completely closed. Let's see if a few hours locked in there makes it rethink its attitude.

There's another brown padded envelope waiting for me when I pass the front door, and a cold chill rushes through me. I tear it open, and this time my anonymous stalker has chosen to send me a Party Hard Posse magazine printed in the band's early days. I hold my breath as I flick through it. A black marker pen has been used to scribble over every one of my photographs. It's tame compared to other 'gifts'. They must be running out of ideas. I stuff it back in the envelope and will put it in the cupboard with the rest later.

I need a drink to settle myself and spend a few minutes in the kitchen failing to locate the remains of the last bottle of red wine. Where the hell is it? Honestly, I'm starting to think I'm going mad at the stuff I'm losing lately. My Kindle, Waitrose loyalty card and

Dior sunglasses have all vanished in this Bermuda Triangle of a house.

There's laughter coming from the garden, so I make my way into the lounge and peer through the patio doors. Nicu is on the other side with his parents. Like Covid, they just keep returning and infecting my world. Frankie and Tommy are with them as they make the most of the surprisingly warm March morning. The whole group laughs again, and loudly, at a joke I'm not party to. Or perhaps I am the joke. It's moments like this when I'm reminded I'm only ever going to be a spectator in this family.

To hell with them, I think. I'd rather be a shot of tequila than everyone's cup of tea. So I leave them to it. Instead, I return to the kitchen, slip a second SIM card into my phone, and cheer myself up by replying to messages from people who do want to pay me the attention I deserve.

CHAPTER 24

LIV

Everyone in my house is still asleep when I leave. I reach the studio just as the 6 a.m. news headlines begin on the radio. My London-based contractors should be here soon, and I like to be here before they arrive to discuss progress. Brandon tells me I'm micromanaging, but he's oblivious to the truth that if I don't control every single aspect of this renovation, there will be no studio. Even with the extra loan I've secured, we are *this* close to running out of money. If there are no hiccups, the opening date I've set is for the first week of June. My family is counting on me to get this right.

I sit cross-legged on the floor of what will be the larger of the two studios and torture myself about how I've financed the studio to date. It's like a hangnail I can't stop myself from pulling. I gave up my video work as soon as I discovered I was pregnant with Ingrid and Rupert. Little did we know that, soon after, a recession would hit the country – and Brandon and me – like a slap to the face.

Escalating mortgage and interest rates meant we struggled soon after the kids were born. My full pay was about to reduce to statutory maternity leave within weeks if I didn't return to work. And many of Brandon's now cash-strapped personal-training clients viewed him as an expendable luxury and cancelled him. He was making much less money than me, but he had an idea of how he might make more.

'Join OnlyFans,' he said. 'Start taking requests and make more films, only this time, step it up and involve me.'

'You mean humiliate you on camera? Very funny, you almost had me for a minute.'

'Why not?' he pressed.

'Oh, you're being serious, aren't you?'

'Yes. What's stopping us?'

'A hundred different reasons! Like you're my partner not my client, like I don't want to humiliate you, and because we have two young children.'

'And they're the reason we should seriously consider it. Desperate times call for desperate measures. And what about the future? Your dream to one day leave London, retrain as a yogi and start your own wellness centre?'

'Yes, but that's a dream, not a reality.'

'But it doesn't have to be. We can change that. Look, you take the lead on most of what we do in the bedroom anyway, so it won't be that much different being told what to do in front of the lens.'

He was right, I'd taken on a more dominant role, which was another reason why I knew Brandon and I were so well matched, because we'd clicked instantly in the bedroom. Occasionally he'd ask me to tie his wrists to the headboard, pull his hair or maybe give him a light slap around the face or bum. We'd also use my sex toys just as frequently on him as we would me. But we were hardly in *Fifty Shades* territory, and I was unsure if I wanted to share our intimacy with the world.

'There's a big difference between telling a stranger he's a worthless piece of shit and hurling abuse at the father of my children,' I insisted. 'You've seen some of the weird and explicit requests I used to get. How far would you be willing to go?'

'I'll represent your subscribers in videos, within reason,' he replied. 'Have them send you suggestions. That's why most men watch porn, isn't it? They get off by pretending it's them on-screen with a beautiful woman.'

The following weekend, and with the twins staying the night with Brandon's sister, we made our first video together, both of our identities hidden behind masks. We drew the line at having full sex on camera. That was going to be kept strictly between ourselves. And each time I felt guilty for what we were doing, I'd remind myself it was for the greater good. For our family's future.

Within a fortnight, subscriber numbers were double those I'd had on my previous website. And so were our earnings. Soon after, following taxes and fees, we were making enough to pay for our mortgage and childcare and were able to save some too. We kept our content fresh by using different locations, and of course we told no one about our extra money-making venture. But opening my own wellness centre was always at the forefront of my mind. So in what little spare time I had, I began a part-time twelve-month yogi course. Two hundred hours of hard work later, I earned my Level 4 Diploma in teaching yoga.

Meanwhile, on returning to the bank, I was soon promoted to a personal assistant role. The money doubled, I became more involved with the bank, I supported the chief executive officers, I was recognised by clients and was a key face at industry events. Sometimes at functions I'd catch myself chatting to a random billionaire financier and wondering what he might think if he knew how else I earned a living.

But when I crunched the figures, I realised there was still a huge shortfall in what we needed to make our dreams a reality.

Brandon was right. Desperate times did call for desperate measures. And I was going to stop at nothing to get what I wanted.

CHAPTER 25

MARGOT

Oh fuck! The bloody cat! I forgot all about it. I wake up with a start at just past 9 a.m. realising that thing has been locked in the garage for the best part of three days. I was going to let it out after a few hours, but I'm easily distracted sometimes and it slipped my mind.

I'm still in my pyjamas when I hurry downstairs from the bedroom and slip into the garage through the side door.

'Cat Face?' I whisper in the most pleasantly apologetic voice I can muster, while realising how stupid I must sound. 'Are you there? I'm really sorry.' I turn on the lights, expecting her to be feral by now, either hissing or rushing past me at breakneck speed, desperate to escape. But neither happens.

'Cat Face?' I repeat, a little louder.

Again, there's nothing.

Ours is a large double garage, but most of the space is taken up with boxes of crap and gardening detritus. It's then I see it, a small pile of vomit on the floor by the Peloton. I cup my hand over my mouth and nose and take a closer look. There's a chunk of something blue in it. It's the poisoned bait we put in here and up in the attic for the mice. Cat Face must have eaten it. So where the hell is she now? I look everywhere but there's no trace of her. I do, however, find her blue collar and tag on a shelf.

I can only assume Nicu must have found her and disposed of her body. It was him who scattered the bait about, so he must've thought he'd killed her, felt guilty about it and decided to keep it to himself.

In any event: RIP Cat Face. The kids will be devastated.

On the other hand, perhaps I'm not the only one to keep secrets from my partner.

APRIL

*SEVEN MONTHS BEFORE BONFIRE
NIGHT*

CHAPTER 26

MARGOT

Anna has been sitting at my kitchen table for much of the morning, slowly working her way through my biscuit barrel and herbal tea caddies. When she turned up earlier unannounced, she mentioned something about self-assessment, tax returns, deadlines and a broken Wi-Fi router. I said that of course she was welcome to use mine, but the village pub also has Wi-Fi and a wonderful breakfast menu. The hint fell on deaf ears.

So I've been stuck indoors, boiling and refilling the kettle like I'm below-stairs staff at Downton Abbey while Countess Hobnob eats her body weight in biscuits.

I need a break from her incessant tap-tap typing and confectionery guzzling, so I disappear upstairs. Last night I had a FaceTime call with Sylvia, a celebrity TV chef, but if I'm being honest, I was hoping to wangle an invitation to her much-sought-after restaurant in the Cotswolds. But some of what she said did make sense. How is Frankie wanting to identify as neither sex actually going to affect me? When I think about it, I suppose it really doesn't. I relayed the conversation earlier to Anna, who gave me an idea of how Frankie's self-identification could benefit both of us. So I drop my agent Geri a line and ask her to put the wheels in motion.

I have time to kill, so I pick up my iPad, sprawl across the bed and scroll through thumbnail photos of clothes for sale on eBay. I've found a loophole in Nicu's tightening of my purse strings and his refusal to allow me to buy anything new. Outfits from eBay are preloved and therefore not new. So I don't have to curtail my spending habits, merely adapt them.

I try and log into my account, but to my frustration, it won't accept my password. I try different combinations but nothing. Bloody stupid technology! Why is it always against me? In the last week, I've been unable to log on to Instagram and Ocado or my banking and Amazon apps. I swear this house has a poltergeist that only has me in its spectral sights.

The doorbell rings just as I'm about to hurl the device at the wall. I want to tell whoever it is to fuck off by the time I reach the bottom of the staircase, but Anna has already let Liv in. She's carrying two bags with the words 'Recycle Me!' on the side in bold print.

'Hi girls,' she begins.

'This is a lovely surprise,' Anna says. 'Would you like a tea?'

'I'd love one,' she replies. 'It's not been a great day. I told you about Cat Face disappearing last week, didn't I?'

'Yes,' says Anna. 'And I saw the reward posters up on lamp posts around the village.'

We all did. Those eyesores are hard to miss.

'We found the kids sitting by the cat flap in the middle of the night. They'd got it into their heads she was coming back. Then this morning they overheard Brandon and I talking about it being likely she'd died somewhere. Now they're besides themselves. We've had to keep them off pre-school today as they're so upset.'

Oh crap, I think. I'm taken back to my own childhood, when an urban fox caught my pet rabbit in its garden pen and I found it torn to shreds one morning. I was inconsolable. Then I picture Rupert and Ingrid's tearful faces as they await the return of a cat who isn't coming home. My conscience isn't even pricked, it's been hit with a sledgehammer. What have I done?

Suddenly Liv thrusts a bag into my chest and I recoil, thinking for a split second that Cat Face might be inside it. 'Anyway, I have something for you.'

Inside are two carefully wrapped items. I open each of them. They contain two LK Bennett skirts and a pair of Miu Miu heels I won in an eBay auction.

'I have got the right order, haven't I?' Liv asks, suddenly concerned. 'They're what you bought?'

'It was your auction?' I ask, jolted by the realisation she was the seller.

'I sell a lot of my old unwanted stuff there,' she explains. 'Every time I have a clear-out, I put what I no longer want online. It's just a waste if you don't, isn't it? Anyway, the skirts were my maternity wear that I won't be needing again. My womb is shutting up shop.'

I'm too mortified to respond. I have bought second-hand maternity wear and I'm not even pregnant. Could this morning get any worse?

'Anyway, I was packaging the orders and noticed it was you who'd won, so I thought I'd save the Royal Mail some carbon footprints and bring them over myself.'

I want the ground to open and swallow me. Has it really come to this? Am I really buying second-hand clothes from the neighbours? What's next? Buying from a catalogue? Putting money aside each week towards a Christmas hamper? Urgh.

'They're not for me,' I'm quick to point out. 'They're for a charity I support that provides emergency shelter for the victims of domestic abuse.'

It's not a complete lie. When I was in the band, we donated some of the sales of one of our singles to support a charity like that. Don't ask me which one though.

'These women often have to leave their homes with only the clothes on their backs,' I continue, 'so it's nice to be able to give them something to make them feel special.'

Liv's face beams. 'That sounds like just the sort of cause I'd love to support. I donate the proceeds of my auctions to different charities and that would be a perfect fit. What's it called?'

Shit.

'What's it called?' I repeat, stalling for time.

'Yes. What's the name of the charity?'

Think, Margot, think. I pluck a name out of thin air.

'The Battered Women's Victim Charity.'

I know it sounds awful even as it's falling clumsily from my mouth.

'I've not heard of that one,' Liv says, puzzled. She begins googling it on her phone. 'Hmm, I can't seem to find it . . .'

'I think they're rebranding,' I reply. 'So they've probably taken their website down for now. I'll find out from my contact.'

'Oh, I don't want to put you to any trouble. Just AirDrop me the number of who I need to speak to.'

She stands with her phone in her hand, waiting.

'I would, but my battery is dead.'

'Later then,' she replies. 'I'll keep an eye open for it.'

I shove her clothes back in the shopping bag where I can't see them. I cannot possibly wear them now. I'd take them to a charity shop, but it's too much effort to drive into town and find a parking space. I'll have to bin them instead.

'Do you mind if I take the bags back with me?' Liv asks. 'I try and reuse them for as long as possible.'

'Of course you do.'

And for a moment I wonder how long I'd need to keep one over her head before she suffocates.

CHAPTER 27

LIV

Of course Margot isn't going to donate to charity the clothes she won from me. Clothes that she could pass off as brand new and that just so happen to be in her size? She ordered them for herself. And there's nothing wrong with that. I buy plenty of second-hand stuff. But once she started making up a charity I wanted to see how far she'd go with her lie. No shelter for domestic abuse survivors has referred to those it houses as victims or battered wives for about fifty years. While her charity might not exist, plenty of others like it do, so I make a mental note to find a local one and donate next month's eBay sales to it.

I suspect that Anna was also aware of the hole Margot was digging for herself, but I note she didn't step in to help her out of it. I assume she was as amused as I was.

'I wasn't sure if you'd be in,' I say, changing the subject. 'I thought you might be doing interviews and promotion for the tour.'

Her face is blank.

'Your old group, the Party Hard Posse, going back on the road,' I prompt. 'You kept that quiet. They were talking about it earlier on *This Morning*. Your fans are very excited, apparently.'

'Oh my God, is that true?' asks Anna. Her eyes are about as wide as they can get.

When Margot's expression remains vacant, it dawns on me she doesn't know the first thing about it.

'Why didn't you say something?' Anna asks Margot. And then she starts typing something into her laptop and I assume she's trying to find out more details.

'"Noughties pop stars the Party Hard Posse have confirmed they are reuniting for a European tour,"' she reads aloud. '"The band has announced tickets will go on sale for the thirty-five-date tour which will be preceded by their first new album together in eighteen years. Singer Gabby Morgan said: 'We can't wait to perform our new material along with our greatest hits in front of fans.' However, it's believed that original member Margot Ward, now Margot Rosetti, won't be rejoining the band . . ."'

I might have my opinions about Margot, but I don't like being deliberately cruel in circumstances that don't warrant it.

'Why?' asks Anna, crestfallen.

'It's in the past,' she says, thinking on her feet. 'And I prefer to move forward than backwards.'

'But you said before that if it ever happened, you'd consider it. That it might be fun?'

'I changed my mind.'

'So when did they approach you?'

Margot turns her back on us as she rinses out a teapot under the tap. 'A while back. I forget.'

I think I'm the only one to notice her shoulders tense. I jump in.

'I don't blame you,' I say. 'I wouldn't want to uproot my life and chase fame second time around. Who'd want to be away from their family and in a different city every night of the week?'

She turns, and although it only lasts for a fleeting moment, I recognise a longing in her, a desire for something more than she already has. It's a feeling I've known all too well in myself.

CHAPTER 28

ANNA

I reach my driveway and am searching my jacket pockets when I realise I've left my keys on Margot's kitchen table.

I turn, ready to knock on her door, when I notice I didn't close it properly. I push it open and am about to call her name when I overhear her upstairs, talking to someone. I think the other person is on her phone's loudspeaker. I can't stop myself from quietly eavesdropping.

'I don't understand,' Margot snaps. 'What do you mean they reached out to me and I turned them down?'

'Their lawyer claims Billy contacted you directly by email and asked if you were interested in returning to the band,' a woman's voice replies. 'You told them absolutely not and never to contact you again.'

'That's a lie!' Margot protests. 'I've not spoken to any of them in fifteen years.'

'That's not what they say.'

'When was this supposed to have happened?'

'Soon after Christmas.'

'No, I'm absolutely sure of it. It didn't happen. And how can they market this tour as "featuring the original line-up" when I'm not in it?'

'Small print,' the woman replies. 'Original line-up means they aren't replacing you with anyone else.'

'Can we take legal action? Stop them using the band's name? They can't be allowed to do it without me. You wouldn't expect the Rolling Stones to perform without Mick Jagger, would you?'

'The remaining six own the trademark to the Party Hard Posse's name, so I'm afraid they can.'

'They own it? As of when?'

'They put in a joint application late last year.'

'Behind my back. The conniving bastards.' There's a pause, and I think Margot might have hung up.

'Are you sure it's not too late for me to rejoin?' she continues suddenly, now more than a trace of desperation in her tone. 'Just think how well ticket sales will do when they announce I'm returning after all.'

'Hun, I'm sorry, but as of an hour ago, the whole tour sold out, along with an extra eleven dates.'

This draws a puffing sound from Margot, as though she's just been punched in the stomach. 'Just call them, Geri,' she says, her voice cracking. 'You're Geri Garland. You created Star People. You made Lightning Strikes the biggest band in the world. People don't want to piss you off. They do what you tell them.'

'That's sweet of you to say, Margot, but I just spoke to their new manager before you called,' she says. 'They're adamant there's no room for you now it's all been announced.'

'But they could make room, couldn't they? Please, call them again. Please. I . . . I . . . I need this.'

'Look Margot,' Geri says, her tone softening, 'reading between the lines, I don't think they really wanted you anyway. They still blame you for what happened at Glastonbury, then for the band splitting up. I was told off the record that it will be, and I quote, "a less toxic environment without her".'

'Toxic?' she repeats, aghast. 'I *carried* those talentless idiots for years.'

'You also have to remember there's still a lot of negative energy attached to your name after what happened to Nicu's ex.'

'That fucking woman made my energy negative!' shouts Margot. 'Before her it was positively positive! She's been rotting in the ground for ten years, so how is she still able to twist the knife? I've lost my career and now I'm raising her fucking kids. What more does she want from me?'

The caller tries placating her and I think the conversation is concluding. I pad softly into the kitchen, grab my keys, turn, and have just reached the front door when Margot speaks again.

'I know where the bodies are buried,' she says. 'If they don't let me back in, then perhaps I'll start digging.'

'Margot,' says Geri slowly. 'You really need to think about this. I've stepped over the line many a time myself, it's par for the course in my job. But it could reflect badly on you if anything negative ever came out and was traced back to you.'

'I have nothing to lose. I'm already toxic, remember?'

When I hear her making her way downstairs, I slip outside and shut the door behind me.

CHAPTER 29

MARGOT

Girls, we have just had the weirdest morning EVER, Liv WhatsApps Anna and me.

I don't have to guess, I know. But I'll have to play along. I let Anna answer first.

What? she messages.

Cat Face is back! Liv replies, and uses several cat emojis to emphasise the point. I know what a cat looks like, thank you.

How amazing, I reply. *Where has she been?*

We have no idea, Liv messages. *But she was wandering around the garden this morning as if she'd never been away, original collar and tag still round her neck.*

I bet the kids are excited, Anna responds.

They won't leave her alone. Although there's something a bit different about her. When she left, she had a small scar above her lip where she once had a scrap with another cat. And now it's not there.

I let out a huff. How was I supposed to know that? Although Cat Face's death was more the result of negligence than malice, I felt bad for the children's loss. Guilt is a funny old thing. Much of the time, it doesn't trouble me, but when it comes to visit, I have an overwhelming urge to repair what I've broken. Finding an identical ragdoll breed the same sex, size, colour and shape as Cat Face proved almost impossible, but I kept referring to images of it posted by Liv on her Instagram page. I spent days searching just about every cat rehoming site I could find online, until I found someone trying to get rid of theirs in Sheffield. After a four-hour round trip and £700 lighter, I brought Cat Face version 2.0 home with me, hid it from my family in the garage – minus the mice bait – and set my alarm for 5 a.m. to let it free in Liv's garden. But I didn't know I needed one with a damn scar.

But that's not all because this is where things get really strange . . . Liv continues.

The dot-dot-dots feel ominous. A minute passes before a photo arrives. It's of her kids with two identical ragdoll cats.

Look who walked through the cat flap an hour ago! Liv messages.

What the actual fuck?

??? writes Anna.

She has no collar but she does have the scar above her lip.

I sit back in my chair. It's only the original bloody Cat Face. I didn't kill her after all. I went to all that trouble, felt all that guilt, for nothing. The damn thing has been staying at some bloody Airbnb or something.

What are you going to do with it? I reply.

Looks like we're a family of six now! writes Liv, and adds a thumbs-up emoji.

I look at the original Cat Face and know just where I'd like to stick that thumb.

CHAPTER 30

JENNY, THE THIRD

I'm not the one who should be dead. And I fucking hate my murderer for it. I detest each and every single molecule that makes up their presence in the world they've taken me from, and I remind them of this fact every single day.

When I first found myself imprisoned here, my captor kept me effectively gagged and paid me not the slightest mind. Out of sight, out of mind. Helpless passenger that I was, all I could do was watch, listen and feel their staggering progress through the days following my killing. At least I had that: a savage price was being paid for the act of ending my life. My murderer vowed their killing days were over. It took too much out of them to kill. For weeks after my death, I watched them stumbling through life, exhausted and barely able to function. Because we were now one, I felt each ache of their body, their fitful sleeps and muddled thoughts, until eventually, they began to heal.

But each time I tried to speak up, my words were batted away like the swatting of mosquitos. However, in time, I realised all I had to do was wait. Because I was never going to remain at the back of someone's mind for long. Especially after what they did. And what they took from me.

The power balance between us shifted during the inquest into my death. I begged my captor not to attend, because as their reluctant hostage, it meant I would be forced to go too. I didn't need to hear any more details than what we both already knew. But my appeals fell on deaf ears. What neither of us expected to hear was that, at the time of my murder, I had been ten weeks pregnant. If I'd known, I'd have used it to barter my way out of being plied with vodka. And, from my husband's tearful reaction at the inquest, he hadn't been aware I was carrying our child, either.

With no evidence to suggest my death was deliberate, the coroner ruled it an accidental overdose. I hate that everyone now believes I died a lapsed addict.

In the corridor on our way out, the two of us watched my husband hug my mum tightly and overheard him ask her if there had been a chance my death was suicide. Had I perhaps known I was pregnant, and couldn't handle the responsibility of juggling motherhood with recovery? She said no. But I'll be forever haunted that he'll always have that niggling doubt.

The revelation of my pregnancy pricked what little remained of the conscience I now find myself sharing. And with my murderer's (OUR murderer's!) defences down, I found myself being listened to. Here was someone to help slake this new thirst for self-punishment, a tireless tor- turer only too happy to bring down the lash! I'd remind them in ever more baroque terms of the depth of my hatred, and catalogue all that they already feared about themselves – that they were worthless and how they would never accomplish anything because they were nothing.

And the longer I've remained inside them, the louder I've become until, now, they just can't handle it anymore. The only way to be free of me is to kill again, despite the toll it will take on them. So they have turned to the next name on their list: Warren.

Shortly before I died that afternoon, I was asked about him.

'Was he the one who pulled the trigger?' came the question. 'I heard a man's voice shouting before the first shot. And I learned later that he was the only one of you who had a criminal record for violence.'

My answer was garbled. By then, the alcohol and ketamine had taken a firm hold.

Perhaps Warren will give a better answer later tonight. Because he's in the car that we're following.

The excitement we are both feeling inside this vehicle is palpable. I feel inside my captor a terrific surge of power when they're in control. They are no longer that helpless kid hiding under the bed as their parents died in the next room. First their mum and then their dad. Two bullets fired, four lives destroyed.

But even though this night has been planned, there are still many elements of chance and luck involved.

Warren is expecting to meet a woman who, for months, was writing to him while he was behind bars. He has no idea that a catfish with a taste for blood exists, and awaits.

We begin by overtaking him, and then, once our car pulls even with his, we swerve into his path. The crunch of metal as our doors collide takes him by surprise and sends him veering towards the kerb. Our vehicle holds steady while he struggles to regain control of his. When he manages it, we immediately swerve into him again. A small car can make a big impact. This time, he loses control and his car leaves the road, ploughs through hedges and, from what we can see in our rear-view mirror, collides with a tree. Then we calmly pull over into a lay-by.

The odours of rubber tyres, acrid smoke and petrol permeate the night air as we approach him. There are no street lights on this country road, so we must rely on a phone's torch to light our way. Warren's vehicle rests on its side, its engine still running, its headlight beams illuminating the trees.

Warren remains inside the car, conscious. He has come to rest against the passenger door. No seatbelt for him. But rules never applied to Warren.

I can barely make out the features of the man I knew so long ago, through the blood pouring from multiple facial lacerations and head wounds. For a second, I forget myself and where I am now, and wonder if he can see me. It's only as the torchlight is held upon him that I can see the force of the collision has pushed his left eyeball from its socket. It hangs by its optic nerve on his cheek.

His voice is little more than a croak and he extends a tattooed arm towards us. His wrist points at an unnatural angle. He is desperate for help but we offer him nothing.

I sense my, and soon to be Warren's, killer wants to stay here for as long as possible, but the risk is too great. It won't be long before another car passes and clocks what has happened. So they lean in through the broken driver's window and turn off his headlights to buy a little more time.

We stroll around the car until the petrol cap is located, then unscrew it. My killer strips a sleeve from a thin hoodie, rolls it into a tight cylindrical shape, and shoves into the hole. After several attempts, a cigarette lighter ignites the material. We should get the hell away, but can't resist one last look at Warren. I feel pity for what's to come for him, but our murderer certainly doesn't. They hope just enough life remains inside him to know that he's about to burn to death. And then we step away.

We make our way towards the car we arrived in, only turning at the sound of the explosion and accompanying fireball that shoots up into the air. We can feel the intensity of the heat on our back when it reaches us. Our murderer's only regret is being unable to hear Warren screaming for help over the noise of shattering glass and the crackles of burning leather and skin.

I only know for certain that Warren is dead when I sense I have been left behind on this road. As our killer's back is illuminated by the flames' orange light, I feel him emerging inside his new home, one I am sure he will detest with the same intensity as I felt. Finally they are both swallowed by the darkness.

As am I.

MAY

SIX MONTHS BEFORE BONFIRE NIGHT

CHAPTER 31

MARGOT

There must be about a hundred faces in our house this afternoon, and at least a third are Frankie's pals. The rest are their parents, and neighbours I invited to make up the numbers. Every one of Nicu's famous friends that I asked him to invite apparently had prior engagements. How convenient.

I follow the photographer around the lounge, and at my request, he's currently shooting the grey and yellow balloons arched over the patio doors. They were the party planner's idea, not mine, but they complement my decor, and when people tell me how great they look, I accept their praise.

If I'm not mistaken, Frankie looks in danger of enjoying being the centre of attention. She treated me with suspicion when I first suggested celebrating her thirteenth birthday with a party. I told her that she could have a say on who was invited, along with a theme if she wanted it, plus she could pick the cake we'd have made for her. Gradually, she warmed to the idea.

However, I failed to mention that I invited *Yeah!* magazine to cover it until two days ago, and it was too late for her to cancel it. Most guests have signed waivers allowing their images to be used in the magazine. I sent on their merry way those who refused. My party, my rules.

First thing this morning, we were assembled by a team of hair and make-up stylists while the photographer, his assistant and a party planner – a fatberg who's clearly spent at least as much time hoovering up buffets as organising them – scanned the house and set up lighting rigs. I think it confused Frankie when I let her choose her own outfit.

Later, the photographer had us living a life so far removed from our own that I barely recognised us. We were pictured playing croquet in the garden (the magazine's team brought its own set – we don't live in Bridgerton); sitting at the kitchen table eating elaborately decorated pastries (the magazine had them delivered) while Frankie opened presents (the magazine bought and wrapped them).

Everyone has been in such good spirits that I've forgotten this house is so often like a battlefield. Today it doesn't feel like me versus them. We feel like, dare I say it, a family. It stirs up something inside me that I can't place.

When the journalist arrives a little later, she asks my opinion on the reunion of the Party Hard Posse. I don't tell her that I've blocked the band's name from appearing on my Google timeline or that I had no knowledge of being invited to the comeback tour.

'That was a lifetime ago,' I tell her. 'If they're happy reliving the past and surfing the nostalgia wave, then I wish them all the best.'

It wasn't until I discovered their invitation in my deleted emails that I believed it had ever been sent. I don't know for how long I must have stared at it. My reply in the sent box told them in no uncertain terms that I wanted nothing to do with it. It was mailed at 1.30 a.m., which suggests I was so drunk that I didn't know what I was doing. The fact I couldn't – and still can't – recollect something so important frightens the hell out of me. So do the things that keep moving around the house, like books, ornaments, wine bottles, etcetera. I want to blame alcohol, so I've cut down a lot lately. I decided a drop won't pass my lips before the clock passes 11 a.m. Now I think I might have to push it back even further.

Anna is here and so is Drew. I see him so rarely these days that I've begun to wonder if he's electronically tagged and on house arrest. Often, his clothes are ill-fitting, his hair messy. It's as if Anna has drawn him with her left hand. But this afternoon, he's reasonably well presented. In the right hands, with the right grooming regimen, hairstylist and personal trainer, he might pass as human.

I kiss Anna on both cheeks – the second one never fails to catch her unawares – and then Drew. I catch a whiff of his aftershave. It's actually pleasant.

'Drew,' I say, trying to imagine him with a personality. 'Nice to see you.'

'And you,' he replies, and takes a large swig from his bottle of beer.

'And how's the . . .' I hesitate as I try and remember what on earth he does for a living. 'The postal business?'

'Haulage,' he corrects, and starts twisting and turning his silver wedding ring. My attention is drawn to that awful tattoo of a lion on his hand.

'Of course,' I reply. 'Haulage.'

'It's good, thanks.'

And that's the extent of our conversation. We literally have nothing else to say to one another.

I spy Liv in the kitchen, talking to Brandon, and he must know my eyes are upon him because he looks at me directly. I turn away, making myself appear busy with my phone. I realise I have left the wrong SIM card in here and curse myself. I need to be more careful, because in the wrong hands, it could get me into a lot of trouble.

I haven't seen Liv much in the last few weeks, as she's been too busy with her wellness cult headquarters to socialise with us commoners. But she was one of the first names on my invitation list. I want her to know she's not the only one who can throw a lavish party. And I want her to realise I'm a progressive parent who puts her child's welfare before her own. It might not be strictly true, but she doesn't need to know that.

I beckon Nicu over and we make our way towards the party planner, who is pouring champagne into glasses in readiness for the toast. The make-up artist gives our faces a little touch-up with an array of brushes in preparation for my speech.

'This is a really kind thing for you to do,' says Nicu as he gently squeezes my hand.

His affection flusters me before I relax into it. Sometimes I forget how much I miss his touch.

I tap my champagne glass with a spoon to get the room's attention. Frankie and Tommy are standing between Nicu and me, and I fleetingly recall how much I once enjoyed commanding an audience. I clear my throat.

'Thank you all for coming here today to help celebrate Frankie's special day,' I begin. 'I remember how special turning thirteen was and how, soon, I would have the world at my feet when fame came calling.' I look to Frankie. 'And while not all of us are destined for great things, I nevertheless wanted to take this opportunity to say how proud we all are of the person Frankie is becoming. And we also wanted to celebrate the arrival of their teens with a special announcement.'

My family turns to me, their faces the same shape of puzzled, and then to the patio doors opening behind us. The party planner brings with her a large white helium balloon and hands it to Frankie.

'What's this?' she asks as she takes it.

I continue addressing my audience.

'Nicu and I support our children with all decisions they make for themselves. And today we want to take this opportunity to share with you, our closest friends, something important. Not only is this a birthday party, it's also a gender reveal party!'

The room goes quieter than I'd expected. I press on.

'Margot,' says Frankie in a tight voice, her face reddening. 'What are you doing?'

'Our beautiful daughter has decided that she no longer wants to be identified by the sex she was born,' I tell everyone, 'which of course Nicu and I completely respect.'

I catch a quick glimpse of Liv, obviously uncomfortable that I'm the one who has everyone's attention and not her. Then I remove a safety pin from my pocket, unhook it and use it to pop the balloon. Frankie is showered in yellow, white, purple and black confetti.

She's perplexed.

'It's your flag!' I enthuse. 'Yellow is for people who identify outside the gender binary, white is for those who identify as all genders, purple is for male and female genders, and black is for agender. See?'

I smile broadly, but it's only when the camera illuminates Frankie's face that I see light reflected in her tears.

Have I done something wrong?

CHAPTER 32

LIV

Oh. My. God.

What has Margot done? The room goes as quiet as a wake. But Margot is persisting like the band that played as the *Titanic* sank. Champagne flutes are reluctantly raised as she leads a toast to Frankie.

'To our Frankie,' she says, and the guests echo her words, although with more murmurs than celebratory tones.

'Is it me, or has she misjudged this very badly?' Brandon whispers to me.

I grimace. 'Very, very badly.'

I must hand it to Frankie, they are being very brave. They wipe their eyes with the sleeve of their T-shirt, paint on a smile, and allow the photographer to tell them where to stand and how to pose. After ten agonising minutes, it's over. Frankie says nothing to their family and pushes their way through their friends and out of the lounge door, swiftly followed by Nicu, while Tommy locates his pals in the garden.

Nobody quite knows what to do or say as Margot remains alone, posing for the camera as the photographer takes close-ups.

She's still holding the safety pin. I think it must also have burst her own bubble, because she's lost the Cheshire cat grin she's been wearing all day. Now her smile is strained.

I catch conversations others are having. Some guests are unsure what it means to be non-binary and ask their phone's operating system to explain it. Others are debating how they might respond if it was their child. All are united in agreeing on one thing: a gender reveal party is up there with Downing Street's bring-a-bottle party during lockdown and *Game of Thrones*' Red Wedding reception as one of the most ill-advised celebrations of all time.

Margot's attention keeps being drawn to the door as if waiting for her family to return. Only they don't. I don't know why, but I'm overtaken by an urge to step in.

So I take her arm and gently lead her into the kitchen where it's quieter.

'I don't get it,' she says, genuinely bewildered. 'I thought she'd love this.'

The way Margot continues to refer to Frankie as 'she' suggests that, despite today's circus, she still doesn't get it. That this was all more for Margot's benefit than her child's.

I approach her with caution. Injured animals can still bite.

'I think an announcement of this kind was for Frankie to decide, not anyone else,' I say gently. 'You've outed them without their permission.'

'But she's already out!' Margot protests. 'Her friends already know. She even told you, for God's sake.'

I take a deep breath.

'Frankie telling people in their own time is different to you telling the world through the pages of a celebrity magazine,' I counter. 'Look, I know what you've done is with the best of intentions.' I might not actually believe that. 'But now you need to convince them of that.'

Margot looks at me like a dog trying to understand a new command.

'Okay,' she says, and exits the room.

I really hope she can sort this mess out and not make it any worse. But I wouldn't count on it.

CHAPTER 33

MARGOT

Once again, my life is available for public consumption. One of the guests at last week's party – I'll probably never know who – leaked what happened to *The Sun* and even sent them photographs they snapped on their phone. Earlier today, *Good Morning Britain* ran a poll on whether I did the right or the wrong thing. Then *Loose Women* played a leaked recording of my speech.

I've spent all day with my phone glued to my hand, reading social media's takes. Some people believe I did it for my own sake and they'd prefer to see my head on a plate rather than across the pages of *Yeah!* magazine. That edition comes out in a few days, so I expect the argument to continue long into the week.

Others reckon I'm trying to show support to my non-binary stepchild and are claiming me as their poster girl for modern mums and blended families. Then there's the anti-woke mob who think I'm a victim, being forced into supporting something I don't truly understand. So I'm either manipulative, a modernist or a moron.

My family are barely talking to me. While I've apologised to Frankie – even though it went against my better judgement – she and I remain as far apart as me and her dad. I hadn't told Nicu in advance about the gender reveal angle, so it was as much of a surprise to him as it was to anyone. But I really thought he'd be on board. Nothing I've said since has changed his belief that my intentions were entirely self-serving. All I've done is push us further apart.

This afternoon I'm distracting myself with a little online maintenance. Every month, some anonymous idiot who's had it in for me for years alters the facts on my Wikipedia page. Then I have to rewrite all the inaccuracies and blatant lies. This time, they've removed the photo I uploaded of me with Britney Spears, taken when the Party Hard Posse supported her on a British tour. And they've replaced it with one that's been edited to give me a gaunt, dead-eyed appearance, and the hint of a moustache.

They've also put a T-shirt on me with the word 'Killer' written across the chest.

I draw in a deep breath as I stare at it, my stomach churning. Who the hell has it in for me? What have I ever done to them? I delete the photo and replace it with a more flattering image, but I know it won't remain there for long.

I reach the section that refers to the *Strictly Come Dancing* fiasco, claiming I was voted out on the first night. Everyone knows that's a lie, because Nicu and I made it to the finals. We were even the bookmakers' favourites to win. Instead of it being a career highlight, it destroyed me.

My life as a pop star had been in the doldrums for years when my agent put my name forward to the show's producers. Geri received an immediate 'no thank you', as they'd already signed up a former pop puppet for that series. But when she was forced to pull out after developing shingles, they invited me to replace her. I've yet to be more grateful to an infection.

Strictly paired me with a handsome Romanian ballroom dancer called Nicu Rosetti. He was smart and sexy and viewers fell in love with him. And soon after our first meeting, so did I.

I knew he had a girlfriend, Ioana, and two young children. I met her several times, and she recoiled around me like a slug in the presence of a salt cellar. It was also clear that any chemistry they might once have shared had fizzled out like day-old Prosecco. Nicu eventually admitted he was only staying with her for the sake of the kids.

Meanwhile, I'd been dating Jerome Maguire, a male model whose career was on the rise thanks to a lucrative contract with British and French fashion houses. He was sweet, intimidatingly handsome and utterly besotted with me. But he was also fluent in stupidity.

Neither Nicu nor I admitted to our mutual attraction at first. However, it was there, an itch waiting to see who'd scratch it first. Then, a month after the series began, we scratched it together after becoming the first couple to have scored a perfect forty that season. The celebrations began in earnest away from the cameras and in my dressing room.

We hated lying to our respective partners, but until we figured out whether it was a fling or something more serious, we did just that. And we were aware of the repercussions if anyone should find out. In a previous series, soap star Ellis Anders had cheated on his girlfriend Mia with a dancer. They were tabloid headlines for weeks. However, I had more sympathy for his ex years later, when she married into the notorious Hunter family. Next time she's looking for love, if I were her, I'd seriously consider lesbianism.

So, Nicu and I were careful. We never visited each other's flats, only meeting at an apartment owned by a dancer friend of his who was away on an eight-month Japanese tour. One of us would enter by the front door and the other through an alleyway, up a fire exit and into the rear of the property.

We kept our relationship under wraps until a week before the *Strictly* final, when our arsehole of a taxi driver turned his dashboard camera around to record us chewing each other's faces off, then sold the footage to a press agency along with the address of where he'd dropped us off. They used their own photographer to catch us sneaking in and out of the flat.

The tabloids and celebrity magazines that I'd once been so desperate to court turned against me quicker than you can say Amber Heard. And even though Nicu had a fiancée and children, I was the one they branded a 'ballroom bitch', the 'foxtrot floozy', and my personal favourite, the 'mambo mistress'.

We followed the BBC press department's advice and issued a grovelling apology, begging our loved ones and viewers to forgive us for our 'error in judgement'. But no one listened. Jerome dumped me and I don't think there was a single publication Ioana didn't sell her story to. She gained a manager and a career, claiming that prior to the affair I'd befriended her (a lie), I'd betrayed her (there was no friendship to betray, except perhaps the illusory 'girl code'), and that she'd even asked me to be chief bridesmaid at her forthcoming wedding to Nicu (there had been no wedding plans or even an engagement).

She also claimed that Nicu had threatened to force her and their children out of their London apartment so I could move in, and how I'd left her hateful, threatening voicemails. Only that last accusation had some truth in it. I did send a couple of angry voice notes that *Daily Star* readers could attest to when the paper set up a premium phoneline for readers to call and listen to just how hateful I was.

Nicu and I were desperate to pull out of that coming weekend's *Strictly* finale, but contractually, we had to remain. Unsurprisingly we came last in the public vote. Incidentally, that episode remains the most viewed in *Strictly*'s history.

'You should think about marriage,' the damage limitations expert we hired advised. 'Prove this isn't a casual affair.'

So that's what we did. And then, just hours after we said 'I do' at a West London register office in front of the remains of our friends and family – plus staff from *Yeah!* magazine who were covering it – our plan for public rehabilitation came crashing to the ground.

It was during our evening party that Nicu's then-manager informed him Ioana's body had been found by a neighbour fifteen storeys below the balcony of her apartment. Later, some salacious online news providers used a photograph of her impaled on railings, the metal spikes protruding through her chest.

Police had broken down Ioana's front door and found two frightened, screaming children locked in the bedroom. And instead of us leaving our reception to fly to our Sicilian honeymoon, Nicu spent the evening in a hospital mortuary identifying Ioana's body while I sat with his bewildered kids and a social worker in a hospital room, wondering what the hell I'd just taken on. Later that night, we drove back to our flat to start our married life as a four, and not a two.

All these years later, I still remember word for word the suicide note Ioana left on her laptop: 'You did this to me, Nicu. You and that bitch took everything. Now I'm going to take it all from you.'

It was one of the only truths she told. I took her love, her life and her children. But in return, she took my career. And, somewhere deep down in hell where she now resides, I get the feeling she's not in any hurry to let go of it.

JUNE

FIVE MONTHS BEFORE BONFIRE NIGHT

CHAPTER 34

LIV

The caterpillars that for weeks have been circling inside my stomach have been waiting until tonight to hatch from their chrysalises and metamorphose. Only they're not butterflies, they're giant bloody pterodactyls. When they aren't swooping and diving and trying to peck their way out of me, they're roosting on my bladder, because I've just had my third nervous wee in the last half an hour.

Leaving the bathroom, I pace the corridor adjacent to the frameless glass wall of the main studio where my classes will rotate. Ingrid and Rupert are tumbling in and out of the rooms, yelping and screaming as they slide across polished floors in their socks. Next to the bathroom is the studio where I'll teach my hot yoga classes. I bend over to place my hand on the floor. It's satisfyingly warm. Which it should be, given how much I've spent on it. And finally there are the healing rooms. One for sound therapy and meditation and the other for massages.

A little further along the corridor is the crèche, then a gym where Brandon will restart his personal training, part-time. I spot him when I reach the café. He finishes pouring orange juice and wine into stemmed glasses. I clock this entrance area and truly believe even the harshest of critics would struggle to deny we've done a damn good job of building something out of nothing. Plants are growing from gaps in the walls, and between them is a floor-to-ceiling mural of a copper-and-yellow meditating Buddha. I still worry the Buddha screams 'You're trying too hard', but the interior designer was adamant it would turn a dull wall into a focal point. Our tables and chairs in the seating area are made from reclaimed wood, and the counter surface is repurposed plastic. I couldn't be any greener if I was Robin Hood.

'You okay?' Brandon asks as he approaches me, putting an arm around my waist and kissing my cheek.

'I think so,' I reply. 'Are you sure we have enough wine? Do we need to pick up another case from Waitrose? I don't want us to run dry. And the canapés? Where are they? Have they been delivered?'

'We have plenty of wine and I was about to take the canapés out of the packaging.'

'But do they look okay? They don't look like we've just bought them from a cash and carry?'

'No, of course not. Trust me, everything is going to be just fine. We've got this.'

Brandon is right, we have got this. There were times when I wondered if we'd ever get here, and what failure would mean. I know I'll never be able to return to my job in the city. Banking is a big business but a small world. And once you're blacklisted, you'll only ever be a persona non grata. That's why I need so desperately for this to work. Because I can still smell smoke from the bridges I've left burning behind me.

Soon after, the room begins to fill. I think everyone who received an invitation is here, chatting to one another and drinking.

It's just as I'm feeling my confidence slowly beginning to return that it happens. I see *him* at the back of the room. His presence is strong and his glare is piercing. I look to Brandon and then back in his direction, but he's gone. I close my eyes, take a deep breath through my nose, exhale through my mouth and open them again. It's my conscience that's the unwelcome guest, not him.

CHAPTER 35

MARGOT

I'm in no mood to celebrate the realisation of anyone's dream by the time I reach Liv's studio.

The last three days have been awful. Nicu has made me – although he'd claim he 'encouraged' me to – accept a job. I only agreed because I hoped he might see how hard I'm trying to repair our relationship. And as a result, I've been locked inside a television studio in Elstree, with a gaggle of fame-hungry nobodies who now believe they're celebs because a few bored kids have favourited their banal videos on social media.

Each had a virtually identical appearance – the girls with their fake tans, fake lips, fake hair, fake teeth and fake tits, and the boys with their pumped-up pecs, sleeves of tattoos, and bodies so waxed they resembled china dolls from their steroid-plumped necks down. Aside from me, the only person over the age of thirty was an actress I vaguely remember from *Casualty*. But she took an instant dislike to me before we'd even been formally introduced.

The title of the pilot show is *Help! I'm In The House From Hell!* and it is every bit as much of a rip-off of *I'm A Celebrity . . . Get Me Out Of Here* as the title suggests. Inside the studio they built a 'haunted' home, and producers paired us up and locked us in different-themed rooms, with names like Deadly Dungeon and Fright Night. And once inside we were forced to face our fears, find a key and escape. The girl I was paired with spent so much time screeching, I've developed tinnitus.

I deadpanned my way through much of it, so much so that the director had a word with me off-camera and asked if I would play up the drama more.

'If you wanted an actress, you should have hired Dame Helen Mirren,' I told him.

'Our budget was for McDonald's, not The Ivy,' he hit back, and was out of earshot by the time I could muster up a catty retort.

Hopefully word will get back to Geri that I'm worth more than this demeaning crap. I need my tank filled with something more in tune with my skillset, because on shows like this, I'm running on the fumes of my talent. One saving grace is that I doubt the programme will ever see the light of day anyway. Pilot episodes rarely amount to anything. And even if it does air, it won't be on a mainstream channel.

The car park outside Liv's studio is almost full, so I make use of an empty disabled space. I check the rearview mirror and refresh my lipstick. I'm still wearing the make-up they put me in for filming, so at least I look on point. I wish Nicu was with me, but I'm flying solo, no surprises there. His tour begins this month and he's rehearsing seven days a week now, so I barely see him.

Inside, I push my way towards a waitress and help myself to two glasses of white wine, pouring one into the other. Then I head for Drew and Anna. Drew and I avoid eye contact.

'How are you?' Anna asks. 'Good day?'

'Fine, thanks.' I want to say my body is here but my spirit has departed, however that would only provoke more questions. And

I'm unwilling to admit just how far down the showbiz ladder I've fallen.

'I love how contemporary it is,' she continues, looking around and easily impressed. 'Liv's done a great job, hasn't she?'

'Liv or her interior designer?' I ask.

'Did I hear someone mentioning my name?'

Liv has appeared from behind us and I almost don't recognise her out of sportswear. Tonight, she's wearing a sky-blue chiffon long-sleeved midi dress and nude high heels. Her make-up is even better than mine. Must she always be the centre of attention?

'I was just saying what a wonderful eye for design you have,' I say quickly, my eyes bypassing Anna's. 'I love how contemporary it is.'

'Oh, that's so sweet of you.' She looks genuinely flattered as she places her hand on my arm.

'It's . . . neat,' I add and smile to myself.

She takes a big sniff. 'What are you wearing?'

'Coco Mademoiselle. Kind of my signature scent. Expensive, but gorgeous.'

'I'd always assumed it was created for the younger market. I didn't realise it was multi-generational.' She turns to Anna before I can defend myself. 'And what do you think of the place?'

'It's amazing,' Anna fawns.

'Oh, and look.' Liv lifts her necklace in her fingers. The pendant is flame-shaped and in two shades of blue.

'It matches your dress perfectly,' says Anna, beaming.

I'd take the compliment with a pinch of salt from someone whose floral dress reminds me of a well-kept grave.

'I really appreciate you making something bespoke for me,' Liv says. 'Are you sure I can't pay you for it?'

'No, absolutely not,' Anna replies. 'My orders have more than trebled since your friend included them on her Instagram page.'

'Just wait until those bracelets appear in *Grazia*. You'll need to take on an apprentice to keep up with demand. You'll have to train Margot.' She laughs, but I know there's a dig somewhere. 'Do you have any skills we don't know about, Margot?'

'Is cynicism a skill?' says Anna a little too quickly.

'More of a blessing,' I retort. 'Actually, I just started a job myself. A little reality show that studio bosses think might be a hit. They needed a name to get it off the ground, so they begged me to . . .'

But before I can sprinkle unicorn glitter over bullshit, Liv's eye is caught by something over my shoulder and she makes her excuses and leaves.

As she wanders away, I catch Brandon's eye. He's chatting to the mayor – well, if it's not the mayor, then it's a man with questionable taste in gold necklaces. Perhaps he could be Anna's apprentice. Brandon is casually dressed in white Converse trainers, smart blue trousers, a blue tux-style fitted jacket with a white vest underneath. I bet it was Liv's idea to coordinate their outfits. She's made them look like the mid-1990s Beckhams.

I linger on Brandon perhaps a little longer than I should, but he's far more interesting than listening to Anna blathering on about a new line of jewellery designs. You can tell by the way he carries himself that he's a confident man. There's also something quite sexy about a stay-at-home dad. He makes his way over to us, and as he kisses my cheek, I recognise his aftershave immediately – Acqua Di Parma Colonia Essenza. My pulse quickens. Nicu used to wear this scent a lot. He might still do, but he never comes close enough for me to get a whiff of it.

'You must be very proud of your wife,' I say.

'I am. Whatever she puts her mind to, she gets.'

'Does that include you?'

He laughs. 'I suppose so.'

'I don't think I've ever asked her. How did you two meet?'

'A mutual friend's leaving dinner,' he recalls. 'We sat next to each other at a restaurant and began talking.'

'I thought you were going to tell me that you swiped left. Isn't that how most couples meet these days?'

'We're a little old-fashioned, I suppose.'

'Yet you're the one who looks after the kids while your wife's working.'

'I'm in an expanding minority.' Brandon shrugs. 'And I wouldn't have it any other way. It's a gift to watch your kids grow up. But I don't need to tell you that. You're a mum, you know what I mean.'

If mine had been a gift, I'd have asked for the receipt and returned them by now.

'But I'll be sort of returning to work here, once I build up my personal-training portfolio,' he adds.

'Oh really? I had a personal trainer once and was thinking of using one again.'

He looks me up and down. 'I don't think it'd take very long to get you in shape,' he says with a smile. 'You already have the framework.'

Brandon looks me dead in the eye and holds my gaze until I am the first to break away. I feel myself flush. Am I imagining things, or is there a spark between us?

CHAPTER 36

LIV

'I'll see you back at the house,' says Brandon as he kisses me goodbye.

Rupert and Ingrid are exhausted, their eyelids half closed as the excitement of the night catches up with them. I wave them off as they walk down the staircase and back to the car.

The two other yogis I've taken on have agreed to join me for a 5 a.m. start tomorrow, when we'll clean up before the first clients arrive. Within a day of advertising on Facebook, classes were fully subscribed for the next seven days. I can breathe easy for now.

Anna has sent me a video clip of the speeches, which I watch as I walk. Brandon told the room how proud he was of me and I told everyone how I couldn't have done any of it without him.

It's then that my new world comes crashing down around me.

'I must say I'm a little disappointed I didn't get a mention in the thank-yous.'

I gasp and retreat two steps when I see him. Harrison is sitting in my office behind the desk, scrolling through his phone. My conscience wasn't playing tricks on me earlier. He was here. He is still here. His head is completely shaved allowing the lighting above to bounce off it. His brow is furrowed, making his dark eyes unreadable. His thin lips hide a tongue as sharp as a razor blade. He is as wide in size as he is in presence. Then I realise he isn't alone. On the sofa in the corner of the room is a dark, bearded man, twenty-something by my guess, whose muscular frame is visible even under his leather jacket. The word 'hate' is tattooed on both sets of knuckles. Neither man is looking at me.

'Quite the little business you've carved out for yourself here, isn't it?' Harrison asks, patting out a crease in his dark pinstriped jacket. 'Found a gap in the market and you've filled it.'

'What . . . what are you doing here?' I stutter.

'I've come to see exactly how you're spending my investment. My invitation to the party must have got lost in the post.'

'I want you to leave.'

The look he gives me is familiar. Disdain.

'Don't worry, Olivia, we won't outstay our welcome.'

He pushes back his chair and stands up, pulling his white shirt cuffs out from beneath his jacket sleeves.

'For what it's worth, I think you've done a wonderful job with the place,' he continues as he approaches me. I take several more steps back until I'm in the centre of the corridor. 'I can see where my money has been spent, and likewise in your beautiful home.'

He nods to the other man, who removes a phone from his pocket, dials a number and thrusts the screen in my direction. He has FaceTimed someone. The footage is dimly lit and it takes a moment for me to realise what I'm seeing. I recognise a painting on the wall. It's in my lounge.

The person he has called is in my house, right now.

'How long will it take your husband and children to get home?' Harrison asks me. 'Fifteen, perhaps twenty minutes?'

My throat is too dry to answer.

'It's been a long night for them all, so I imagine it won't take them long to fall asleep. And probably a deep one. Children can sleep through anything, can't they? Sometimes they won't so much as stir, no matter who is in their room.'

My hand trembles as I try to swipe the phone from him. He pulls it away and squares up to me. I back down.

'What do you want?' I ask him.

'Our relationship has reached its end, Olivia.' He slips his phone back into his pocket. 'My visit, and that of my associate, signifies the end of an arrangement you forced upon me. Do you understand? And count yourself lucky I am giving you this warning at all. Because if I ever hear from or see you again, I promise you that my associate and *his* associates will be only too happy to visit you. When they do, you will not have a family to return home to. And I am nothing if not a man of my word.'

His accomplice shoves me, hard, against the wall. I lose my balance and fall to the floor. I can barely breathe as I watch them leave.

CHAPTER 37

WARREN, THE FOURTH

I wish I could say I'd turned my life around before I was run off the road and left to burn to death in my car. But if I did, I'd be lying. Because I'm the same worthless piece of shit in death as I was in life.

At least, that's the version of me my killer chooses to believe.

I'd spent seven years behind bars. And while it might not have been for killing their parents – it was for a drugs bust, actually – it was still a sentence. But it wasn't enough for them. Only an eye for an eye would do.

A year before I could apply for parole, the first letter arrived, via some do-gooder charity where strangers with sod all better to do with their time write to blokes like me. Some days I was locked in that cell for twenty-three hours straight, so I wrote back to break the monotony.

The other lads told me about birds like her. Can't find a man in the real world, so in desperation, they start looking elsewhere. And we're sitting ducks in there, aren't we? It didn't matter to me; she was a distraction.

We had stuff in common, despite our age difference. In her letters, she told me about her office job for some energy company, that she was divorced, that she didn't have any kids but wanted them. I told her

I couldn't remember the last time I'd had a regular bird and that I'd assumed I'd have kids one day, but it never happened. We wrote about the telly programmes and films we liked (me, anything with Jason Statham or Nic Cage, and her, animated Disney rubbish), music (that twat Olly Murs for her, Kasabian for me), and about how neither of us had families anymore (I'd long been disowned by mine, while a drunk driver had wiped out hers).

She was also fascinated by my life behind bars, who I spent time with, who I avoided and why. She wanted to know if it was like the prisons you saw on the telly. She asked me if there were murderers in my wing. Of course there were, I said, this was HMP Manchester, not summer camp. She asked if I ever got scared and I told her yes, sometimes, but explained you can never show fear or you'll get hurt. She admitted that sometimes she worried about me and hoped that I was looking after myself. It was weird to think that, somewhere, someone cared about me. The more often we wrote, the more I looked forward to when the screws called out the mail each day.

Eventually she admitted she was starting to develop feelings for me. I said I thought about her too and it was true. I told her that in the nights when I struggled to sleep, like when one of the other lads in the wing was screaming his way through darkness 'til daybreak, I'd wonder what life might be like with her on the outside. From the photos she sent, she wasn't my type. Not much to look at, skinny and no arse, but beggars couldn't be choosers.

She also got me thinking about how much of my life I'd wasted. I'd heard through the grapevine that Zain and Jenny were dead, and unless I made some changes, I'd probably end up the same way. Could she be my clean slate?

When I asked if we could meet in person when I got out, she said she'd love to. It was the first time she signed an 'x' after her name.

Two days after I was released, we agreed to meet at a country pub. But the first time we clapped eyes on each other, one of mine was hanging out of its socket as I lay crumpled up in the passenger seat of a mate's car I'd borrowed. And I knew I'd been lied to about everything.

When I moved into my killer, I wanted them to understand what it feels like being burned alive. The pain as the smoke chokes you, the unbearable heat on your skin as your clothes catch light. But it turned out they knew this already. They had killed me so that I could understand what they went through, not the other way around.

The next name atop their kill list has been there forever. But as time's passed and I've been in here a while, I've sensed a change of heart. Murder is no longer a prime motivation. It's more fun to toy with their prey than to eat it. And I reckon the person who has borne the brunt of all this rage for so long has actually become a reason to live. Deep down, there's a hidden fear: fear that once the list is empty, it'll take with it any sense of purpose. And all that'll remain will be a black hole of loneliness that's impossible to fill. So, some time ago, I reluctantly came to terms with remaining in here indefinitely.

But tonight, a shift is happening. And in this unguarded moment, inspiration dawns on me.

I'm a third party, listening to an argument inside Ioana's flat. She's a nasty piece of work, so both parties are well matched. Ioana's saying a lot of shitty things and the cloud of red mist has begun to cover our shared vision.

Suddenly there's a flashpoint, a bubbling over of emotions and thoughts firing in all directions. They're leaving themselves vulnerable, out of control. And this is my opportunity to take charge. I don't care that Ioana isn't on a list. She's going to be my way out. Taking my captor's wheel, so to speak, I charge us toward Ioana and shove her so hard that she loses her balance and topples over the balcony and down into the darkness of the night.

The realisation of what's just happened begins to sink in for both my captor and me as we peer down over the balcony and find Ioana impaled on the railings below.

'No!' my killer shouts aloud, before I can force a hand over their mouth.

Then they hurry back into the lounge – and I don't follow. Don't want to, and couldn't even if I did. I remain on the balcony and hear, back in the lounge, Ioana talking once again. This is where my journey ends and hers begins. And I can't think of two people who deserve each more.

And now it's me falling backwards over the balcony and into darkness.

JULY

FOUR MONTHS BEFORE BONFIRE NIGHT

CHAPTER 38

MARGOT

They loved it. It doesn't make sense. But what makes even less sense is that they loved it because they loved *me*.

My excited manager Geri FaceTimed me with the news that the producers of the godawful reality show pilot I was forced to make just three weeks ago, *Help! I'm In The House From Hell!*, had been in touch. It was supposed to be for E4, the digital channel no one over the age of twenty-one watches. Well, because another reality show was scrapped at the last minute on its parent station Channel 4, they needed something fast to fill a gap in the schedule. Bosses saw a rough cut and guess what they chose?

That's not the worst of it. Those bright sparks want me to return as a series regular. Frankie's disastrous gender reveal party has apparently renewed the public's interest in me and they want to capitalise on it. So instead of humiliating and degrading myself in just one episode, they've asked me to do it another five times.

'Not a chance,' I told Geri in no uncertain terms. 'All they want is a pantomime villain to get their show trending on social media. I was cancelled once, and I won't be cancelled again. It's too humiliating.'

'But they're offering you £20,000 an episode,' she countered.

I thought about it for all of two seconds.

'When do we start filming?'

I texted Nicu with the expectation he'd be proud of me, but his response was a simple *Great*. Not even an 'x' after it. *Well to hell with him*, I thought. I've had enough of trying to keep his interest and make him proud of me.

Now here I am, sitting in a trailer, waiting to get my hair and make-up done by a girl who resembles the ghost of Amy Winehouse, complete with battered ballet pumps and bird's nest beehive. God knows what's living inside it. Next to me is one of the stars of *Knightsbridge Knights*, a scripted reality show, a little like *Made in Chelsea* but with a cast with bigger bank balances. Myself and Tonya triple-barrelled-something-or-other are waiting to be called on set and be locked in a pretend house to face our fears.

Of the other 'luminaries' I've met in the last two days of filming, Tonya is by far the best. She likes to gossip, for one thing. I particularly liked one salacious story about her castmate, a private members' club and a lazy Susan.

'I've also heard some stories about her,' I offer. 'Apparently she's a little light-fingered, but no shop ever presses charges because her father always steps in to settle the bills.'

'OMG yes!' Tonya chirps. 'Who told you that?'

'One of my neighbours. She was a Chelsea girl before she moved to Northampton.'

'Do I know her?'

'Liv Barton-Aldridge.'

'Liv! Oh yes, we all know Live Wire Liv.'

I'm unsure how to interpret the wink that accompanies this remark.

'What's she doing these days?' asks Tonya.

'She's opened her own wellness studio. So she must have had a successful banking career to fund that.'

She cocks her head. 'Is that what she told you? She worked *at* a bank, but she wasn't actually *in* banking.'

'Oh really?'

'She was a secretary, maybe even a PA, I can't quite remember. But what I do recall is that it wasn't her day job that paid the bills.'

'So what did?'

I wait as Tanya taps her finger with her chin as if she's wrestling with whether to tell me something. She's play-acting. Of course she's going to tell me.

'Well,' I say afterwards and with a theatrical brow wipe and broad smile, 'I was not expecting that.'

CHAPTER 39

MARGOT

'Fuck!'

I'm cursing aloud to an empty house when the doorbell rings.

'Come in,' I shout, 'the door's unlocked.'

I'm on my hands and knees searching the cupboard under the stairs when Anna appears. She said in a text that she'd call for me before we meet Liv for coffee.

'Morning,' she says as I turn to face her.

Even for Anna, she's looking exceptionally beige today. Her T-shirt has a brown stain on her right breast, her leggings are too small, and that bob went out of style at the same time as UGGs paired with denim miniskirts. Many times I've offered to take her out clothes shopping, even to – God help me – Primark. She can chuck as much as she wants in a basket there and it will never break the £30 barrier. Each time, it has fallen on deaf ears.

'Lost something?' she asks.

'My white Florent lace-ups.'

'Your white what?'

'Trainers, Anna, Florents are trainers. Surely even you have heard of Jimmy Choo?'

She looks at me blankly. I might as well be talking fashion with a bag of rocks.

'I'm sure I left them in a box in here, but I can't find them anywhere.'

I wonder if Frankie has hidden them in retaliation for me tossing her Crocs in the recycling bin all those months ago? Much to my annoyance, she found them before it was emptied.

'Where have you been hiding yourself the last few days?' Anna asks.

'Oh, just a little life admin,' I say.

There's a lot I can't tell her, as I'm not in the mood for a lecture. I also can't mention how many hours I've spent trawling through the website OnlyFans, searching for an account that apparently belongs to Liv.

Tonya, the *Knightsbridge Knights* star I met on the set of *Help!*, revealed an ex-flatmate of Liv's told her Liv has funded her lifestyle and business through money made in the online sex industry. Well, telling me that was like throwing a seal at a shark and expecting the shark to refrain from taking a bite. Of course I was going to search for it. However, with two-million-plus content providers, it's been impossible to find. She might even have taken her page down, now that she thinks she's Gwyneth Paltrow in full lifestyle provocateur mode.

Anna glances at two stacks of brown padded envelopes behind me that I've taken out of the cupboard. She spots one with a box poking out from the top, containing two tiny plastic feet.

'Oh wow,' she says, pulling it out. 'Is this one of the Party Hard Posse dolls?'

'Yes, but that one's been a little modified,' I reply as she removes the rest of it.

'Oh,' she says suddenly. 'Where's the head gone?'

'My stalker has kept it as a souvenir.'

'Your what?'

'My stalker. You know you've really made it when you have an obsessive.' I direct her attention to the rest of the envelopes. I try and play it cool and make out that it doesn't bother me, but of course it does. 'Have a look at the other little treats he's sent me. There's another decapitated one, but most times, I'm allowed to keep my head.'

I give up searching for my elusive footwear and watch her reaction as she reopens random envelopes. Her face creases: they're disturbing her as much as they do me. In one, she finds the remains of a Margot mug, in another there's a T-shirt with red paint covering my face and my eyes have been cut out. A third has a watch with a broken face, and yet another includes a smashed-up signed CD.

'How long have you been getting them?' she asks.

'Eighteen months or so, I think.'

'And what do the police say?'

'I don't bother reporting them anymore. I did when they first started arriving and they took them away and fingerprinted them. But everything had been wiped clean. And the products were so mass-manufactured that there's nothing the police can do. They suggested I keep hold of them, so I store them in here. Like a macabre retrospective of my life.'

'You should post something about this online.'

'And give the creep the attention he's looking for? No. It'd probably encourage a bunch of brand-new fuckwits to come out of the woodwork and join him.'

Anna appears genuinely concerned for me. And if I'm not mistaken, there are tears forming.

'Sorry,' she says. 'I just think after all you've been through, it's unfair.'

I'm uncertain how to respond as she dabs her eyes while watching me. Normally when people stare at me this long, they're making notes. But not her. I'm unused to this depth of connection. Yet I'm more surprised by how much I appreciate it.

A short time later, we're at Liv's house and Brandon ushers us towards the patio chairs. It's a gorgeous day, and I struggle to tear my line of vision away from his sports shorts and black vest. Those thighs could crack billiard balls. Both Liv and I are fortunate to have husbands who look after themselves because their bodies are their careers. No one pays to see a fat dancer in tight clothing prancing around a ballroom and firing sequins through the air like bullets, or a personal trainer stuffed into Lycra like too much pork in a sausage skin.

I'm suddenly aware of Anna's glare. She's caught me staring at Brandon.

'What?' I mouth.

She gives me a withering glance. If only she knew.

Two Cat Faces brush past us. One turns – version 1.0 I think – and I swear it's laughing at me. Surely they've renamed 2.0, but I don't care enough to inquire.

'Sorry to keep you waiting, girls,' Liv begins when she appears.

I hate how she refers to us as 'girls'. We're not in *Sex and the City*. And if we were, she'd be one of the new characters in the reboot that no one gives a toss about.

Now she's staring at her phone and clenching her jaw.

'Everything okay?' asks Anna.

'Problems with the orangery,' she sighs.

She's referring to the extension she and Brandon are building on the back of their house. The way she talks about it, you'd think she was recreating the Palace of Versailles.

'Brandon was in construction before he became a personal trainer, so he's been working on it himself, but now the council's planning officers are telling us we've gone over the agreed boundary by ten centimetres.'

'Is that all?' says Anna.

'I know. But it's enough for someone to have reported us. How in hell could they have known? Anyway, now we either keep on building, return to the planning department and put in a retrospective application with no guarantee of it being approved, and risk having to demolish it. Or Brandon has to dig out what we've already done and start again.'

'Who complained?' Anna asks.

'It was anonymous.'

Liv looks at me for a beat too long. I think she's studying my reaction.

'Some people aren't happy unless they're making other people miserable,' I suggest.

The 'people' I'm referring to is just one person. Me, of course. While Liv and the family were out one afternoon, I snuck into their back garden to measure their *conservatory* before comparing it with the planning application listed on the council's website. It was larger than they'd been granted permission for. If people like Liv are given an inch, they'll take a mile. And then probably build on that as well. Not this time.

'What are you going to do?' asks Anna.

'I think we'll have to take it down,' Liv acquiesces. 'I'm starting to wonder if someone has a vendetta against us, because the studio had six one-star reviews appear on Trustpilot last night. That's brought my average down to two and a half out of five. I checked the names of the reviewers against past bookings, and unless they've changed their identities, I don't think they've been to any of my classes. And they were all posted within half an hour of each other.'

Once more, Liv's gaze lingers on me. *Guilty as charged*, I think. There's one thing she has yet to learn about me, and that is if you poke your nose into my business, then I will retaliate in kind. By offering Frankie advice about her non-binary phase, Liv overstepped the mark. And don't get me started on how she tried to humiliate me in front of Anna with that eBay auction. Or led me to believe that she was treating me and not just Anna to the spa weekend. Since she moved here, she has been gaslighting me so often I'm thinking of carrying a caged canary to detect each whiff of deceit.

'Perhaps Anna and I can leave you five-star reviews?' I suggest. 'And if we get Nicu and Drew to do the same, that should push your average back up, shouldn't it?'

'Yes,' she says, a little thrown by my offer. 'That'd be really kind of you.'

'Anything for a friend,' I reply.

CHAPTER 40

ANNA

'Did someone have fun on their night out?' Liv asks Margot suddenly. Margot looks at me blankly, then back at Liv. 'Last night,' Liv prompts. 'That Turkish restaurant on the Wellingborough Road, I saw you leaving, all dressed up.'

'It wasn't me,' she replies.

'You must have a lookalike then. She was even in the same-style Donna Karan dress you wore to our New Year's Eve party.'

'Nope.' Margot shrugs. Her cheeks are reddening. She pushes her chair back and stands up. 'Little girls' room,' she says, as if she can't get away quickly enough.

This little paroxysm of weirdness doesn't go unnoticed by either Liv or me.

My buzzing phone distracts me. It's so bright out here that I squint to read the screen. It's a text message from Drew to say he's working late again tonight. That's four nights in the last two weeks, but I don't mind. I'm glad he's finally found a job he's taking seriously.

Things have been better between us lately, but that's probably down to us seeing each other less rather than being more emotionally aligned. Our absence from one another's lives has taken away our conversation and therefore a reason to bicker. It's more of an Elastoplast to cover the cracks than a solution. But when I do see him, he appears happier and less angry than he has been, and he's stopped taking out his petty frustrations on me.

I look up from my phone as Margot returns from the bathroom. Her expression isn't the same one she left wearing and the atmosphere has chilled by several degrees. Liv has picked up on it too.

'Everything okay, Margot?' she asks.

'Yes.' A smile arrives a second too late.

'Only you look a little flustered,' Liv adds.

Liv's phone rings before Margot replies. Liv makes her excuses and leaves the garden to answer it.

'What's wrong?' I whisper.

Her eyes follow Liv back inside the house until she is out of sight.

'I found something in the bathroom,' she hisses.

'What?'

'An envelope. A padded envelope. In the bin.'

'What kind of padded envelope?'

She cocks her head to one side and raises her eyebrows, waiting for me to play catch-up. My own eyebrows arch when the penny drops.

'Yes,' she continues, '*that* kind of padded envelope. Same brand, same printed label with my name and address on the front.'

'What was inside? Did you look?'

'It was empty and folded in half.'

'Perhaps she found it outside. Maybe it came out of your recycling bin during the high winds at the weekend and ended up in her garden.'

'I don't throw them away, remember?' she fires back. 'The police told me not to.'

'There has to be an explanation.'

Margot folds her arms and throws herself back into her seat.

'Well, the only one I can think of right now is that I am having coffee in the garden of the psychopath who's stalking me.'

CHAPTER 41

MARGOT

Predictably, glass-half-full Anna is jumping to BFF Liv's defence.

'It's just not in her to . . .' She trails off.

'Stalk someone? Send them hate mail?'

'Well, yes. She's a good person. She has children.'

'And so does Rosemary West, but I don't hear anyone calling her mother of the year.'

'You're being silly. Liv's the furthest thing from a serial killer.'

'Are you not just scared to admit you might be a very poor judge of character?'

'Liv doesn't have a malicious bone in her body. And you said those packages started arriving about eighteen months ago, yes?' I nod. 'And Liv only moved here just before Christmas, didn't she?'

'Which is even more of a concern,' I say. 'Because it means she arrived in this street knowing full well who I was and pretended she didn't.'

'But why?'

'How do I know?' I reply, exasperated. 'I'm not privy to the inner workings of a psychopath's mind! Perhaps our paths once crossed and I pissed her off. Believe me, there are many skeletons in my closet.'

'Such as?'

Caught off guard and in the moment, I almost lose myself and say something I'd regret. I gather myself quickly.

'All that matters is what I found,' I say. 'That bloody envelope.'

'Liv could have had that envelope for any number of reasons. Maybe Brandon found it in the street. It could have been posted by mistake to their house instead of yours. Whatever was inside it could've fallen out in transit. It happens all the time. Look at my order of gemstones. You found the box dumped by the side of the road.'

I can't tell her why that's a poor argument.

'Well let's see how you feel if someone starts smashing your jewellery to pieces and posting it back to you, shall we?' I reply instead. 'And do you really believe she just happened to be driving past me on the Wellingborough Road? There are many different routes she could have chosen.'

'I thought you said that wasn't you?'

Shit.

'The point is, how well do we really know her? Because I've heard things about Liv she's kept quiet from us that might surprise you.'

'Like what?'

'That she didn't really work in banking, but as a PA.'

'So? Most people embellish their CVs.'

'Not all of us have needed to,' I say with a hint of superiority. 'From what I hear, she's airbrushed from hers how she funded her studio by making sex videos.'

'What?' exclaims Anna in a way that again says she doesn't believe me. 'Who told you that?'

'A very reliable source.'

'And have you seen these videos yourself?'

'Well, no, but I'm assured they're out there.'

'I'm sorry, but no.'

Liv makes her way back into the garden and takes a seat with us.

'Sorry about that. Wellness studio stuff. What have I missed?'

'Nothing,' we say together.

When the truth is, everything.

CHAPTER 42

MARGOT

I wait inside my car, twisting my neck and glancing nervously through each of the windows until I'm assured I've not been spotted by anyone familiar. Now that I know Liv uses this road to drive home, I need to be more careful. And that's not the only reason my vigilance detector is on full alert.

I give the road outside my car one last look before I exit and make my way into the Turkish restaurant. It's only just opened for the night and, aside from the staff, I'm alone. I order a vodka and orange from the bar and flick through my phone as I wait. Nicu is currently in Stockport on his tour and the kids are doing their homework at friends' houses.

I check the calendar on my phone and realise filming starts soon for the *Help! I'm In The House From Hell!* series. My jaw tightens at the prospect, but the money will give me more financial independence from my husband.

My company is late. I don't care that it's only by five minutes. I despise tardiness. Unless I'm the one who's running behind. I'd have checked my watch if I'd been able to find the damn thing when I searched for it earlier. I'm misplacing more and more things lately, which I'm reluctant to admit is becoming less of an irritation and more of a worry. I pass the time by using my phone to go online and search for the symptoms of early-onset dementia. I stop reading when I find symptoms I share with victims of that disease. But what if . . . no, it doesn't bear thinking about. I'd rather be dead. I put the device face down on the bar.

Another seven minutes pass and a handful of diners are being shown to their seats by a waitress. One of the customers catches my eye. Large, hooped gold earrings, hand and neck tattoos, stripper stilettos, and a midi dress that's a size too small for someone with the arms of a mariner. Somewhere out there is a street corner waiting patiently for its hooker to return. She has the same gaudy dress sense as Nicu's ex-partner. I whisper the name, '*Ioana.*'

If there has ever been a person put on this earth for me to despise more than Ioana, I have yet to find them. Later this month it'll be the eleventh anniversary of her fifteen-storey plunge from her apartment balcony.

And all these years later, I remain the only person in the world who knows I was there that night.

I'd taken my cue from the movies and waited in the street outside her building until someone else exited the key-coded doors. Then I slipped in unnoticed before they shut, and in my large coat, hair tied up and tucked into a baseball cap with the brim lowered, I made my way into the lobby, sure my face wouldn't be caught by CCTV. The last thing I needed was Ioana selling stills to a newspaper alongside a made-up story of how I turned up at her flat uninvited and threatened her. Because that wasn't what I planned to do. Quite the opposite, in fact.

'What the hell do you want?' she snapped as she opened her door to me.

Her Romanian accent was stronger than Nicu's. His was more melodic, but hers was always sharper, the words exiting her mouth like rapid-fire bullets being spat out from a machine gun.

She flicked ash from the cigarette in her hand on to the bare wood floor. Behind her, the room was thick with smoke, which explained why Nicu changed their kids into fresh clothing every time he picked them up from there.

'I'd like to talk to you,' I replied nervously.

'Haven't you got better things to do, like stealing husbands from their wives?'

'You and Nicu were never married.'

'We were as good as.'

'Look Ioana, I'd rather not do this in the corridor. Can I come in?'

'What for?'

'I want to listen to you.'

Her surprise was evident by her short, sharp snort. Then she turned and made her way inside, leaving the door open for me to follow. I closed it behind me.

The rental apartment she'd once shared with Nicu was in disarray. Empty food wrappers, dirty clothes and children's toys were strewn across the floor or piled on to two sofas. One bedroom door was open, and the other, where I assumed a toddler Frankie and baby Tommy were sleeping, was closed.

Ioana and I were standing opposite one another like boxers eyeing each other up and down at a press conference. Only I wasn't there to fight.

'Whether you like it or not, Nicu and I are getting married tomorrow,' I began calmly. 'And I am genuinely sorry for the hurt it's caused you.'

'Oh please. You are only marrying him for public rehabilitation.'

It wasn't far from the truth. But I was also in love with Nicu.

'We're getting married because I want to spend the rest of my life with him,' I said. 'And that means you and I are going to be in one another's lives for a long time to come. So I need you to tell me what I can do to make things easier for us all to coexist. Doesn't this negative energy exhaust you? Because I know it's draining me.'

'It's fuelling me,' she snorted.

I balled my fists. What had Nicu ever seen in this witch? She must have been an Olympic champion in the bedroom.

'It can't fuel you forever,' I replied. 'Can't we find a compromise?'

'Like what? We share him? I have him weekdays, you have him weekends? Here's a better idea: why don't I drive up to your little party tomorrow and we can both marry him?'

'You know what it would mean to him to have his kids at the wedding. Would you be willing to reconsider?'

She threw her head back and laughed.

'So that's why you're here. To beg me to let his kids watch him promise to throw his life away on a *curvă*.'

I didn't know what a *curvă* was, but I assumed it didn't translate into 'beautiful bride'.

'No,' I said, but once again, she'd assumed correctly.

Of course it would sadden him not to have his children with him on his big day, which is why, without his knowledge, I'd taken a black cab across London to beg Ioana to change her mind. Personally, I wasn't fussed if the kids were going to be there or not. But I did want to make my husband-to-be happy.

'What can I do to make your life easier?' I asked.

'Die.'

I rolled my eyes. 'Apart from die.'

'There is no apart from die,' she smirked. 'That's it. That's all I wish from you.'

'How can you hate me that much?'

She walked towards a Juliet balcony and flicked her cigarette over the side, and immediately lit another.

'Actually, hating you is the easy part,' she said as I followed her. 'It takes a lot less effort than you might imagine.'

I hadn't smoked in nine years, but a few minutes in her company was enough to reactivate the craving. I took one from the packet without asking and lit it.

'Tell me what else you think of me,' I said.

'What are you, a fucking psychiatrist?'

She laughed, but there was no humour in her tone.

'I told you I was here to listen, so now's your chance. Get it off your chest, woman to woman.'

'You are no woman,' she jibed. 'Someone like you could never understand what you've done.'

'And who exactly do you think I am?'

'You're a *moroaică*,' she replied.

Another word lost on me.

She rolled her eyes. 'It's a ghost, a type of vampire in Romanian folklore. They use their charms to steal the milk from cattle, leaving them empty. You do the same to people. You take what is not yours because you can and because you're greedy. Nicu was, and still is, the love of my life. And then you, the *moroaică*, appear and steal him away from me and drain him of all he felt for me. I bet you thought I'd have faded into the background by now until eventually I disappeared. Well, Margot, that is not going to happen. Ever. Because I am a vindictive bitch and I will spend the rest of my life making sure you two can never be happy together. I'm going to make it hard for Nicu to see his children, I am going to sell every story I can about you, I will publicly criticise all you do and I will ensure people never forget what you did to my family. I am going to be your worst nightmare until I destroy any love that might remain between you and my Nicu. And then you will know how it feels to be me. To be left with nothing.'

I took one last deep drag from my cigarette as her words sank in, then stubbed it out on the floor.

And in the split second it took for Ioana to look away, I moved like lightning.

A voice comes from behind, snapping me back to the present.

'I'm so, so sorry,' he says.

'You're late,' I snip as he approaches me and apologises again.

I finish my vodka and orange in two gulps and set an alarm on my phone. I need to be home in an hour and a half with no one any the wiser as to where I have been.

Or who I have been with.

CHAPTER 43

ANNA

I'm not expecting anyone when the doorbell rings. I huff, as I'm in the middle of some intricate work shaping a cut stone, and no matter how many times I try, it isn't going well. The man standing on my doorstep must be in his fifties, is smartly dressed in a shirt, V-neck jumper and casual trousers, and has a rucksack over his shoulder. He offers me a crooked smile and brushes a salt-and-pepper fringe across his forehead.

'Miss Khan?' he asks.

His use of my old name catches me unawares.

'Not for a long time,' I reply. 'Do I know you?'

'We have met, once, yes, some years ago. Detective Sergeant Roger Fenton.'

I stare at him blankly, still none the wiser. He realises this.

'I had been asked to come to your house to talk to you about an accusation you had made.'

I feel a sudden chill pass through me. Yes, I remember him now. And why we spoke.

'Hi,' I say awkwardly.

'May I come in?'

'What's this about?'

'It's probably better to have this conversation inside, if that's possible?'

I hesitate, then move to one side. I glance at his car, relieved it's unmarked. Then I close the door behind him. I feel my legs beginning to tremble as he follows me into the kitchen. He places his briefcase on the kitchen table as we sit.

I try my hardest to appear calm.

'I wanted to chat to you about something,' he says. 'Do you remember the circumstances of how and when we first met? It stemmed from a phone call we received about—'

'I know what it was about,' I reply. I don't need him to go over old ground.

'I remember it well, because I don't think I had ever met someone your age who was more desperate to be believed.'

'Because I was telling the truth,' I say. 'But nobody would listen to me.'

For a moment, I allow myself to imagine how different my life might have been had he accepted what I told him. Had justice been served.

'And for that, I apologise,' he says, and he looks as if he might mean it. 'You probably assume I forgot about you after that day, but I didn't. In fact I made a lot of inquiries as to whether there might be something in your accusations. But I was never able to find any evidence to back up your claims.'

This should offer me a little comfort, but too much time has passed.

'So why are you here today?'

'Are you aware that, at the time, four people were arrested? They were questioned but later released without charge.'

I shake my head as I struggle to maintain control over my breathing. I can't let him see that I am lying.

'Of those four, three are now dead,' he continues.

I don't know what he expects me to say. That I'm glad they're dead or that I'm sorry they didn't face justice for their crime. Instead, I give nothing away but a nod.

He pauses before removing from his briefcase a familiar magazine, opening it up to a page that's been bookmarked with a coloured Post-it note.

When I see the photograph, I know exactly why he is here. How could I have been so stupid?

'So,' he continues, 'you can imagine my surprise when I saw this.'

He points to the image and is about to speak again. But those are his last words. Because without warning, Drew appears from behind him. A hammer he brandishes above his head swings so fast and hits the detective with such force, it drives him face first on to the tabletop, the tool still embedded in his skull. Drew needs to use both hands to pull it out, twisting it from side to side until it's released, and taking fragments of bone and brain matter with it.

CHAPTER 44

IOANA, THE FIFTH

She thought she had the strength to permanently silence me. But no one can shut out the little voice in the back of their head completely. Especially when that voice belongs to someone else. And being trapped inside her has allowed me to sense her weaknesses and exploit them. For the last ten years, I have been able to manipulate her when I feel like it, make her pay for doing what she did to me. Today is one of those days, when she will do what I say because, if she doesn't, I'll take her over completely. And I don't deliver empty threats.

She's changed a lot since her first occupant joined her on this journey. Her mother, I have learned. I suppose she only wanted the best for her daughter. To encourage her to take charge of her life. To give her a reason to continue when she was at her bleakest. And she is grateful for that. But her mother would be mortified if she realised she'd left the gates open for the rest of us to jump on board the crazy train. I assume she thought she'd be the only one to guide her child, not to then be replaced with the next fresh kill, and so on and so forth.

Of course, Zain, Jenny and Warren all wanted out of her head the moment they arrived. Why would anyone in their right mind – excuse the pun – want to be anywhere near her? They didn't think twice about killing their friends as a means to escape her. Warren even murdered me, a stranger to him, just to free himself from her toxicity. But she knows me well enough to know I'm different.

Because I want to stay here.

I'm not going to encourage her to kill anyone else. Given the choice of being out there in the real world or here, of course I'd pick out there. But being here is better than being dead and forgotten. It gives me the opportunity to continue where I left off. She and I have a common enemy and if I urged her to kill the final name on her list, what would happen to me? I'd vanish and be replaced. And I'm not ready to go anywhere.

The second counsellor she saw told her there's a diagnosis for what she has.

'A dissociative identity disorder that can evolve as an extreme reaction to bereavement in adolescence,' they said.

She doesn't agree with that evaluation, but I think it's because accepting it means she'd be forced to admit there's something wrong with her. That me and the others are not real. That we are in her imagination. By denying it, she can continue to blame her passengers for making her kill. Anyone but herself.

If she thought about it, she'd realise she's lucky to have me. We're the perfect match. However, for our relationship to work, she knows there has to be give and take. And now it's my turn to take. I need her to listen and to do as I say. And only when I'm completely satisfied will I retire, at least for a time, to the shadows.

'Start gathering your equipment and preparing yourself for what is to come,' I tell her now. 'Because later this week, all you'll hear is my voice giving you instructions. And you're going to follow them to the letter.'

Silence.

'I hope you're listening to me,' I continue. 'Because there will be consequences if you aren't, Anna.'

PART TWO

AUGUST

THREE MONTHS BEFORE BONFIRE NIGHT

CHAPTER 45

ANNA

I hear voices. I have done since I was a teenager, standing at the top of a cliff face, preparing to throw myself from it. First it was Mum and then, over time, came the others. All of them urging me to kill those who have wronged me, and I listen to them because I have no choice. Once I act out their wishes, they disappear and are replaced by the next one.

Of all my inhabitants, Ioana has spent the longest time with me, which is ironic, as she was never on my list. She is the result of me letting my guard down and allowing someone else to take advantage. She and I go through quiet and noisy spells, and for a while, I tuned her out. However, when I'm stressed or distracted, and my guard is lowered, she exploits the situation. Like now, in the aftermath of that detective's death. It has brought about it a tension between Drew and I that exceeds anything we've ever experienced before. And Ioana has seeped back into me like a slow-releasing poison.

It hasn't only taken that man's death. The build-up to today has probably been months in the making. Ioana began her approach subtly – a stray thought here, a quiet word there, progressing every so often to a snatched sentence before I even realised these were not my thoughts but hers. Even then, I naively assumed I could take back control at will, and certainly didn't imagine she could harm me to the degree she did a few years back, when she was at her most vocal. But slowly and surely, her quiet voice has loudened to a roar that I can't ignore. She reminds me again and again of who I really am, the woman who people like Liv and Margot can't see because I'm so well hidden.

And now she wants to punish me for not listening to her. She has worn me down. Today, I'm admitting defeat.

I have the house to myself. Drew is working, but to put my mind at ease, I check the Find My iPhone app and see he's still on a delivery somewhere between Coventry and Birmingham. I assume that somewhere en route he will find a place to dump that detective's body.

Then I make my way along the hallway and into the bathroom. There's no need to lock the door. I remove my socks first, then jogging bottoms, fold them up neatly then place them on the lid of the wash basket. Then I position myself on the side of the bath, both feet resting in the tub. The shower head is next to me and the tap is within easy reach. Resting on the toilet tank is a box of super-absorbent sanitary pads, gauze and tape.

And my trusted Stanley knife.

I hate myself for giving in to Ioana but her voice turns the inside of my head into a pressure cooker. The only way to release the strain is to do as she says and cut myself. Only then is she appeased and I'm back in control of my life. Until next time.

I take the knife with the freshly attached blade and position it halfway down my left thigh, placing the tip upon one of my old, raised, diagonal scars.

'Are you ready?' Ioana asks.

I nod. I don't know if it's her pulse or mine pounding in my ears, and it doesn't matter. Because after this moment, we are united by the same cause. Slowly, I begin to cut. The pain is sharp and I gasp, until the warm blood rises to the surface, leaving scarlet candle-wax drips down each side of my thigh. I'm slow and methodical and the relief is instant. And when I finish that line, I start on a second.

'Keep going,' she urges. 'I need to feel how sorry you are for what you did to me.'

I do as she asks, daring to cut a little deeper, three or perhaps four millimetres under the surface now, and suddenly I'm no longer in control of my own hand. Now Ioana is guiding me, pushing me forward, controlling everything.

'You can go deeper,' she says. 'It won't do any harm, will it?'

'No it won't,' I reply.

But we are both wrong. It does cause harm. Because without warning, I'm wrenched from my hypnotic state and thrust back into the reality of what I've just done. The pain is no longer pleasurable, and when I dare to look down through half-closed eyes, my blood is seeping to the surface like oil from a well.

Shit, I think, and drop the knife into the bath with a clatter. I grab a sanitary pad from the toilet lid and press it firmly against the wound, angry at myself for allowing Ioana's influence to get the better of me. It's been years since I last cut this deep, which put paid to me doing it again for a long time.

The room is silent aside from my short, sharp gasps. I know that Ioana has got what she wanted and has left me to clear up the mess. Immediately I regret being so weak. Why did I give in? Why do I keep allowing her to hurt me?

I lift the pad and again the blood flows. And this time, panic accompanies it.

I think about the explanations I'll have to give, the lies I'll be forced to tell. I was supposed to go lightly, so I could allow my thigh time to heal before my plastic surgery procedure on my large scar seven weeks from now. The letter arrived seven months ago with the appointment date. Today's wound won't recover in time. The surgeon will see what I've done to myself and she'll delay the operation, because why would she waste her time putting me back together again when I keep finding ways to tear myself apart? She'll refer me back to my GP, who will recommend another psychiatrist, but the NHS waiting list will be at least a year to eighteen months long. And when I do finally get to see someone, they'll be another person I'm dishonest with and I'll make false promises to, to get me back on the surgery waiting list. In three years' time, I will be exactly where I am now, waiting for an operation and trying to shield myself from Ioana's influence.

I momentarily consider calling Drew and asking him to come home and help me. He is the only person who knows my truths and vice versa. Despite all that divides us, he was protecting me from that detective, from the accusations that were about to come, the explanations I'd have to give. In one swift hammer blow, he provided us with a solution to a problem I hadn't ever predicted. Then I decide against it. I can't let him see me like this again.

I reach for the shower head and turn the tap on to wash away the blood dripping down my leg and from my still-seeping wound. I grab a towel and wish I hadn't only bought white ones because I know from experience that blood stains won't come out, no matter how many times I put them through a cold wash. I'll have to replace them before Drew notices. I clamp it against my leg with one hand and rinse the bath with the other. I lift the towel up and still the blood rises. And now I feel tears pouring down my cheeks.

It's then when the voice appears.

And this time, it's not coming from inside my head.

CHAPTER 46

LIV

It wasn't long past 5.30 a.m. when I pulled into the car park. Me and the two yogis I've taken on rotate who unlocks and closes the studio each day, and today it's my turn for the early bird start.

The novelty of walking through these corridors and knowing this place is mine has yet to wear off. Brandon and I have stepped far from our comfort zones to be where we need to be, and I've done things he isn't aware of to push us over the line. But as I gaze at what I've accomplished, I am convinced the end has justified the means. It doesn't stop the hairs on the back of my neck from prickling each time I'm alone here though. Whenever I open the closed door to my office, I am hesitant just in case Harrison has returned. It's unlikely, as he made his point with his last visit. But I can never be a hundred per cent sure.

I still don't miss my life in the capital. Bow's gentrification enabled us to make a huge profit on our flat two years after moving in. That, alongside my bank job and online work, afforded us a decent deposit on a small house and a suitable building to use as a studio in our commuter belt of choice, Northamptonshire. But we still needed to take out a loan. Our only obstacle was Brandon, who, along with a friend, ended up bankrupt when a gym they had invested in before we met proved unsuccessful. So I had to secure a loan on my own.

I applied to each of the high-street banks because I didn't want my employers knowing I was planning to quit my job. And one by one, they declined. Their excuses echoed: I was newly qualified with an unproven track record in the health and well-being industry; I didn't have a sufficient back-up plan; I lacked collateral; my debt-to-income ratio was too high. And they never allowed me to forget that I was married to a bankrupt.

Harrison, Murray & Kline was my last resort. I was PA to Michael Murray, grandson of one of the founders. But internal regulations meant that Murray deciding upon my application for a loan would be a conflict of interest, so instead I was interviewed by Lord Robert Harrison, an arrogant bulldog of a man who couldn't have looked any more like the Monopoly mascot Uncle Pennybags than if he had worn a top hat and monocle. I'd remained in touch with his former secretary, Mary, who, before resigning, had been signed off on long-term sick leave due to the stress he put her under. She loathed the man.

'He will turn your application down,' she'd warned me weeks earlier when we met at a café far from the bank. 'But he'll make you feel as awkward as possible before he does it. He might even make you beg, because he gets off on humiliating women.'

'So I'm wasting my time?' I asked, deflated.

'That depends. How far are you willing to go?'

'How far will I need to go?'

Her response was a wry smile.

For ten long minutes, Harrison silently pored over my accounts in his wood-panelled office as I shifted from buttock to buttock opposite him. For reasons I had yet to learn, he'd invited two lawyers with him into our meeting.

'You've saved a lot of money, particularly over the last three years,' he began.

'My husband Brandon has a lot of social media followers who subscribe to his personal-training videos,' I explained. It was a part-truth. 'His earnings are paid into my account because of the bankruptcy I mentioned earlier. Next year he hopes to be discharged from his debts.'

'Will he be joining you as a director in your proposed business?'

'No, he will be a paid employee.'

'*A paid employee*,' he scoffed.

One lawyer smirked.

'So your earnings, beyond the generous wage we pay you, are actually your husband's?' he continued.

'Yes, and of course I pay tax on them.'

'So just to clarify, this money has nothing to do with the adult content you also provide for an OnlyFans page?'

He pushed his glasses down his nose and glared at me. I swallowed hard.

'Olivia,' began one of his po-faced lawyers. 'Background checks on your income revenues have revealed you provide services of an adult nature which contravene your contract with Harrison, Murray & Kline, as they risk bringing our business into disrepute.'

I was readying myself to protest when Harrison swivelled his laptop in my direction and played a video of Brandon and me. It was a two-year-old clip of him naked and handcuffed to a hook on the wall while I slapped his buttocks with a wooden paddle. Our faces may not have been identifiable, but our voices were. How on earth had they discovered this?

I don't know if it was out of nervousness or if the video was a prime example of the absurdity of what Brandon and I were prepared to do to follow our dreams, but I laughed. A proper, vocal laugh out loud.

'You find this funny?' Harrison asked.

'Of course it is,' I replied. By this point, I had nothing to lose. 'This business means everything to us and we've been willing to do anything to reach our goal. Do you think I'm happy we've had to raise money this way? Of course I'm not. But can I see the funny side of it? Yes, I can.'

Harrison shook his head in dismay.

'As an executive personal assistant, you are one of the faces of this business,' the lawyer continued. 'If a client was to recognise you, how do you think that might reflect upon our image?'

'I'd be more interested to know how they recognised me,' I replied, perhaps a little too flippantly. 'So I assume my application has been refused.'

Without waiting for an answer, I gathered the paperwork I'd brought with me and slipped it back inside my folder.

'It's more serious than that,' the second lawyer said. 'I'm afraid what you have been doing is a terminable offence.'

Now that came as a surprise.

'You're sacking me for something I've done that has nothing to do with my actual job?'

'Not if you are willing to resign with immediate effect and sign a non-disclosure agreement. Lord Harrison has more than generously agreed to pay you for the next three months, and you will also receive a generous reference.'

'And if I don't?'

'Then we will suspend you without pay and begin disciplinary procedures. What's it to be, Olivia?'

For a moment I wished I'd brought the wooden paddle I'd used on Brandon to knock twelve shades of shit out of Harrison and his cronies. I looked to him, his arrogant, fat face radiating smugness. Then I gave them my answer.

'I'd like to speak to Lord Harrison alone, please,' I said calmly.

Both lawyers shook their heads vigorously.

'That's not possible,' said the first.

I directed my attention towards their employer.

'I think you'll find it is possible,' I told him.

I took a breath as I removed my phone from my handbag, accessed my photographs and showed Lord Harrison an image.

His face paled and he slowly balled his fists.

'Give us a moment,' he ordered his lawyers.

'I would strongly advise—' began the second one.

'Now!' he yelled.

He waited until the door had closed before he spoke again.

Eight days later, I received a severance offer including two years of full pay, a guaranteed investment from the bank in an empty studio property, and a favourable mortgage on the family home of my dreams. In return, I signed a non-disclosure agreement in which I agreed never to make public the online conversation he and I had where I'd pretended to be a fifteen-year-old boy and he had solicited me for sex. It had occurred a week before our meeting, in a chatroom that Mary, his former secretary, had informed me she'd found in his computer's search history.

I'd saved the explicit images of himself he'd sent to my alter ego, and messages where he'd offered money for the boy's photos. The stupid old fool had even paid for a train ticket for the lad to travel to London to meet him. Mary had also supplied me with details of the apartment Harrison rented in central London and regularly used to entertain young male sex workers. Neither the bank – which footed the bill – nor his wife and four children had any idea of the arrangement.

Brandon still doesn't know our new life was mostly funded by blackmail. Not once but twice. I was forced to go back to Harrison when the heated flooring needed to be replaced. It's the only secret I've ever kept from my husband. But that's not what pricks my conscience. It's that Harrison is a paedophile and I've chosen to keep that quiet, to benefit myself. I'm a mother. I should know better. My moral compass is highly questionable, to say the least.

Inside my office, I open the windows to allow in August's fresh early morning air. I take deep breaths to try and rid my mind of the memory of Harrison, but he stubbornly remains. I know that to my friends and the outside world, I'm a self-made woman. But inside, I hate that I'm not. Blackmail alongside my OnlyFans work means that my little empire has been built on the foundations paid to me by the parts of myself I have sold to men.

And that leaves a very bitter taste in my mouth.

CHAPTER 47

ANNA

'It looks like an abattoir in here,' she begins.

I turn quickly and Margot is standing there. She is calmly surveying the room: the bloody towel, the Stanley knife in the bath, the sanitary pads and me in the middle of it all, crying and with snot dripping from my nose. I don't know how to explain my way out of this.

'How did you get in?' is all I can think of to say.

'Garage door,' she says. 'You keep moaning about Drew leaving it open. I was making sure you hadn't been burgled.'

She approaches me. I don't try and stop her as she lifts up my towel and examines the damage I've done to my leg. She grimaces ever so slightly and reaches for a second towel, takes a seat on the edge of the bath and uses it to clamp down heavily over my wound. Five minutes must pass where neither of us says a word. Finally, she unpeels it and the bleeding has all but stopped. Then she spots a cord from a bathrobe hanging from the door, and ties it around my leg. At first I think she's using it as a torniquet until I realise it's thick enough to cover the gash.

'Right, let's get you out of here,' she says. 'Keep your leg straight.'

I lean on her shoulder and hobble into the bedroom, where she lays me down on the bed. She returns to the bathroom and comes back with the gauze, tape, sanitary pads and a wet flannel. She patches me up and wipes the remaining blood from my legs and feet.

I can barely look her in the eye.

'I assume you don't want me to take you to hospital?' she asks and I shake my head. 'And you also won't want me calling your Drew?'

'No,' I mutter.

'Do you have any camomile tea?'

'In the cupboard above the dishwasher.'

She's back ten minutes later with two cups, passes one to me, then she lies next to me, our heads and shoulders propped up by pillows.

'You haven't asked me why,' I say eventually.

'You'll tell me if you want to.'

There's a pause, and I'm unsure if she is expecting me to volunteer my trigger, but I don't. That would be a step too far, and I can't tell where it might take our relationship.

'Look Anna,' she continues. 'I don't need to tell you that you should probably speak to someone about this. So all I'm going to say is that we all have demons. There are things that have happened to me and that I've done in the past to others that I spent years trying to run away from. But I've learned that sooner or later you have to own your fuck-ups and make your peace with them. Otherwise you will never stop hurting yourself. And the next time, it could be a lot worse.'

'So you have regrets?'

'Don't we all,' she says with a faraway look in her eye. 'But you must find a way to draw a line under them. If you don't, your past will always define your present and ruin your future.'

There's a lot to unpack in what she says, but now is not the time. She reaches out to hold my hand. Her skin is soft and warm and I allow her to entwine her fingers with mine. The tenderness she shows takes me aback, and that, along with my fragile state, makes me cry like a burst dam. Try as I might, I cannot stop sobbing. Margot doesn't say a word; she literally provides me with a shoulder to cry on and I'm too weak to refuse. For the first time in I can't recall how long, I remember how it feels to be a child being comforted by her mother. It's the purest form of love, utterly unconditional and reassuring. I don't want to let her go. So I don't, until I drift off to sleep.

I awake sometime later in the afternoon, only realising I haven't dreamed the whole episode when I spot my bandaged thigh. I check the Find My iPhone app: Drew will be home in about thirty minutes. So I limp into the bathroom to clear up the scene of the crime. But it's immaculate. You'd never know what I did in there. Margot must be responsible. And she has also left four brand-new neatly folded white towels on the rail.

I take three painkillers from the bathroom cabinet and swallow them with tap water. Until today, Margot and I had not truly met one another. We had never seen these sides to each other.

I've spent my whole adult life hating that woman. And now I have invited the enemy to my side, I don't know how to feel.

Because Margot has always been the final name on my kill list.

CHAPTER 48

2000 – TWENTY-FIVE YEARS EARLIER

MARGOT

I feel the pinch of the cold night air on my cheeks. I smell the spices from a curry house a little further along the road and hear the leaves crunching under my feet as I hop from foot to foot, trying to rid myself of nervous energy.

I steal a glance at the people waiting with me. We're all trying to keep a distance between us and the street light above, hiding in the anonymity of an estate agent's doorway.

Jenny is fourteen too, and I know her better than I do the others, even though we only met properly for the first time during a lunchtime detention when our teacher slipped on his headphones and ignored us for an hour. She and I have similar tastes in music, celebrities, TV shows and the hottest guys in school. I get the impression that, like my parents, hers have checked out. My mum isn't a bad person – neither is Dad. We're all just mismatched. They have the wrong daughter and I have the wrong parents. Mum as much as admitted the only thing stopping her and Dad from formally giving up and handing me over to social services is the shame it'd bring them in front of their friends.

For a few months, Jenny's been dating Warren Jones, a boy four years older than us. What Jenny sees in him is beyond me. He has acne, is missing a front tooth, and the stench of weed and Lynx Africa follows him around like a noxious cloud. But with nothing better to do, I hang out with her and an older group Warren is desperate to be accepted by.

These twenty-plus-year-olds smuggle us into grimy, spit-and-sawdust pubs, they buy us booze and gave us our first taste of speed and ecstasy. They drive us around in souped-up cars with spoiler upon spoiler fixed to the back, and while none of them work, they're never without money. They in turn worship Eddie, a much older man they'll do anything for. He's both charm and menace in one. You don't need a shark to introduce itself to understand he'll rip you to shreds if he feels like it.

'Eddie has a job for us,' Warren informed us last week. His wiry frame was hunched over the table in a pub garden, his pupils dilated.

'Really? What?' Zain asked, trying to hide his excitement at finally being asked to step up.

'Supermarket,' Warren continued, speaking as ever in clipped sentences. 'Owners live upstairs. Cash will be left on the premises.'

'How does Eddie know this?' I asked.

'Have you ever met Andy?'

We all shook our heads.

'A kid who owes Eddie money. Was about to have the shit kicked out of him when he spilled. This is how he's paying off his debt.'

Warren opened his jacket ever so slightly to reveal the black grip of a gun tucked in his inside pocket.

Zain gasped. 'That thing real?'

'For sure.'

I felt the blood drain from my face. 'Why do we need it if the place is empty?'

Warren shrugged. 'Just in case.'

Zain slumped in his chair. 'Nah, man. I ain't going down for a ten stretch if this goes wrong.'

Warren shook his head. 'It won't, mate. In and out in five minutes. Promise.'

He went on to explain how, most evenings, the supermarket owner deposited the daily takings into the bank, leaving only a small float on the premises. But on the night we were to enter, the shop would be closing early, as the owners were attending a family event. The cash was to be left overnight in a safe.

'Victimless crime,' Warren concluded. 'Insurance will pay out. And Eddie will know we're for real.'

As the others thought about what it might mean if we pulled this off, I was busy trying to find a way out without losing face. Jenny was my only real friend, but if I backed out, she'd choose Warren over me and I'd be locked out of that group. There would be no second chances.

Which is why, following a sleepless night and countless toilet trips, the four of us now find ourselves walking down an alleyway towards the back entrance of a SupaSaver supermarket in an unfamiliar part of town.

As I'm the smallest and most agile, Warren hoists me through a storeroom window, the one Eddie told him would be unlocked. Once inside, I locate the key to the reinforced rear door. It's on a shelf, as his informant said it would be. Within five minutes we're making our way through the shop by torchlight until we find a door that leads upstairs to the owners' flat. Then, once in the flat, we make a beeline for the concealed safe, hidden under a rug in the corner of the living room.

'Why can't we turn the lights on?' Zain asks.

'We don't want to be seen from outside,' Warren replies, shining his torch at a console table. 'The key should be over there by the telephone.'

Jenny approaches it first, looking under old newspapers and a Yellow Pages business directory. 'I can't find it,' she says.

'Look again,' Warren barks. 'Check the drawer.'

It's the same outcome: there is no key inside. Warren pushes her to one side and checks it himself, and when he realises she's right, his temper flares. He curses as he yanks the table hard, sending it toppling to the floor.

'Are you sure Eddie said the keys were in there?' Zain asks, brow furrowed.

'I'm not a fucking idiot.'

'So what happens if we can't get into the safe?' asks Jenny.

If she's anything like me, she's hoping we'll give up and get the hell out of here.

Instead, Warren flashes his light around the room until he spots a framed cricket bat hanging from the wall. He pulls it down to the floor and its glass shatters. He grabs the bat, lifts it above his head and starts pounding it against the metal safe. It's a hopeless cause. Safes were built to withstand more than a man armed with a piece of wood.

'Mate, you're wasting your time,' says Zain.

Warren doesn't answer, and instead goes on hitting it repeatedly.

'Give up,' Zain says. 'Let's go, man.'

'No!' yells Warren, striking it another half-dozen times before hurling the bat at the wall. 'I can't fail Eddie. It's my only—'

Our lives as we know it change with the flicking on of a light switch, and the appearance of a man in a doorway. He's glaring wild-eyed at us and holding a bedside lamp above his head. He looks furious.

CHAPTER 49

2000

ANNA

I wake up to find my brother's hand across my mouth and he's whispering in my ear.

'Get up,' he hisses.

Before he gives me the chance to ask why, he's yanking me by my arm and dragging me out of bed. He's eight years older than me and a lot stronger. He leads me across the room, into the bathroom I share with Mum and Dad, then into their bedroom. Through light coming from a crack in the curtains, I can just make out Dad standing by a closed second door leading into the lounge. Behind us, Mum is in the corner of the room, holding something close to her chest.

'Under the bed,' Dad whispers and my brother pulls me to the floor. 'Keep your sister safe.'

I'm only six but even I know something is very, very wrong. Not just because of what's happening, but because my brother doesn't argue. And he never does anything Dad tells him to do.

Suddenly from beneath the door, glimmers of moving lights catch our eyes. The next thing I see are Dad's bare feet approaching the door, it opening, a light being switched on, the door closing again, followed by a deafening bang that rings throughout the flat.

CHAPTER 50

2000

MARGOT

The sound of the gunshot is deafening. My ears ring as I cower, and when I dare to look up, Warren is towering over the man, now slumped on the floor, much of his right cheek and an eye missing. Behind him, blood trickles down the wall like syrup. I look to Jenny and Zain, frozen in time. Even Warren remains sealed in a stunned, numb silence, watching the last flicker of movement in the man's remaining eyelid.

But Warren is the first to regain his senses.

'Why did he close the door?' he asks slowly.

We are all still too much in shock to answer him.

He walks slowly towards it, opens it and disappears inside. We hear a woman's voice talking at first, then soon escalating into a panicked, frightened shriek. I edge towards the door and the light in the lounge illuminates something held up to her chest. From this distance it looks like a can of hairspray. She fumbles, trying to spray it in Warren's face, but in her panic, she drops it to the floor.

He grabs her by the neck and frogmarches her out into the lounge. She is sobbing.

'Shut up,' Warren yells, and slaps her hard across the side of the head. 'Where's the key to the safe?'

Now she's coughing, choking on her tears, her words unintelligible.

'Where is it?' he screams at the top of his lungs.

None of us have met this version of Warren before. He points the muzzle of the gun at the centre of her forehead.

'I don't know,' she sobs. 'Sanjay hides it in different places.'

'Tell me!' he demands.

'I don't know!' she cries. 'I promise.'

This time, when Warren pulls the trigger, it isn't reactive. It's deliberate, brought about by rage and frustration. The woman falls into a console table then crashes to the floor, landing on her side. Blood oozes from the hole in her throat. She clasps it but bleeds out in less than half a minute.

It's too much for Zain. He grabs Jenny's wrist and pulls her towards the staircase, the two of them disappearing in an instant. Warren is too slow to react and they are already out of his eyeline when he fires the gun twice in their direction. I should follow, but I'm too far away from the stairs to make a dash for it.

Now it's just me, Warren and two dead bodies.

His eyes dart around the room, lizard-like, unsure of what to do next, before they settle upon me. The only remaining witness. I watch as the hand holding the gun begins to rise and point in my direction. I don't think either of us knows what he's going to do next.

And then it's like someone flicks a switch in my brain which pushes me to take charge. I spot a tin of cigarette lighter fuel on the floor by the overturned console table. I point to it.

'Go find more,' I order Warren, as if ignorant of the gun aimed at me. 'Our fingerprints are everywhere. We need to burn this place down.'

Warren casts a curious eye over me before acknowledging I'm on his side and I might be right. He lowers his weapon, disappears downstairs, re-emerging moments later brandishing three two-litre bottles of white spirits.

'Pour them over the curtains and sofa,' I tell him. 'Anything that might be flammable.'

I clock a box of firelighters by the side of the fireplace, so I break them into cubes, enter the bedroom, then toss them around like chunks of confetti. Warren throws me a bottle and I empty the liquid across the bed and curtains in a zigzag pattern.

I'm so nervous that when I remove the tin of lighter fuel from my pocket, it falls to the floor. I crouch to find it, shining my torch across the floor and under the bed.

And that's when I see them.

Two young faces.

Wide-eyed and staring back at me.

CHAPTER 51

2000

ANNA

Hot tears pour down my cheeks and pool in the collar of my nightie. I cover my ears while my brother slips his hand over my mouth as we remain hidden under the bed. I feel him shaking just as much as me. Nothing happens for the longest time, until the door is suddenly thrown open again, and Mum's shrill screams echo throughout the room as she's dragged into the lounge. I'm so scared I pee myself.

A man's muffled voice shouts at her, demanding she tells him where something is. And then there's a second banging sound, much louder than the last because the door is still open.

I pull my hands from my ears just in time to hear a thump on the ground and, soon after, feet running down the stairs and more bangs, one after the other. And there are voices too. People are still out there. A few moments pass as I hear them moving around and then two strong, familiar smells arrive in the bedroom: white spirits, which Mum used when she decorated the lounge last Easter, and the fluid Dad uses to fill his cigarette lighter.

Suddenly a tin falls to the floor and bounces under the bed. A pair of knees press into the carpet. A hand enters our safe space and fingers fumble round for it. Finally a face appears. Her surprise mirrors ours.

Our eye contact holds for only a few fleeting seconds, but it's long enough for me to take in every inch of her, imprinting it into a memory before she scrambles to her feet. A handful of seconds pass and the lighter fluid falls once again, only this time, the flame is clearly visible. We watch helplessly as line after line of fuel spreads across the floor in zigzagging ribbons.

I'm petrified, caught somewhere between fear and fire. Meanwhile, my brother pushes himself backwards under the bed to make his escape, grabs me by the ankle and drags me out, the friction from the carpet burning my thighs and belly as my nightie rises. The duvet and curtains are already well ablaze by the time he hauls me through the room and into the fiery lounge. We have no choice but to navigate our way through the flames or die. We cough and splutter as the acrid smoke fills our lungs until we've almost reached the door leading to the stairs.

Disorientated, I trip over an object on the floor, my nose taking the brunt of the impact. Blood trickles down my throat as I turn to discover Mum's body. The orange and yellow flames threatening us reflect in a line of blood originating at a dark hole in the middle of her neck.

Before I can scream again, my brother is pulling me back towards the staircase. It's only then he realises the lower part of my nightie is ablaze, so he grabs a coat from a hook and holds it over the flames to snuff them out. Then he carries me in his arms as he runs the length of the stairs, stumbling down the final few and sending us both into a crashing heap.

I just about struggle to my feet, but he remains on the floor, dazed and coughing more intensely than me. I try to help him as he helped me, but he is far too big for a six-year-old to shift. I'm struggling to breathe, but the adrenaline must have quashed the pain from my burns as I stumble to open the back door and draw in as much air as my scorched lungs will allow. I'm preparing to return to him when two police patrol officers appear from nowhere. I frantically tell them my brother is behind me and my parents are upstairs, but they only reach as far as him, carrying his unconscious body to safety.

I watch him being laid on his back as they desperately try to revive him, their large hands pressing down hard upon his chest over and over again until one exchanges a solemn glance with the other, then shakes his head.

If my brother is dead, I want to be dead too.

SEPTEMBER

TWO MONTHS BEFORE BONFIRE NIGHT

CHAPTER 52

2025 – PRESENT DAY

ANNA

The soldering iron rests on a rack as I attach clasps to both ends of a bracelet. It's intricate work, so I've decamped to the kitchen where the lighting is better. As much as I used to enjoy working from home, these days it's become harder. Especially being in this room. Knowing that detective died in the chair opposite me, his blood spilling over the tabletop I'm using now, and across the floor under my feet. I still find myself checking my fingernails for blood from Drew and my clean-up operation. All we used was a garden waste bag cinched tightly around the detective's neck to prevent more blood from leaking, before Drew hoisted him over his shoulder and drove him away in the car. I don't know where to and I didn't ask.

More than ever it's made me want to be like Liv and able to afford a place of my own to work. Nothing grand like her studio, just a little workshop somewhere and perhaps an apprentice to help me when demand is high. Three months ago, Deja, one of Liv's friends, styled a photoshoot for *Elle* magazine and a handful of her models wore my bracelets and necklaces. The issue finally hit the shelves this week, including credits of who provided the jewellery, along with my website address. That, plus appearances on her influencer friends' Instagram pages, means my inbox has been flooded with orders.

I rest my tired eyes from this intricate work and they settle upon the soldering iron. I briefly imagine the pain of pressing the tip against my skin, the smell of burning flesh, the wetness of tears running down my cheeks and the sting of antiseptic wipes as I clean my wound afterwards. I blink hard and the fantasy dissolves. I remember that I don't need to hurt myself because Ioana isn't here. Wherever she is, she's been suspiciously quiet of late.

Margot came over again this morning without texting or calling first. She's got into the habit of checking up on me. Perhaps she thinks I won't cut again if she doesn't announce when she's coming. She doesn't know that it's not up to me if and when it happens, that other forces control me. However, it feels strange to have someone care about my well-being, especially her of all people, as she's the one to blame for so much of this.

Neither of us have mentioned how she caught me, quite literally, red-handed. Although I've spotted her glancing at my thigh a few times. Even today, I sensed I was being watched as I made her a coffee. My healing skin is tight and thin, and when I'm alone, I've started keeping my leg as straight as I can when I walk, pulling it behind me like a reluctant dog on a lead. When I'm with others, I bend it like I'm supposed to, but it hurts.

'That thing stinks,' says Drew, pointing at the soldering iron as he enters the room.

He removes his green uniform jacket and tosses it towards the back of a chair. He doesn't bother to pick it up when it falls to the floor.

'I could say the same about you,' I say, catching a sourness from his shirt. 'You need to shower before we go to the party.'

'What party?'

'Liv's birthday. She's invited a few of us over for drinks.'

'And why should I care?'

He's in a combative mood, but for once, he won't be putting a dampener on my day.

'Two words,' I reply. 'Free bar.'

He makes his way to the fridge and removes a bottle of Estrella from an open box. I doubt it's his first drink of the day. But I've given up trying to manage his alcohol consumption, especially since that detective's death. I need to take care of myself, not him. I spoke too soon when I thought things were a little better between us back in the summer. Something he won't talk about is casting a shadow over him. I assume it's what he did to that man, which came as just as much of a surprise to me as it did to the detective. But each time I've asked what's troubling him, he stonewalls me.

He clocks the two coffee cups on the draining board.

'Company?' he asks.

I nod without looking at him.

'Who?' But he already knows the answer.

'Margot,' I say.

He takes a long swig of his beer, then starts tapping his silver wedding ring against the glass bottle. The lion tattoo on the back of his hand is supposed to represent strength, courage and wisdom. I don't see any of those things in him. Once, perhaps. But not anymore.

'Why was she here?' he continues.

'She stopped by for a catch-up.'

'You mean a check-up.'

That catches me off guard. 'What's that supposed to mean?'

'My phone is linked to the doorbell camera, remember? And she's over here daily. Sometimes twice. We've got all-new white towels and those blades have vanished – the ones you don't think

223

I know are hidden in the tampon box in the bathroom cabinet. You went too deep again, didn't you? You bled out and called her for help.'

My voice cracks ever so slightly as I deny it. 'I didn't call anyone for anything.'

Drew offers a humourless laugh and continues tapping the bottle. The clink is growing louder.

'But she was here,' he continues. 'And she's been back every day since, to make sure you haven't killed yourself.'

'She helped me,' I concede.

'Oh did she? That's so kind of her. So neighbourly.'

To my surprise, I find myself jumping to the defence of a woman I have hated since I was six years old.

'Yes, she was kind to me.'

'Kind?' he repeats. 'She was being *kind* to you? Jesus, Joanna!'

He only uses my full name when he's angry.

'Have you forgotten why you're like this in the first place?' he argues as he slams the bottle of beer down, its contents frothing over the rim. 'You've lost all perspective.'

'No, I haven't forgotten,' I say, but I can't deny that I'm conflicted. However, I can't admit that to him because he won't understand. He wouldn't even try.

'Don't lie to me,' he snaps.

'I'm not!'

'I can see it in your eyes,' he yells. 'You don't know who you are anymore.'

Drew's normally pallid complexion is now puce, and spit flies like bullets from his mouth when he speaks. He moves towards me, and before I can defend myself, he grabs my arm so hard that I yelp. He pulls me off the chair and yanks down my jogging bottoms to reveal the bandages I'm still applying twice daily to my injuries. He tears them off to uncover the patchwork of scabs and scars beneath.

'Look at yourself!' he roars, and I'm too frightened and crying too hard from the pain of his grip to say anything but 'Please let go.'

He grabs the back of my head and pushes it down towards my thigh. I whimper.

'Look at yourself!' he repeats. 'You're a mess. You're a fucking mess. And it's all because of her. You're no use to me, no use to anyone.'

He's never behaved like this before. He is furious: his breath is as hot as his skin. I've only just pulled up my joggers when he forcibly moves me to the kitchen window and pushes my face so hard against the Venetian blinds that I feel like the metal slats are going to slice through my cheek.

'And *her*,' he snarls. 'Every day I have to look at that house opposite, knowing who is really living under that roof. And you have the gall to say "she was nice to me" when it was her who made you like this.'

'Let go of me,' I whimper, and finally, he does.

'If it wasn't for her and if you did what you were supposed to do, we wouldn't still be here and that copper would be alive.'

'I had it under control,' I protest.

'Don't kid yourself. He didn't know everything, but he would've got there in the end if it wasn't for my intervention. I did it to protect you, and how do you show your gratitude? By making friends with *her*.'

There's so much I still don't know about what happened after he loaded the body on to the back of his delivery truck. Where he dumped the detective, what he did with the man's car and his phone. I can only assume the policeman hadn't told his boss he was coming to our house that day, because his colleagues haven't come to question us. And I've refrained from googling him to see if the media has reported on his disappearance. I carry enough information about my own passengers without adding to the load.

Drew grabs a second bottle of beer from the fridge and opens the back door. My whole body is shaking as I hold on to the countertop for dear life, scared that if I let go, my leg will give way and I'll collapse. He looks me up and down with disgust.

'Where are you going?' I gasp.

'Liv's party,' he adds. 'Before I do something here that we'll both regret.'

And I don't doubt him.

CHAPTER 53

MARGOT

His attention flits towards me again. I don't think he realises I can see his reflection in the dining room mirror. He's talking to Nigel the dullard from number thirty-seven. That man should come with a health warning. His bug eyes, combover and grey complexion give him a Gollum-esque appearance. But the way Brandon rocks back and forth on his heels in time with the music suggests he's distracted. And I just know he'd rather be talking to me.

We're all here to celebrate what his wife is trying to convince us is her thirty-first birthday party. Until I see Liv's birth certificate, I can only assume that's her Botox age.

This soirée is a very different affair from the one she threw when she first arrived in the cul-de-sac ten months ago. There are no London imports here as far as I can tell, just neighbours, playgroup mums and a few clients. And she hasn't splashed the cash either. Which makes me wonder how much cash there is left. Because there's no such thing as an infinite well. Perhaps someone needs to go back on OnlyFans to top up their coffers. My search for her profile has continued, but I've yet to find it.

Although we've seen each other a fair few times since I found that envelope in her bathroom bin, I still don't trust her. I haven't been sent any more anonymous packages, and I wonder if the two things are related. And until I have absolute proof she's not to blame, my guard remains up.

I check the mirror again and Brandon's attention moves quickly from me and back to the Gollum. I don't blame him for checking me out, because I'm looking damn good tonight. My hair is natural and relaxed, this new bodycon dress is pushing up my boobs almost to chin level and is giving me a Nicki Minaj bum lift. Being with Liv, he must have forgotten what a curve looks like.

I'm flying solo tonight. Nicu is at home getting an early night. His tour came to a close last week, and tomorrow morning he's off to London to start rehearsals for the new series of *Strictly*. So that's potentially another three months where we'll barely see one another.

I made a fool of myself with him earlier. Lately I've found myself picking arguments with him just to prompt a reaction. Tonight we bickered over sex. I was desperate for a connection with him – just a kiss would've been enough, and now I think about it, that's all I should've asked for. He was in the bath when I made my move, hoping the hot water might help with his sore knee. I slipped my hand under the bubbles but, despite my best attempts, his knee was the only thing to remain swollen.

'Do you not find me attractive anymore?' I snapped. 'Is that why you keep pushing me away?'

'We're just a little out of sync,' he replied. 'I have a lot going on for when *Strictly* returns and I need to keep my focus on that.'

'And I'm, what, expected to wait until you can squeeze me in between your other commitments? I'm not your mistress, Nicu.'

'Not anymore.'

I glared at him and he apologised. I took my hand from beneath the water and splashed bubbles in his face. 'Fine. If you're not interested, I'm sure I can find someone else who is.'

'Knock yourself out.'

'Knock one out yourself while you're in there,' I replied and stormed off downstairs for my first drink of the night.

Now, as I look around Liv's perfect house, with her perfect husband and with her perfect life, I find myself resenting her more than ever. Maybe it's unfair, but I can't help myself. I should have a better life than the one I'm living. All I did was fall in love with the wrong person. One who I don't think loves me back anymore.

Anna also rejected me tonight when I dropped by to pick her up, blaming a headache. But after catching her hacking at her leg like a butcher carving a pork tenderloin, I'm being vigilant when it comes to that one. As she lay with her head pressed against my shoulder sobbing her heart out that night, I really felt for that girl. The emotional pain she goes through every time she hurts herself must be immeasurable.

I top up my glass from an open bottle of Shiraz. And after an hour here, I'm positively buzzing. Suddenly I recognise the scent of Acqua Di Parma and turn to find Brandon behind me. He leans in to kiss me on both cheeks and there's something about his soft stubble brushing against me that makes me want to grab the back of his head and devour him.

'How's your night?' he asks.

I try and find something positive to say about it, but the wine has blurred my vocabulary.

'It's neat,' I reply.

'Oh no, is it really that bad?'

'No,' I correct, 'I said it was neat.'

'*Truth or Dare: In Bed with Madonna*.' He winks and I feel my cheeks blaze.

He has correctly sourced my dig. In the film, Kevin Costner describes one of Madonna's concerts as 'neat', and when he leaves her dressing room, cameras catch her repeating the word and sticking her fingers down her throat. Ever since seeing the movie, that's been my go-to word when I'm having as much fun as I would in a dental hygienist's chair. An in-joke that nobody gets but me. Or so I thought.

'I have two older sisters who worshipped her,' he says. 'They made me watch that movie as a kid and forced me to learn the dance routines. I defy you to find another straight bloke on this planet who can vogue like me.'

'Now that I need to see.'

'It's okay, though,' Brandon continues. 'You're allowed not to have fun. Just between us, I'd rather be upstairs.'

'Oh would you now?' I reply without thinking.

He grins. 'Set myself up there, didn't I?' He looks around. 'Where's Nicu?'

'At home.' I shrug. 'Probably asleep by now.'

'Can I pour you another one?' But before I can answer, he reaches for the bottle and tops up my glass.

'Where's your wife?' I ask.

'Fluttering about like the social butterfly she is. When we throw a party, we barely see each other.'

'And doesn't that bother you? That she leaves you all alone to fend for yourself?'

'But I'm not alone, am I? Besides, I'm a big boy.'

And when he smiles at me, I know exactly what's on his mind, because it's exactly the same thing I am thinking. He's going to be showing me more than just his vogue moves before the night is through.

CHAPTER 54

MARGOT

'Get up,' comes Nicu's voice. It's the first thing he's said to me this morning and he already sounds irritated. I assume I've slept in past noon again.

'What time is it?' I reply.

'Nine o'clock.'

I slip my eye mask up on to my forehead and turn to face him. He's standing under the doorway, his arms tightly folded and his forehead knitted.

'Nine o'clock on a Sunday morning?' I ask, a little dramatically. 'Unless the house is on fire, why would you be so cruel?'

'I know what you did.'

'Last summer? It's too early for a movie quiz.'

I roll back to face the wall.

'I know about you and him.'

He can't see my eyes ping wide open. There's a sharp twinge in my belly.

'About who?' I ask.

'About *him*. About what you've been doing behind my back. You're a fucking arsehole.'

He turns to leave the room and I sit up in the bed. But I've moved too fast, and when my brain catches up with me, dizziness strikes. I half dash, half stumble to the en-suite to be sick. Only I can't reach the toilet in time, and I vomit on the bedroom wall and skirting boards. I manage to reach the bowl when the second and third waves hit.

Shit, shit, shit! How could he know? We were careful. We made sure to go somewhere we wouldn't be seen.

I splash water across my face and gargle mouthwash, but that only makes me retch again. How am I going to get out of this?

I quickly rub with a towel the mess I've made on the wall, throw on some joggers and a T-shirt and find Nicu downstairs in the lounge. His hands rest on his hips as he stands with his back to me. He stares from the patio doors out into the garden. He is framed by glowing September sunlight which shines through his T-shirt, accentuating the muscles in his back and arms. I need to take control of this situation, but first, I need to understand what he believes he knows.

'Where are the kids?' I begin.

'Hockey and football.'

'Nicu,' I say, softly. 'I don't know what you think you—'

'I don't "think" anything, Margot,' he interrupts. 'I've seen it with my own eyes.'

How? Did he follow me? And when? Has he found my second SIM card? I've deleted any incriminating text messages, then deleted them from the deleted folder.

'What did you see?' I ask.

'You and him together.'

'Me and who?'

He turns around sharply. The whites of his eyes are red. He's been crying. I've really, really hurt him.

'Don't you dare,' he replies. 'Don't you dare deny it. How long has it been going on for?'

I open my mouth, firming up another lie, before stopping myself. I don't know whether it's the hangover or if I'm just too weary to fight. I owe it to him to admit my mistakes and take responsibility. I take a deep breath.

'Not long,' I say quietly.

The truth disarms him, albeit briefly.

'Not long? How long is not long?'

'I don't know. I haven't been counting.'

'Jesus, Margot!' he shouts. 'Why would you do this to me? To our family? Our marriage?'

'What marriage?' I shoot back, triggered by his use of the word. 'We are two people who share space under the same roof. What did you think was going to happen if you kept rejecting me? You know the kind of person I am. I need to know that I'm cared for, that I'm loved. You had no interest in doing that and someone else did.'

'So it's all my fault?'

'No, it's not all your fault. But that's my truth.'

'Well I have a very different definition of truth to yours. Do you love him?'

'No.'

'Then what was the point?'

I look down at my stomach. The twinge there is now so intense that, for a second, I wonder if I've been stabbed. The guilt of thinking I'd killed Cat Face is nothing compared to this.

'It's over between me and him anyway,' I say, hoping it might offer Nicu a little comfort.

'Who ended it?' he asks. 'You or him?'

'Me.'

'Why?'

'Because I knew it was wrong. He has a wife, but they're separated and they don't have kids. He had nothing to lose and I did.'

Nicu's brow furrows again. 'What do you mean?'

'I meant that having an affair with me wasn't a big deal for him.'

'But he has two children,' he says.

'No he doesn't,' I reply, perplexed.

And that's when he shows me his phone. Nicu is referring to a text message with a video attached.

It's of me in Liv's kitchen, kissing her husband Brandon. I think I want to be sick again.

With the force of a tsunami, the video prompts images from last night to flood back. In my hungover state, I'd forgotten all about it, and now I've just made things a hell of a lot worse.

'If you don't mean Brandon, then who do you mean?' Nicu asks.

Until this moment, Nicu knew nothing about me and the man I've spent the last three months having an affair with.

CHAPTER 55

ANNA

Margot is like the weather. You can't be one hundred per cent sure what you'll get from one day to the next. Catty, funny, resentful, theatrical, melancholic . . . She slips into moods as effortlessly as she might slip on one of her designer dresses. But tears? No, that's not her style. However, they're already running when I open my front door. Her hair is piled up on her head and her skin is red and blotchy.

'What's wrong?' I ask, failing to hide my surprise.

'It's Nicu,' she sobs.

'Has something happened?'

'He's walked out on me.' She exhales sharply from her nose and a thick line of snot falls, resting above her upper lip. She wipes it away with the back of her hand. 'He's packed his bags, taken the kids and gone.'

'Why?'

Now she's sobbing too hard to be understood.

I invite her in, step out to close the garage door that Drew left open, then follow her into the lounge. I hand her a box of tissues. She grabs a bunch and wipes her tears, nose and hand. Behind her,

I spy Drew descending the stairs. He catches a glimpse of the back of her head, scowls and creeps out, quietly shutting the front door behind him.

When I offer Margot a hug, she hangs on to me for dear life. Only weeks ago we were the other way around. I feel the dampness of her cheek against my neck.

'Anna, I've messed up,' she admits as she lets go of me and sinks into the sofa.

I sit next to her.

'You have no idea what a terrible person I can be,' she says.

Oh I think I do.

'It can't be that bad,' I reply. And then I twist the knife. 'It's not like you've killed anyone, have you?'

She hesitates for the length of a heartbeat before shaking her head.

'Then whatever could it be?' I persist.

'I don't want you to think badly of me.'

The horse bolted from that stable a long, long time ago.

'I've been cheating on Nicu,' she continues.

'Who with?' I ask.

'Someone I met online. On an app.'

She recounts how things haven't been great between her and her husband for some time, and so she sought attention from others. I ask how Nicu found out.

'That's the thing, he didn't. I told him.'

'Wow,' I say. 'That's brave.'

She shakes her head. 'Brave has nothing to do with it. We'd been talking at cross-purposes. I was admitting to a fling with another guy, but he was talking about Brandon.'

'Brandon?' I repeat. 'As in Liv's husband, Brandon?'

Margot breaks eye contact.

'What does Brandon have to do with this?' I ask.

'Liv's birthday party on Saturday night. We kissed.'

'You did what?'

'Don't judge me!' she cries.

'I'm sorry,' I say, then wonder why I'm the one apologising. 'You kissed?'

'Yes . . . well . . . not exactly. It wasn't what I'd call mutual.' Her face reddens. 'I kissed him and he pulled away. I was drunk, and Nicu and I'd had another argument before I left the house and Brandon was flirting with me . . .'

'That's no reason to kiss your friend's husband.'

Her tone switches to defensive. 'I know, but it's not like he didn't offer me any encouragement, Anna. He was leading me on.'

I can't explain why, but I feel disappointed by her behaviour. I shouldn't, given what I know she's capable of. But I thought I'd witnessed a different side to her when she found me in trouble. A nurturing side that was genuinely worried about another human being. And now she's reverted to type. I half expect to hear Ioana's voice chirp up with a 'told you so', but she maintains her silence.

'And who is this other man you were having an affair with?'

Margot looks shifty. 'It doesn't matter. *He* doesn't matter. Again, I was lonely and it was stupid.'

She admits it lasted a few months before she ended it when her mysterious other man began to fall for her.

'And you definitely haven't been having an affair with Brandon?' I ask. 'What happened on Saturday night was a one-off?'

'Yes.'

'Does Liv know about it?'

'I have no idea,' Margot groans. 'I didn't recognise the number of the person who sent Nicu the video.'

'There's a video?'

'Yes. Someone recorded what I did but edited out the part where Brandon pushed me away and left me alone, looking like an idiot.'

'The party was two days ago and you've not heard from Liv?'

'No.'

'I think if she knew, she'd have confronted you about it by now.'

'Perhaps. Unless she was the one who recorded it.'

'I think she'd be more inclined to slap you than take the time to record you.'

'Well she's never really liked me, has she?' Margot argues.

'Of course she does.'

'Come on, Anna. You've turned a blind eye to all the things she's done and said to undermine me. And we never got to the bottom of that envelope in her bin, did we? Some women are just naturally jealous of others.'

'I don't mean any offence, but look at her. I don't think she has much to be jealous of.'

'Well surprise surprise, you're taking her side again.'

'I'm not taking anyone's side,' I protest. But she's not listening.

'I shouldn't have come here. I was expecting too much from my so-called friend.'

Margot picks herself up off the sofa and makes a beeline for the front door.

'Sit down,' I say. 'Don't go home like this.'

But before I know it, the door slams and the same whirlwind that brought her here carries her home again.

CHAPTER 56

MARGOT

My head is swimming. I can't focus on any one thing at a time. I look at my watch to remind myself what day of the week it is. Wednesday, apparently. The last day of what has been a pretty shitty month. It feels so much longer than three days since Nicu left with the kids. My family, the three people closest to me but whom I have pushed away for so long, are now all I can think about.

I check my phone. None of them have messaged me today. Tommy and I have had the occasional Snapchat, but Frankie's ignoring me. Nicu won't answer my phone calls, insisting he only wants to communicate by text until he's ready to talk. I've asked myself if I could forgive him for cheating and I don't know if I could. Yet I'm hoping that's what he'll do for me. I need him to know I'm sorry. But each time I type those words in all their variations and press send, they go unacknowledged.

The three of them are staying at the home of Nicu's dance partner Kristina and her wife in Milton Keynes, about forty minutes from here. He drives the kids to school each day before catching a train to London to rehearse for *Strictly*, and then he's back in time to pick them up from school. I volunteered to help while we're in this transitory period but he offered a firm 'no thanks'.

As I lie on this empty bed I realise that, for the first time in as long as I can remember, I am completely alone. I didn't understand how much I'd miss the chaos and mess that comes with having a family until I threw it away. Not even my double dose of antidepressants or alcohol is diluting the pain.

Anna has been in contact, which is kind of her, considering the way I left things. But I've not replied to her texts and voice notes and I didn't answer the door when she called earlier. I'm not punishing her for taking Liv's side, I'm just too ashamed to face her. So I remain hidden behind closed shutters like a modern-day Miss Havisham.

I've downed a bottle and a half of Pinot Grigio this afternoon, and the more I drink, the angrier I feel towards Liv. No matter what Anna says, I'm convinced it was Liv who made that video of me kissing her husband and sent it to Nicu. The number of ways she has screwed me over is as long as her hair extensions. She's plagued me with hate mail, interfered in my relationship with Frankie, she's driven subtle wedges between Anna and me, and now this.

Liv should have had the decency to confront me about coming on to Brandon, woman to woman, not break up me and Nicu. Yes, I'm partly responsible, but I will go to my grave convinced Brandon was leading me on.

I know I should sleep it off and tomorrow, with a sober head, come up with a plan to rescue my marriage. But the longer I wait, the harder fear grips me. What if tomorrow is too late? What if I'm giving Nicu too much time to dwell on what I've done? Perhaps if I turned up unannounced on Kristina's doorstep today, I could persuade him to talk this through? I might just say the one thing that makes him realise we can resolve this. It's got to be worth a try, hasn't it?

I sit up, wait for my head to stop spinning, shower, then throw open the wardrobe doors. I can't arrive overdressed and have Nicu think his absence has had no effect on me. So I slip on a dark pair of trousers and top, apply a minimal amount of make-up and a handful of sprays from a bottle of Chanel Coco Mademoiselle, Nicu's favourite. The orange, jasmine and bergamot notes cling to my neck. Then I head downstairs and guzzle two cups of industrial-strength black coffee to sharpen my mind. Finally, I'm ready.

Once inside my own car, I take a few swigs from a canister of water that's been in here for days. It's warm and musty but I need to dilute the wine still coursing through me. On Nicu's insistence, we've had this electric vehicle for two years now and I still don't have the first clue how to charge it. I think there's enough power to get me to Milton Keynes and back. I wind the window down, fill my lungs with fresh air and set off to save my marriage.

I've only just passed a road sign informing me I've left the village when I spot a familiar figure running up ahead.

Liv.

There's nobody else around here who runs in skintight outfits or who has the figure of a street light. So even from behind, I know it's her. I gently press the brakes and glare at her. Her hair is tied back into a ponytail and she is wearing a pair of large over-the-ear headphones that I assume cancel outside noise. They, along with the whisper-quiet engine of this car, mean I doubt she knows there's anyone behind her. There are no paths on either side of this road, only verges.

I'm drawing closer to her, the so-called friend who destroyed my life with one text. Everything has turned to shit because of her. I feel the rage gradually building inside me. And slowly, I accelerate.

I glance into the rearview mirror to check no one is following me. But it's just Liv and me on this road. I apply a little more pressure upon the pedal and the car speeds up, then its sensors beep, warning me I'm too close to an object. I press a button to override the automatic braking system and pull wide so that a third of the car is on the other side of the road, close enough to brush up against her and scare the hell out of her. But before I get the chance to think twice, it happens. I clip her.

Liv flies off the road like a skittle hit by a ten-pin bowling ball. I've knocked her into a ditch.

It wasn't the plan, but after the initial surprise, I burst into laughter. And the rush of adrenaline that soars through me is immeasurable.

I slow down, glancing again into my rearview mirror, waiting for her to appear, caked in mud, clambering to her feet and wiping herself down. There was a good rainfall last night, so I bet she's soaked to the skin.

Only there's no sign of her.

I slow the car to barely a crawl. Perhaps she's a little dazed and is taking a minute before she rises to her feet like Lazarus in Adidas. Still, nothing.

So then I stop and wait. She is still nowhere to be seen. I hang around a little longer, and gradually, a sense of dread wells up inside me.

'Get up you stupid cow!' I shout aloud. 'Come on! Stop being so dramatic.'

Two interminably long minutes pass in which a car appears ahead and I spread out across the passenger seat so as not to be spotted. When it passes, I manoeuvre my own car into a three-point turn and drive, stopping at where I clipped her. I look out from the driver's window and spot a pink and silver trainer lying on its side on the verge.

Not even the strongest coffee will sober you up as quickly as the realisation you might have just killed someone. Instinct is telling me to get the hell out of there, but my controlling side warns me

I can't leave until I know for certain what's happened. So I exit the car and walk slowly across the road.

And there I find her. Liv is lying face up, half her body in the watery ditch, half of it out. Her arm is unnaturally bent backwards and her head is resting against a wooden fence post. Blood seeps from a gash to her forehead.

'Liv,' I say. 'Are you alright?'

There's no response. I repeat her name. Then I say it again, waiting for a spark of life to ignite inside her. But there's no flicker of animation.

All I know about first aid is what I've seen on TV, so I search for a pulse in her wrists, then her neck. There's nothing. I even place my palm in the centre of her chest to find a heartbeat. But she is completely motionless.

I think I've killed her. I think I have bloody well killed her.

I steady myself against the fence post as the ground beneath me gives way. Then, when I'm able to, I hurry back to the car and drive.

OCTOBER

ONE MONTH BEFORE BONFIRE NIGHT

CHAPTER 57

ANNA

I'm sure I spot a shadow moving behind the shutters in Margot's lounge. I know Nicu and the kids haven't returned, so it can only be her. But she's not answering the door. And she hasn't replied to my messages for days.

It takes two more knocks – much louder this time – before finally the door opens a crack. In even this limited view of her, she looks worse than she did the last time I saw her. Her eyes are bloodshot, her make-up smeared and her unruly hair makes her looks like something the cat dragged in, ate, then vomited up. It's clear she's taking the split with Nicu badly.

However, I'm struggling to revel in her misery like I once would have. And I don't know if it's because my resolve has weakened or because, today, there's something bigger than both of us to deal with.

'Anna,' she says huskily, but doesn't invite me in.

'Did you get my messages?' I ask.

'I've had a bug and haven't left the house in a couple of days or turned on my—'

'It's Liv. She's been hurt.'

Margot blinks rapidly, her red eyes opening wide.

'Car accident,' I continue. 'Hit-and-run, the police think. She was out jogging yesterday afternoon when it happened. Brandon found her using a phone-tracking app. She's in a bad way apparently.'

'But she's still alive?'

'Yes.'

She releases a long breath that reeks of vinegar, and I pull my head back. 'Oh thank God,' she says. And for a moment, I think she might be about to cry.

'She's in hospital,' I continue. 'Brandon says she's being kept in a medically induced coma until the swelling on her brain shrinks. She also has a broken arm, ribs and a leg.'

Margot steadies herself against the doorframe with her hand.

'Are you alright?' I ask. 'You don't look well.'

'I'm okay.'

'Brandon has asked if we can help him. The kids don't know what's happened and he's asked if we can pick them up from nursery tonight and keep them until his mum can get here. She's driving up from Cornwall.'

Margot's face turns an even more ghostly shade of grey.

'I don't know . . .'

'Why?' I ask, a little irritated. 'Do you have something more important to do?'

I'm being pushy. And I know why. I'm overcompensating because I'm terrified. I smelled alcohol on Drew when he returned home yesterday. He always takes the back road to the village and he was passing along it at the time the police told Brandon his wife was likely hit. I begged Drew to tell me he wasn't responsible. He denied it, adamant it wasn't him. And when I pressed further, he reacted by punching a hole in the dining room wall. I still don't know if I believe him.

'You're right,' Margot backtracks. 'What can I do?'

'I thought you could have the twins for a couple of hours, as you have more experience with kids than I do, and I'll go to Aldi and make sure there's plenty of food in their house.'

'You're sure Brandon wants my help?' she asks hesitantly.

'What happened between you and him will be the last thing on his mind right now. I'll text you later about times, etcetera.'

'Anna,' Margot says as I'm about to leave. 'Is Liv going to be alright?'

'I don't know,' I reply. 'All we can do is keep our fingers crossed.'

CHAPTER 58

MARGOT

I've barely budged from behind the bedroom window this week. All morning Liv's house has been a hive of activity, from police officers in marked cars to friends stopping by with meals stuffed into casserole dishes and Tupperware pots. To add insult to injury, I watch Cat Face versions 1.0 and 2.0 shitting together in my borders.

Brandon texted me earlier to thank me in advance for picking the twins up from nursery. I replied politely with an *If there's anything else I can do, just ask.* But now I'm questioning whether he might misinterpret what was supposed to be an innocent offer. Not even I'd try coming on to the husband of someone I almost killed.

A week after the accident – for that's what I'm calling it – I've got into the habit of checking my car daily to reassure myself there's no evidence of Liv on it. The moment I returned home, I checked the front bumper and wing for dents, chipped paint or traces of Liv's hair, blood or clothing. I've watched enough true-life crime documentaries on Netflix to know that all it might take is a microscopic droplet of plasma to send me to prison.

I found nothing. But just to be sure, early the next morning, I paid for it to be professionally valeted – then, on my return home, I deleted the journey from my sat nav history.

A grumbling stomach reminds me I haven't eaten since yesterday afternoon. But all I find in the kitchen cupboard are slices of blue-speckled bread and a couple of croissants that are more flaky than pastry.

My thoughts drift back to when I approached Liv's body in that ditch. I was convinced she was dead – there was no pulse, no breathing and no heartbeat – so I didn't call for help. I play it out in my head. If I had, how would I have explained why I spotted her from my car, off road and lying in a ditch? If a suspicious police officer had breathalysed me, I'd have been well over the legal drink-drive limit. And it wouldn't have been long before they'd have discovered the video Liv sent to Nicu, giving me a motive to hurt her. The tabloid exposé of Nicu's affair with me almost twelve years ago would pale into insignificance compared to the headlines that would generate. So what else could I do but leave?

I have considered begging Nicu for his help in sorting this mess out. I know he still loves me, because if he didn't care, he wouldn't have been so hurt by my affair. But both times I've picked up my phone to dial him, I've changed my mind. It's unfair to expect him to try and bail me out. Besides, he's not like me. He'd insist I do the right thing when I'm convinced that, by leaving her, I already did.

The phone's alarm sounds – it's time to get the twins. The nursery is a ten-minute walk from my house and one of the teaching assistants is waiting for me by the door when I arrive. It's my fourth pick-up, so she recognises me and explains that Rupert has been upset, saying he's missing his mum. I feel just awful. I can only stop his tears by FaceTiming Brandon, who's at the hospital with Liv. He calms his son down with promises of a trip to the playpark later before Brandon and I share a brief, perfunctory exchange. Apparently Liv remains stable, the swelling to her brain has subsided, and now it's a waiting game until when she regains consciousness.

I honestly hope she pulls through. And it's not just to alleviate my guilt. It's for the sake of the kids I'm now watching in the dining room playing with Tommy's old toys. I hate to think how losing their mother at such an early age might affect them. Then I'm reminded that's exactly what happened to Frankie and Tommy. They've spent most of their lives with me, not Ioana.

Back then, it felt so unfair. They were thrust upon me without anyone asking if it was what I wanted. I was less concerned for the welfare of two frightened, confused kids and more bothered by the aftermath of being accused by the press and social media of driving a young mum to take her own life. I didn't want to be a mother to any child, let alone those spawned by a vindictive bitch who, even in death, was out to ruin me. Only now can I admit how phenomenally selfish I was.

Suddenly, my phone rings. Nicu's face lights up the screen. We've had text conversations about Liv but we've not actually spoken. I hurry into the other room, leaving the door open so I can keep an eye on the twins as they play with an Octonauts boat.

'How's Liv?' he says without asking how I am first.

I run through Brandon's update. Nicu hears the children's laughter and I tell him I'm looking after them again.

'Do you need my help?' he asks.

I want to say yes, that while I'm not struggling with them, I am struggling with just about everything else in my life since he left. But I don't. I need him to see that I have got this.

'Thank you, but we'll be okay,' I reply instead.

A brief silence follows. I need to fill the gap.

'Look,' I continue, 'when you're ready to talk, I'm here to listen. And I don't mean that I'm going to talk over you or try and justify what I did, I just want to hear what you have to say.'

'Thank you,' he replies before we say our goodbyes.

I take a moment to myself, dab the corner of my eyes, perform a few cleansing breaths and return to the twins. At this very moment, they might well be the only two people in this world who want to be around me.

CHAPTER 59

MARGOT

The hospital is the last place I want to be. But Anna was adamant I join her. Apparently, she hates these places. She muttered something about spending too much time in them when she was a girl, but I wasn't wearing the appropriate footwear for a trip down memory lane. I was preoccupied by trying to find a way out of this. Short of faking a heart attack or stroke, she gave me little choice but to come.

Truth be told, I'd rather be spending time with Liv's kids than their mum. They have no expectations of me, and all I'm required to do is keep them fed, safe and entertained for a few hours until I hand them back to Brandon or their grandma. They seem to enjoy my company, and when we arrive at their home, they always hug me goodbye without being told to. They've shown me this is how it should've been between me, Frankie and Tommy when they first came into my life. They deserved attention. They received resentment. I wish I'd been better.

I've started trying to build inroads with them, which is difficult when you're living under separate roofs. And to do that, I've decided to be honest with them. I've admitted it's my fault their dad and I have separated, and they're old enough to understand what an affair is. I've promised I'm going to do my best to make it up to them all. Frankie will be harder to convince than their brother – I'm training myself to use their chosen pronouns – but I'm willing to put the work in. I've allowed too much water to pass under the bridge to call myself their mother, but I can be their friend.

I'm hoping it'll be easier next month, as that's when they're all moving back. The new series of *Strictly* starts soon, so Nicu will be away in London from Wednesday to Saturday each week. He'll stay at ours the rest of the time, although we'll have our own bedrooms.

But first, I need to get this morning out of the way. Anna senses my trepidation.

'Are you still worried about that video?' she asks.

'You think?' I say dryly.

'We don't even know if she's aware of what happened that night.'

'Then who sent Nicu the video?'

'I have no idea. Given what's happened since, it doesn't matter anymore. If Brandon hasn't mentioned it already, he's not going to now.'

'Perhaps I should just take the bull by the horns and apologise for what I did?'

Anna shakes her head vigorously. 'Or perhaps you shouldn't. Perhaps you should let sleeping dogs lie and keep your mouth shut.'

Her bluntness surprises me.

'I was expecting you to tell me to be honest,' I reply.

'In my experience, people only admit the truth to ease their conscience. Don't make yourself feel better by making her feel worse.'

Anna leads the way to Liv's floor. It's a private hospital so she has a room to herself. My body stiffens when I catch sight of her.

She's awake, sitting upright on top of the bedcovers, watching an afternoon quiz show on a wall-mounted television. She is casually dressed, in a sweatsuit. Even without make-up, she doesn't look as if, just over two weeks ago, I left her at death's door. Her arm and leg are in plaster casts and there is a bandage taped to her forehead.

'Oh my God!' she yelps as Anna approaches.

She leans over the bed and gives Anna a hug, and Anna places a box of chocolates and a bouquet of October blooms on a cupboard by her bedside. My heart is racing when her eyes meet with mine.

'Margot.' She grins and hugs me next. 'It's so good to see you.'

I wait for a sign that this is an act, but it doesn't surface. She pats the side of her bed and beckons us to sit.

'How are you feeling?' asks Anna.

'You know what, I'm doing pretty good, I think,' she says. 'At least that's what the doctors keep telling me. They can't find any significant brain damage. Well, no more than I had before the accident.'

I laugh nervously.

'When are they discharging you?' Anna continues.

'All being well, in a couple of days.'

'Oh that's wonderful.'

'I know. I can't wait to sleep in my own bed.'

I look around at this plush room and think that, compared to an NHS patient, she's hardly roughing it. Then I remind myself why she's here in the first place.

'Do you remember anything about the accident?' I ask. I should've waited for her to bring it up. But my mouth is operating faster than my brain.

'Nope, not a thing.' She shrugs. 'The last thing I recall is leaving the house to go for a run and then waking up in here, missing a few days and with the headache from hell.'

'You didn't see who hit you?'

256

'I don't think I even heard the car. Apparently, I was even dead for a while.'

'Dead?' Anna asks.

'Brandon could barely locate my pulse when he found me, and by the time the ambulance arrived, it'd disappeared.'

Yes! I almost want to punch the air with joy. I was right to believe she was dead.

'They had to resuscitate me with a defibrillator,' she continues.

'And do the police have any leads?' I say.

She shakes her head. 'And unless any witnesses come forward, they can't put any more man-hours into the case. They don't have the resources.'

'Well, you're alive and that's what counts,' I reply, and I mean it. And not only for my sake.

'And you're expected to make a full recovery?' Anna asks.

'My fractures are healing well, but I'll probably need to grow my fringe out until I can have surgery on the scar under this bandage.'

She removes her phone from the cabinet next to her bed and locates a photograph of the stitches in her forehead. They're in the shape of a crescent. Blood was oozing from that wound the last time I saw her.

'I told Brandon I might keep the scar, as it gives me an edge,' she jokes. 'He said it makes me look like an ageing Harry Potter.'

I laugh dutifully.

'The only lasting effect is that my memory isn't great,' Liv continues. 'The week or so leading up to the accident is fuzzy. I can't remember much about it.'

I wonder if she remembers recording a certain video and sending it to my husband?

'It might come back or it might not,' she adds. 'It's only a week out of my life so it could've been a lot worse.' She turns to us both.

'I hate to ask, but could one of you help me into the bathroom? My legs are still weak and I'm not used to the crutches.'

I am grateful when Anna offers to help. When they disappear behind the closed door, I seize my opportunity. Liv's phone remains unlocked so I open her photo reel and search for the incriminating video footage. If her memory of that week is so hazy, there's a chance she might not recall me and Brandon. It's not here. I rack my brain to remember the format it was in when Nicu showed it to me. But in my hungover state, all that registered were the images. I check her WhatsApps, texts, iMessages, emails and Facebook Messenger, but it's not there either.

It's when I jump in and out of other folders that a handful of video clips in the same folder catch my eye. I can't work out what I'm watching until a few moments in. It's porn. Well, that's a surprise. I turn the volume down a couple of notches. There's a masked man having wax poured over his buttocks while a masked woman smacks him with a wooden paddle. I'm surprised this is Liv's cup of tea, but we all have our quirks.

And then I hear this kinky couple's voices.

'Do you want me to stop?' she screams.

'Yes, mistress, yes,' he shouts back at her.

'Oh my God!' I say aloud when I realise what, or who, I'm viewing. These are the elusive OnlyFans videos I've been searching for. I press stop and go further back. There are dozens more like this. I randomly select a few, then AirDrop them to my phone so there's no trace of them being sent to me. The toilet flushes just as the last one appears on my screen.

Then I return her device to the home screen, place it back where it was and position myself in front of the window facing the lawned gardens that she has an uninterrupted view of.

My back is to her, so she doesn't spot the smile I can't peel from my face.

CHAPTER 60

LIV

Margot and Anna stay with me for the best part of an hour before they sense I'm growing tired. They slip their jackets on and prepare to leave.

'Thank you so much for coming,' I say as Anna leans over the bed and hugs me. 'And thanks to both of you for helping Brandon and his mum with the kids. You've been amazing.'

'You're very welcome,' Anna replies. 'You'd do the same for us.'

'I'm lucky to have you as friends.'

Margot looks away when I say this. I always assumed she was one of those people who revelled in a compliment. Who actively fished for them. I guess I was wrong. Actually, I think I might be wrong about a few things when it comes to her. She has been there for my family when it really matters. She has her faults, but she has come through for us.

She picks up her handbag and checks her phone.

There's so much about the day of my hit-and-run that I don't remember. I don't recall hearing or seeing the car that knocked me into the ditch or the driver who left me there. I don't remember my husband finding my body or the paramedics who resuscitated me. I don't recall hearing the hospital doctors and consultants discussing putting me into a coma to help alleviate my swelling brain. And I don't remember them bringing me out of it.

There is, however, one tiny detail that I do recall. And it only comes to me as Margot is hugging me goodbye. And that's a smell. A pungent, citrusy scent that's out of place in the roadside ditch where I was left for dead. Yet I remember it as clear as day.

And I think I have just smelled it again.

CHAPTER 61

ANNA

'Where have you been?' snaps Drew the moment I enter the kitchen.

I've barely set foot over the threshold and he's already gunning for me. His tone creates a tension in my body, and the intensity of just those few words is like a weight pressing down on my chest. I hold up four bulging bags of supermarket shopping.

'Where do you think?' I reply casually, trying to defuse a situation before it arises.

'You need to see this.'

He thrusts his iPad in front of my face like a weapon. It's too close to make out what's on it.

'Let me put these away first,' I say and place the bags on the countertop. 'The rest are in the car if you want to help?'

'Joanna!' he says with a raised voice. I bristle and his last aggressive outburst jumps to mind. I placate him because I don't want to risk a repeat performance.

'Okay, what's so important?'

We take seats at the kitchen table. He is where that detective was when Drew killed him. We never talk about it but I wonder if he replays it in his head as often as I do?

Drew's face and body are animated. A chapter from our long-shared history reappears, a time when amphetamines were part of his day-to-day routine and long before alcohol became the norm. Is he using again?

'The evening of Liv's hit-and-run,' he begins. 'You know I was on my way home from work and drove past the spot where they later found her?'

We argued about this previously when I asked if he had any involvement. I remain unconvinced by his angry denials because he is often all too willing to climb behind the wheel of a vehicle while over the drink-drive limit. If he hasn't hurt Liv, it'll be someone else.

'And?' I ask.

'This morning, I woke up remembering something. A car parked by the side of the road.'

'Whose car?'

His irises widen, like unnavigable black holes. 'Margot's,' he says.

'Margot's?' I repeat.

Now he's like one of those toy nodding dogs.

'And you suddenly remembered this today. Three weeks after the accident.'

'You think I'm lying?' he asks in disbelief, throwing himself back in his seat.

'No, but sometimes you misremember things, especially if you've been drinking.'

My body tenses again as I prepare for him to fly into another rage.

'I know I'm not always reliable,' he says, his admission catching me off guard. 'And the day of the hit-and-run had been shitty, so yeah, I'd had a couple of drinks and I probably shouldn't have driven. But I didn't hit Liv, and now I remember passing a car that looked exactly like Margot's.'

'Wait, was it Margot's car or a car that *looked* like hers?'

'It *was* hers,' says Drew. 'Did she tell you where she was the afternoon when Liv was hit?'

I remember going to her house the next morning to tell her about Liv's accident. 'I think she said she'd caught a bug and hadn't been out in days,' I recall. 'But Nicu had walked out on her earlier that weekend, so I think she'd been drowning her sorrows.'

If I'm not mistaken, there's a hint of a smile at the mention of Nicu's departure.

'Well, she was lying,' Drew says adamantly.

He opens the Doorbell app on his iPad, and the timestamp in the top right-hand corner of the screen is the day of Liv's accident.

'Look,' he says, and as clear as day, Liv goes past in running gear. Soon after, Margot also exits across the road. She stumbles – either she's lost her footing or she's drunk. Seconds later, her car pulls out of the camera's range.

'So she goes out,' I say. 'Perhaps she went to pick up some groceries.'

'Now watch this,' he says and moves to another saved clip.

It's of the car he and I share pulling on to the drive. He fast-forwards, and ten minutes later, Margot returns in her vehicle and hurries into her house. In a third and final clip taken the same night, the screen is much darker but I watch as a figure leaves her house and spends time at the front end of Margot's car. It's too dark to tell, but they're hunched over the front, slowly moving around it, section by section.

'I think she's cleaning the bumpers, trying to get rid of evidence,' Drew says triumphantly. 'She ran over Liv, hung around on that road to see if she was dead, then returned home, panicked there might be evidence left, and tried to cover her tracks.'

I watch the clips again in order. Could he be right?

'But it doesn't make sense,' I protest. 'Margot wouldn't leave two kids without a mum. She has no reason to hurt Liv.'

But of course she does. The video of her kissing Brandon which she believes Liv filmed and sent to Nicu.

'You haven't seen what she's been like since the accident,' I add, now arguing with myself. 'She's been brilliant with Liv's kids, better than she is with her own. She even came to the hospital with me to visit her. Why would she do that to someone she tried to kill?'

'Because she's a fucking psychopath!' Drew roars. 'You already know this! She's trying to cover her back.'

'But she cared about me when I . . . hurt myself.'

'And I bet Vladimir Putin bought his mum flowers on Mother's Day,' he replies. 'That doesn't make him a good person either.'

'You weren't there,' I say. 'You didn't see her.'

I close the app and return to the shopping bags. I'm only just coming to terms with seeing a different side to Margot and now Drew is hitting me with this. Have I lowered my guard too far? Has she been pulling the wool over my eyes? I'm aware I'm being watched as I unpack.

'So that's it?' Drew asks.

'What do you want me to say?' I reply.

'That you believe Margot drove into Liv and left her for dead.'

'I think you're desperate for it to be her,' I argue. 'It's too much of a stretch.'

'Stop being so fucking blind!' he continues. 'Margot has you hoodwinked. The leopard hasn't changed its spots, it's just hiding them under a different coat. And let's not forget, long before Liv, she tried to kill you first. She tried to kill *both* of us. You need to stop listening to her and start listening to me.'

'Why?'

'Because she is a fucking sociopath and I am your brother.'

CHAPTER 62

ANNA

I want to argue with Drew but I can't. He's right. Margot did try and murder us the night she and her gang broke into our home. That version of us, Andrew and Joanna, feels strange to me now.

After he and I sought refuge under our parents' bed, it was Margot's face I saw moments before she set the room ablaze. Our eyes locked: her expression mirrored the shock I felt at seeing her. I took in her curly auburn hair, her green pupils, her silver nose ring and eyebrow piercings. Then she vanished out of sight, jumping to her feet, and seconds later the trail of lighter fuel she had squirted across the carpet and above us on the bed was zigzagging like flaming ribbons.

I remember everything about that night with such clarity. The aftermath of our escape. Watching my brother being brought back to life on the cold pavement outside our burning home. Screaming in fear and pain while paramedics treated my burns. Crying long into the night in our separate hospital wards. My bewildered aunt and uncle appearing the following day after a flight from Pakistan, the two of them forced to come to terms with both the death of family members and having to care for two children. The days, weeks and months that followed. The skin grafts, the infections, my brother's rasp through smoke-damaged lungs, moving into a new home in a new county with a new school and new parents.

The transition was difficult for us all, our worlds turned upside down and inside out. The rebellious streak that had blighted Andrew's relationship with our dad burned alongside his body in the fire. Confrontations and clashes were replaced by long periods of silence and deep depressions. He became a shadow of the brother I remembered. I adapted to change better, but fragments of me would always remain under that blazing bed.

While arrests were made, there were no charges. All evidence had been destroyed by the fire, and anything left against the four suspects was circumstantial. It wasn't enough that I picked out Margot's face from a dozen mugshots they showed us, because Andrew was too traumatised to corroborate. At six and testifying alone, I was not considered a reliable witness for the prosecution.

It took another seven years before I crossed paths with Margot for a second time.

I was in my bedroom watching *Ant & Dec's Saturday Night Takeaway* when the presenters introduced a brand-new seven-piece pop group made up of four boys and three girls. Their song had an instant hook, the band's outfits were bright and colourful and their personalities excitable as they each chased the camera for attention. They were perfect fodder for a thirteen-year-old me. But it was the post-performance interview when my already fragile world spun another hundred and eighty degrees.

'I'm Margot,' chirped a brash redhead with green eyes and a wide smile. Although her physical appearance had altered with age and maturity, I instantly recognised her. Her eyes shone with the same intensity as when our gazes had met as I hid under that bed.

It was her. It was *definitely* her.

I screamed Andrew's name until he came into my room, then I tried to make him see what I saw. I thought there was a glimmer of recognition, then he shook his head. He didn't remember her. The commotion brought the attention of my aunt and uncle, but they were equally sceptical of my accusations. Only after days of pestering them did they finally relent and contact our case's investigating officer.

Later in the week, a lower-ranking police officer was sent to talk to me. Detective Sergeant Roger Fenton – the same man who, years later, would turn up at our house, and whom my brother had killed ten weeks ago. He'd recognised the adult version of myself in the pages of *Yeah!* magazine at Frankie's awful gender reveal party, realising 'Anna' on the picture caption was short for Joanna, and that my surname had changed from Khan to Mason when our aunt and uncle formally adopted me and Drew.

Considering my allegations against Margot, he was surprised to find me not only at her party but living in a house opposite her. And after a little investigative work, he learned the other members of Margot's gang – who, like her, had been questioned but released without charge – were now dead.

But back then, I'd know immediately he was only there to pay me lip service.

'Look, Joanna, I have every sympathy with you,' he said, 'but you were only six years old at the time, a kid. You were traumatised. You don't know what you saw through the darkness under that bed. This pop star might look a little like her, but it isn't. Your mind is playing tricks on you.'

I argued and argued but still he wouldn't believe me. Only, it turned out a part of him quietly had. I hated them all for doubting me, especially my brother. The person closest to me hadn't even offered me the benefit of the doubt.

The frustration became intolerable, particularly once the Party Hard Posse began climbing the charts. But I wasn't going to give up trying to be heard. I called the *News of the World*'s news desk to tell them what she'd done, but they hung up on me. I made it through to the band's record company's press office, but they told me not to call again.

I had one option left. To confront Margot in person. Because if I hadn't forgotten her, surely she hadn't forgotten me either? So one morning I played truant at school and hopped on a London-bound train to spend four hours outside Oxford Street's HMV store with hundreds of Party Hard Posse fans, patiently waiting for the band to sign their latest CD.

And when I eventually approached the front of the line, I'd never been more certain of anything in my life. Margot's hair might have been styled and coloured differently, her face might have lost its puppy fat and her nose might have been thinner, but her green eyes remained as sharp and distinguishable as when I'd seen her that night.

My heart pounded in my throat when I stepped up to the band, sitting behind a table, taking it in turns to sign my CD case and poster. Then, for the first time in seven years, Margot and I were face to face. I was close enough to spot a small hole in the side of her nose and another in her left eyebrow where she'd once had the piercings I remembered. It was all I could do to stop my legs from buckling beneath me. I could barely say my own name when she asked. Only the second syllable came out.

'Anna,' I muttered.

As her black marker pen glided across the merchandise, I realised that if I didn't say anything else, everything I wished would happen would not. I had to feed her ego to make her really see me.

'You're my favourite,' I said.

It worked. She looked up at me. But instead of a flicker of recognition, panic, or better still, sheer terror, there was only a smile.

'Thanks,' she said. 'That's neat.'

Then her attention was diverted to the girl behind me and staff ushered me away.

I was sick in an alley as soon as I left the shop. Margot had obliterated everything I had loved. But I did not exist in her memory.

What else could I do?

The years that followed were beyond difficult. I'd lost my parents, Drew was living away from home, and my aunt and uncle were discussing returning to their native Pakistan after relocating here for our sake. I had nobody and nothing. I saw a counsellor, but instead of being honest about my feelings, I told her what I thought she wanted to hear. Then, just as I reached my lowest point, standing on the cliff edge at Beachy Head and giving serious consideration as to whether I wanted to live anymore, my mum spoke to me. She gave me a purpose. She steered me towards a path that would redefine my life. And when her work was complete, other passengers joined me. No matter what it took and who might fall to the wayside, I promised myself that, one day, Margot would know who I was. Then she would die and I could get on with the rest of my life.

But now I've gotten to know her. And while she has many, many faults, she is no longer the devil who haunted a six-year-old's dreams. She is a human being – a deeply flawed one, but one capable of kindness too. I want to hate her with the same passion I once did, but it's not in me anymore. I no longer want to be that person. Even if she did hurt Liv, be it by accident or on purpose, I don't want to go back to how I was. It's exhausting, being so many people at once.

'So what are you going to do about her?' Drew asks.

I clench my fists to stop my hands from trembling and clear my throat. 'Nothing,' I say. 'Liv can choose her own battles if that's what she wants. But I'm done.'

'So, what?' he says, looking around him. 'Everything we've worked for, putting our lives on hold, moving here, reinventing ourselves, pretending we're a married couple, it's all been for nothing?'

I swallow hard but say nothing, waiting for either a physical or a verbal assault. Neither happens. Instead, he kicks his chair backwards and it falls to the ground with a clatter as he storms out of the room.

NOVEMBER

BONFIRE NIGHT

CHAPTER 63

ANNA

I rifle through the odds-and-ends drawer, searching for where I might have left my red woollen gloves. The BBC weather app warns it'll drop to zero degrees tonight, so I want to wrap up warm for the village Bonfire Night.

I need to leave the house in about an hour. I check my phone to see if I've missed Margot's response to my texts but I've yet to hear from her. The last message she sent was just after 9 p.m. yesterday. We had a loose arrangement for me to call at hers. She offered to come here, but I don't want her anywhere near Drew at the moment. I don't want to be around him either. Not that he's been here very often since our confrontation almost two weeks ago. Sometimes days pass when he doesn't return. I have no idea where he goes or who he's with and I'm past caring. I'm less on edge when he's missing.

I know that I need to confront Margot about her involvement in Liv's accident, but I'm putting it off. Because if I do, I know that Ioana will have to kill her. It's been years since her death and I'm out of practice. The aftermath drains me of everything and I don't know if I have the strength to fight back one more time.

I suddenly remember when I last saw my gloves. I wore them as I swept leaves from the driveway at the weekend. They were wet and dirty so I put them in the washing machine. I rummage around inside it and find them along with some of Drew's damp clothes. So he has been here. He must have returned and put a load on when I was out.

As I remove them, a silver-coloured key falls from the pocket of his overalls and clinks as it hits the utility room's floor tiles. I take a closer look at it and draw a sharp intake of breath when I spot a concave mark from where I once purposely jabbed the soldering iron against it. It was to distinguish it from all the other keys in the drawer. It's one that nobody else is supposed to know I have.

I let out a gasp when a shadow moves over me.

I whirl around to meet Drew's glare. He looks at the key in my hand and I take a step back.

'What's this?' I ask, trying to mask my unease.

'Looks like a key.'

'A key to what?'

'Buckingham Palace?' he deadpans. 'Hogwarts? You tell me.'

We glare at each other and I make a snap decision not to play games.

'Why do you have Margot's front door key?'

'Shouldn't the question be why do *you* have Margot's front door key?' he replies.

'You know why.'

'Ah that's right. To break in when she's not there and move stuff around her house so she thinks she's losing the plot.'

'Why was it in your pocket?'

Drew folds his arms. 'You took too long,' he says. 'You've gone soft, Joanna. You forgot why you're here. Instead of making her life hell, you've made her your friend.'

'That's untrue,' I say. 'You know the things I've done.'

He slowly shakes his head. 'Well, I'm afraid it's no longer enough.'

'Then what would you have me do?'

'There's no need for you to do anything because I've taken care of it.'

I'm filled with fear by the coldness of his smile.

'What have you done?'

'You'll see.'

'Have you hurt her?'

'Why do you care? Because your conscience didn't seem to bother you when you killed Ioana. Or Zain, for that matter. How about Jenny? Or Warren?'

It was the aftermath of Ioana's death when I confessed to Drew what I'd done to her and the others. I'd been struggling to think straight for weeks. Day after day, night after night, she'd be shouting in my ear, never allowing me a moment's peace. She wanted her pound of flesh for killing her. And that involved me cutting mine. The more often I cut and the deeper the blade went, the quieter she became. And one morning, she pushed me too far.

I was desperate when I called my brother for help, and he found me in the bedroom of my London flat, barely conscious after nicking an artery. I sobbed uncontrollably as I waited to be patched up in the Accident & Emergency department he'd driven me to. And later, concealed behind the blue curtain of a bay, I broke down and admitted what I'd done to the others who killed our parents, plus the extent of my obsession with Margot. I remember his face draining of colour as, gradually, he became aware of what his baby sister was capable of.

But to my surprise, he began to accept it. And for the first time in our lives, he took me seriously.

'Have you hurt Margot?' I ask again now.

'No.' He smiles smugly. 'At least not for another forty-five minutes.'

Then he turns to leave. I lurch towards him, grabbing his shoulder, spinning him around. But his forceful shove is so hard that it sends me staggering from the kitchen back into the utility room. I lose my footing on his damp overalls and I slip, hitting my forehead on the corner of the washing machine. I land awkwardly on my back. I try and clamber to my feet but my spinning head hampers me and it's too late to stop him from locking the door.

I bang on it with my fists, begging to be let out. But when the lights switch off, leaving me in darkness, and I hear the back door slamming shut, I know I'm on my own.

CHAPTER 64

LIV

Five weeks after my accident, I'm still a little wobbly on my feet. So I make my way slowly up the cul-de-sac and into the high street with my hand gripped tightly around my walking stick. It was an ugly wooden thing before the kids gave it a glow-up with stickers, sparkly paints and glitter. Now I love it. Well, for the time being, at least. Because the sooner I can walk unaided, the better. I'm probably imagining it, but sometimes I think I can feel the metal pin pushing against the bone inside my leg when I move. They cut the plaster cast off my arm last week and I'm slowly regaining strength in it. My spare arm is looped through Brandon's as he walks with the twins.

'What is Bomfire Night?' asks Rupert.

'Bonfire Night,' I correct. 'Hundreds of years ago a naughty man called Guy Fawkes tried to kill the King by blowing up the Houses of Parliament. It didn't work, so once a year, we celebrate by lighting bonfires and having fireworks.'

A hundred more questions follow, but Brandon answers as I'm busy keeping an eye out for Margot while we walk along the road and up the hill. She hasn't been answering her phone, and for some reason Anna was being vague about her plans when I invited her to join us. Aside from their hospital visit, I can't remember when the three of us were last in one room together.

I took my first solo walk outside yesterday. Brandon insisted he come with me but I put my foot down – the good one – and told him I'd take my phone and call him if I got into any difficulties. Alone, I had only one destination in my sights: the place where I was knocked over and left for dead. A yellow metal board left by police on the verge was the only reminder of the sorry affair.

WITNESS APPEAL. CAN YOU HELP US? HIT-AND-RUN OCCURRED HERE ON SEPTEMBER 30 AT APPROX. 6PM. PLEASE CONTACT THE POLICE WITH ANY INFORMATION ON (01604) 60016.

I was there for a reason – to find something the police didn't realise existed. And that I'd only recalled the day before. And eventually, I spotted it, submerged in the stream running at the bottom of the ditch and partially hidden behind autumn leaf fall. It's been drying out in my airing cupboard. It's another of my secrets Brandon is unaware of.

I need to put it out of my mind for tonight. Likewise the studio. I'm out of action and one of the other two instructors has left to take on a job as a resident yogi on a Caribbean cruise liner. So that leaves only one other staff member. Brandon has been forced to pass on some of his personal-training clients to instructor friends as he helps to look after me. He keeps telling me not to worry and that everything will sort itself out. But what we're earning falls woefully short of what we need to break even. And I've exhausted my options of where to go for help. Harrison is out of the question. Even with the proof I have he's a paedophile, he's made it clear that if I try and blackmail him again, I'll be putting my family at risk. I just wish my leg would heal quicker.

Finally, the four of us reach the community centre, and I take a seat under a portable heater. Up ahead, I spot Anna's husband Drew leaning against the wall, a bottle in his hand. He's wearing a baseball cap that shields much of his face but he's still recognisable by his oversized parka coat and trainers. He must be waiting for her. I'm about to wave when Brandon returns from the café with steaming paper cups of hot chocolate. By the time I look back, Drew has gone.

The kids persuade their dad to buy them brightly coloured neon glow sticks and head off in search of a vendor. Meanwhile, ahead of me, final preparations are being made to light the bonfire. Fire marshals in hi-vis yellow jackets make their way towards it, and one, using a blowtorch, lights a towel doused in something flammable on the end of a long stick. The bonfire itself is made up mainly of packing crates and pallets that an unknown Good Samaritan donated and assembled in the early hours of this morning, according to a conversation I overheard behind me.

Suddenly I spot Anna up ahead, hurrying through the crowds as if searching for someone. I call her name.

'Oh hi,' she says, flustered.

She's panting, and plumes of white breath escaping her mouth become visible against the night sky.

'Your hands must be freezing,' I say, pointing to them. 'Do you want to borrow my gloves?'

'They're fine,' she says, failing to hide a shiver. 'Have you seen Margot?'

'No, I tried calling earlier but I couldn't get hold of her. Perhaps she's with Nicu?'

Anna's preoccupied by something. Her eyes flit nervously across the throngs of people.

'You and Drew are welcome to come back to ours for some supper after the display if you fancy it?' I ask.

'He's working tonight.'

'Oh. I was sure I saw him a few minutes ago.'

She glares at me. 'Where?'

'Over there,' I say and point to the community centre wall.

I spot something trickling down her forehead.

'Anna, is that blood?' I ask, pointing to it. She moves her fingers towards it. 'What's happened?'

A loud crack and a bang interrupt us, followed by two yellow fireworks illuminating the sky and leaving ribbons in their wake.

I turn back to her just in time to catch the swish of her coat before she disappears as quickly as she arrived.

CHAPTER 65

MARGOT

It's a commotion of crackling and sputtering noises that brings me back to life.

I open my eyes but it's close to pitch-black in here, and when I try and focus on anything, it's blurred. Even when I have had the hangover from hell it hasn't felt as bad as this. Am I injured? Have I had a stroke or a brain tumour? Am I in hospital?

A scent of smoke swiftly follows and grabs my attention. It's vague at first and I can't be sure if it's getting stronger because I'm regaining my senses or something is on fire. Is it the house? The fear of God flashes through me.

Hurriedly, I try and sit up in my bed but I barely budge. I can feel my hands, fingers and feet moving from side to side but they won't lift up. Something is stopping them, a weight pushing all of me down.

And then I realise this isn't a mattress I'm lying on. It's way too firm, it's freezing and my clothes are damp. As my vision gradually returns, I know that I need to get out of here, wherever here is. I curl my fingers in on themselves and there is something binding them together – it feels like cling film but it won't stretch or tear. It's more like a plastic wrap.

Wherever I am, I've been put here deliberately. Something around me explodes, but as I scream I realise my mouth isn't opening as it should. There's a gag tied around my head, stretching tightly across my face each time my jaw opens and my lips part. I want to be sick but stop myself. I twist and turn my head, and finally the gag is pushed down to my chin.

'Help me!' I yell, but my throat is hoarse and I sound pathetic.

I start coughing as the smoke slowly grows thicker. I wriggle and squirm in a bid to breathe in unpolluted air until I can just about turn my head. And it's only when my ear reaches the ground that I realise something is lodged inside it. Before I can figure out what it is, there are more thunderous outbursts, and through gaps in whatever I'm trapped inside, I spot flickers of multicoloured bright lights.

Only then do I know exactly where I am and why I can't escape.

I'm trapped in the centre of a burning bonfire.

I scream and toss back and forth, contorting my body, but I'm limited in my movements because of the wrap I'm cocooned inside. Suddenly, something in my pocket makes my thigh vibrate, quickly followed by a resounding ringing in my ear. I realise something is both inside it and balancing on my ear, like a hearing aid. It must be one of those hands-free Bluetooth devices, but I'm powerless to answer it. Then I remember they often have touch-sensitive tabs attached to them, so with one press, you can answer the call. I rub my ear as far as I can upon the ground beneath. When nothing happens, I lift my head up and slam it down on the ground, over and over again, my ear stinging with each slap. Meanwhile all around me there are more and more explosions as the heat becomes more intense.

And then I hear a voice through the headphones.

'You're conscious then.'

'Please help me,' I cry, barely able to get my words out. 'Someone is trying to kill me and I need you to . . .'

My voice trails as his words sink in. *You're conscious then.* He knows where I am.

'Please get me out of here,' I beg.

'Do you think I'd go to all this trouble just to free you?'

'I'll do anything.'

It's only when he laughs that I recognise his voice.

It's Anna's husband, Drew.

'I'm begging you, I'll do anything. Just help me.'

'I'm sorry, but I can't. You are going to burn alive in a bonfire of your own making.'

'*What?* Why?' My mind whirls pointlessly for a moment and then I come out with it. 'What did I do to you?'

He laughs again.

'I'll tell you what you did. You killed me first.'

CHAPTER 66

ANNA

I wipe away the blood that keeps dripping down my forehead as I hurry in the direction of where Liv saw my brother. I don't think my wound needs stitches, but it's flashing hard and hot. And so is my shoulder, from fruitlessly charging the door to the utility room that he locked me inside. I must have been trapped for about twenty minutes before I remembered the toolbox in the cupboard under the sink. Fumbling around in the dark I opened it, hoping to find a screwdriver with the right-sized tip to take apart the lock. Instead, I found a hammer, and a few thwacks later, the handle clattered to the floor. Once free, I washed away the blood streaming down my face with a wet tea towel, and stuck three Band-Aids over my wound while dialling and redialling Margot. Each time my call went to voicemail.

I was still calling her as I dashed out of the house. And that was when I heard her ringtone, the distinctive, bouncy opening sounds of Madonna's 'Material Girl'. It was coming from inside the works van Drew had left on the drive. I opened the unlocked door and caught the glimmer of light coming from the central arm rest. The screensaver of a much younger Margot confirmed it definitely belonged to her. Hesitantly, I moved around to the back doors, holding my breath as I opened them.

The van was empty, save for a couple of wooden pallets, some dead leaves and an axe. I was closing the doors when I paused. Why would Drew have branches in the back of his van?

And then I realised what he'd meant when he told me Margot was safe, for at least another forty-five minutes. Because that was when the bonfire was going to be lit.

I ran as fast as my legs could carry me through the village until I reached the playing fields. I didn't have time to make small talk with Liv once she confirmed she'd seen Drew. And now, as I squeeze my way through the crowds, I can just about make out a solitary figure lurking at the back by the tennis courts, with a clear view of the bonfire, and his hand held up to his ear.

'Where is she?' I yell as I run towards him. 'What have you done with Margot?'

He lowers his phone and presses it against his chest.

'Why do you care?' he asks, attempting to conceal his surprise at seeing me.

I point to his device. 'Who are you talking to?' He doesn't answer.

I need that phone, but Drew is bigger and stronger than me so there's nothing for it but to dip into my bag of tricks. I let my gaze shift over his shoulder and widen my eyes.

'Over here!' I yell. 'Help!'

When he wrenches his head around to see who I'm talking to, I slap the bottom of his hand holding the phone and it pops up into the air. I snatch it and race past him with it jammed to my ear.

'Who's this?' I ask, shouting above the airborne explosions.

'Anna, is that you?' comes the desperate reply.

I recognise Margot's voice immediately. She's crying.

'Where are you?'

'In the bonfire.'

'What?'

'I'm going to die,' she sobs. 'I'm sorry for what I did to you, but please help me.'

Margot knows. She knows who Drew and I are. And I know that, despite everything, I can't allow her to die like this.

Without thinking, I run hell for leather towards the event's organisers and the fire marshals in their yellow vests as Drew shouts after me. His voice is becoming distant, so I assume he's no longer following me. My exposed cheeks feel the rising heat of the flames like those Drew and I were almost burned alive by. I clench my fists to stop the panic from consuming me.

'Put it out!' I gasp as I point to the bonfire. 'Someone is in there.'

'What?' one of the men replies.

'There's someone trapped inside the bonfire,' I yell. 'You have to help them!'

Understandably he looks baffled. 'You think someone is in the bonfire?'

Now I'm screaming like a madwoman. 'Listen to me! You have to get them out.'

He glares at me as if I'm insane. But he knows he can't take the risk of ignoring me. He grabs his two colleagues by the arms and they run towards a hose reel drum and hosepipe attached to the wall of the community centre. Then, in front of a bewildered crowd, they push people to one side and get as close as they can to the flames, and set about dousing them with a thick jet of water.

'What's happening?' someone asks.

'Margot's in the bonfire!' I reply, and I know how ridiculous it sounds as soon as I say it.

Once the blaze is out, one of the marshals continues firing water at the burnt pile to prevent it from reigniting. Word spreads quickly and dozens of people rush towards it. They become soaked by the freezing spray but that doesn't dissuade them from pulling at the smouldering embers and tossing them to one side.

Please be alive, please be alive, I repeat until they reach the lower portion of the bonfire.

'I've found her!' a voice shouts just as the crowd parts for the arriving ambulance and paramedics that someone must have called. 'She's breathing,' the voice continues, and I'm flooded with relief, grateful that despite his best efforts, my brother hasn't killed her.

Time stands still for I don't know how long, and I can't see what the paramedics are doing until they lift a body on to a stretcher and carry it towards the waiting ambulance. Margot is barely recognisable. Soot has blackened her face and clothes and she's coughing and spluttering as oxygen is pumped into a mask they've affixed to her face. As she passes me, she opens her eyes. They are stark and white and in contrast to the rest of her shadowy face. Her hand suddenly reaches out, grabs my coat and pulls me towards her with unexpected strength. She won't let go and I'm forced to join her as she is wheeled across the grass and towards the open rear doors of the ambulance. Then she beckons me closer. Now she's holding my hand and mutters something. Her voice is so hoarse.

'I'm sorry, I can't understand you,' I say.

She pulls me closer still and pushes up her mask until her blackened lips brush my ear.

And when she speaks, I know that nothing in my life is ever going to be the same again.

CHAPTER 67

ANNA

There are no lights on inside my house as I approach it. Drew's work van is no longer parked on the drive and the back door to the house remains how I left it, unlocked. I enter, quietly closing and locking it behind me. I remain still, listening for any signs of life in the eerie silence, in case my brother is actually here. My hands are trembling, partly down to the biting cold and partly from the shock of the night's events. I clench and unclench my fists but it doesn't stop the persistent shakes.

Upstairs in the bathroom, I strip out of my clothes, leaving them in a heap on the floor. Bonfire smoke has seeped into the threads and stuck to my skin. I turn the shower up to a medium heat and wince when a jet of water hits the wound on my forehead. I rinse matted blood out of my hair, then shampoo it twice. When I'm finished, I turn the heat up a few more notches until it's almost unbearable. It scalds the scars on my thigh but I don't budge despite how much it hurts. Then I find myself crying, slapping the tiles over and over again to distract from the pain. And only when the rest of my skin feels as if it wants to slide off my body do I turn the temperature down and attack myself with a body scrub, using most of a bottle. I rub the grit into my scar, encouraging it to hurt more. Finally, I slump against the wall, slide down into the shower tray and allow the water to cascade over me.

I'm not sure how long I remain there because I'm busy replaying the police interview from earlier. Our conversation was more a fact-finding mission than a formal statement. I'll have to make that at the station tomorrow. I hope what I told them was convincing, but the more I think about it, the less convinced I am.

I told the detectives I'd picked up a phone with an illuminated screen which I found near the playing field's tennis court. Margot's voice had come out of the blue. I'd been trying to get hold of her all day but she hadn't returned my calls. I explained how, to begin with, I couldn't make sense of what she was telling me, something about being trapped in the bonfire. I said I'd thought she was drunk, as she'd found it tough after the recent separation from her husband. Then, when I knew she was being serious, I dropped the phone and ran to alert the fire marshals.

I failed to mention I took the phone with me. I've since turned it off and removed the battery and SIM card, and as soon as it gets light and I can see what I'm doing, I'll hide it inside a waterproof bag and tie it to a conifer branch a couple of metres high in the back garden where it won't be seen.

The DS asked who I thought might want to hurt Margot and I mentioned a stalker who sends her macabre gifts.

I said nothing about my brother.

Eventually I turn the shower off and dry my red, pimpled skin. As I put on fresh clothes, I return to the last thing Margot told me as she was being stretchered into the back of the ambulance. I know that she exaggerates, but I'm a hundred per cent certain that tonight, she didn't. You don't lie when you think you're about to die.

'You know what you have to do,' Ioana now whispers in my ear.

I jump when her voice appears without warning and after weeks of silence.

But for once, it doesn't feel ominous, because she doesn't want me to hurt myself. She knows what I'm thinking, and she agrees.

I make my way downstairs. And when I find what I need, I am ready.

DECEMBER

ONE MONTH AFTER BONFIRE NIGHT

CHAPTER 68

LIV

'She's back,' Brandon yells from the lounge.

I hear him from my home office and know immediately who he means. My shoulders tense.

'How does she look?' I shout back.

'Like she's about to accept an Academy Award for best actress.'

We're under siege from news crews scattered about the village. Some have tried to park in the cul-de-sac, but a group of neighbours fed up of being caught in the eye of this media storm have taken action. Word went round that Margot was being discharged from hospital this morning, so they've made a human chain across the entrance to our street like those Just Stop Oil protesters, to keep press vehicles out.

Instead of joining Brandon by the window, I remain in front of my Mac. I replay a video I've been watching since I uploaded it earlier today. This time, I slow it down to about a quarter of its speed and take in everything I see, frame by frame. Goosebumps cover my back and arms.

I hear Brandon's footsteps approaching the office so I close down one of the two windows open on my screen, leaving just the spreadsheet.

'When are you going over to see Dame Judi Dench?' he asks.

'I'll text Nicu later to see how she's doing then give her a couple of days to settle in.'

Brandon was one of those helping to pull away smouldering wood from Margot's pyre on Bonfire Night. We then made a swift return home as we didn't want the kids any more confused than they were already as to why the display had come to a swift halt.

Something wasn't right when I visited Anna the next morning. At first, I blamed it on the trauma of almost losing a close friend. But when I look back on it now, I'm not so sure. Her explanation of how she had known where to find Margot felt rehearsed and implausible.

The more Brandon and I have discussed it, the more we're in agreement there are too many holes in her story. How did Anna just so happen to stumble across a telephone with Margot on the other end? Why was Anna's head bleeding? And why did she tell me Drew was working when he was already there?

'Oh, did I tell you I've booked the concrete delivery?' Brandon continues.

'Concrete?' I repeat.

'For the orangery floor.'

'Of course,' I say and try to appear enthusiastic. 'When?'

'Last week in January is the earliest I can get it.'

It took us weeks to make a decision about the orangery after council planners were tipped off that we'd breached regulations. Brandon has since demolished it and has dug out replacement foundations and built most of it by himself. I haven't been able to bring myself to admit we're not in a financial position to be going ahead with anything beyond the flooring.

He peers over my shoulder at my screen. He won't be able to read what's on the spreadsheets without his contact lenses. And even then, he's unlikely to make sense of what any of it means. Excel isn't one of my husband's fortes.

'What's got your attention?' he asks.

'Nothing,' I lie. 'Just checking a few figures.'

'And we're all good?'

'Yep.'

He kisses me on the crown. 'See?' he says. 'I told you we would be.'

Shouting coming from the hallway takes him back to the children.

I wish I had Brandon's naivety. He wouldn't be so carefree if he knew how close we are to slipping into the red. But I want to spare him the truth. It's my fault I didn't take out business interruption insurance. If I had, I could make a claim for my two months of recovery. I'm sure a high-street bank would have required me to take one out as a condition of a loan. But mine was organised through blackmail.

So it's up to me to dig my way out of this hole. I'm not going to fail my family like my parents did me and my siblings when we were moved from pillar to post for unpaid rent or mortgage defaults. I am keeping this roof over our heads come hell or high water. I will find a way.

I reopen the minimised window on my screen and watch the video one more time. I don't know what to do with it.

But I know it's going to be the complete opposite of what I should do.

CHAPTER 69

ANNA

It smells of Christmas in here. Two candles are burning behind me, one bay and rosemary and the other cinnamon and orange. Their scents are so strong, they're cloying in my throat. But I don't blow them out.

I'm perched by the kitchen window, staring at Margot's house. Drew is with me. The media interest following her attempted murder has yet to die down. I've been a casualty of it too, finding myself at the centre of much unwanted attention. My name was leaked to the press as the person who discovered Margot was trapped in the bonfire. I've been doorstepped by journalists and photographers who took photos of me before I could give them a 'no comment' then close the front door. They've been persistent and have made many attempts since, calling me or pushing notes through the letterbox. Perhaps Margot being discharged will shift this news cycle in the direction of somewhere else tomorrow. Because I can't move on until it does.

I've yet to speak to her and I don't know what she's told the police. I made an official statement at the station, and the fact they haven't come to the house to question me further in the last four weeks or to arrest Drew suggests they don't know what she knows. That my brother tried to murder her in one of the most horrific ways imaginable.

I both want to see her and don't. She must have so many questions, but then, so do I. I'm still unaware of how or when Drew got Margot into that bonfire, but according to a story in the *Mail Online*, her blood tests revealed the presence of a powerful sedative in her system. In fact, the measure was so high that it was a miracle she hadn't died from an overdose, let alone the fire.

I stop looking at her house and scroll through the news on my iPad. Margot's life continues to be picked apart, feasted upon, the past rehashed and the future speculated about. The haters are still as vocal as ever, posting bonfire memes with an effigy of Margot superimposed on top like Guy Fawkes. But they're diminishing. After so many years as an outcast, the court of public sympathy finally appears to be welcoming Margot back with open arms.

Outside, a car catches the corner of my eye.

'It's Nicu,' Drew says before there's a rush of movement and photographers run down the street, trying to be the first to grab sellable images of Margot. My heart moves up a gear as Nicu opens the rear door like he is her chauffeur. I can just about make her out through the crowd as she exits. She is wearing sunglasses and a headscarf like an old Hollywood idol. I switch my iPad to camera mode, zooming in for a closer look. She pauses and grasps the door as if weak and in need of an object to steady herself.

'Once again, we're in the audience of *The Margot Show*,' says Drew dryly.

Nicu leads her slowly into the house, but before entering, she turns to wave. Then she slips her sunglasses down ever so slightly until her green eyes can be seen, and even though I'm sure I'm imagining it, I feel the weight of her stare. It's as if she knows I am hiding in here, watching and waiting for her return. I shrink into myself. She turns one last time and the door closes behind her.

'In a twisted way, she should be thanking me,' adds Drew. 'I've given her everything she wanted. A second stab at fame and public forgiveness.'

I don't respond. Even if, for once, I agree with him.

CHAPTER 70

MARGOT

I spit another mouthful of dark brown mucus into a paper tissue. It's disgusting. I'm like a miner with black lung and a sixty-a-day cigarette habit. My specialist told me I should be grateful the majority of debris used for the fire was wood-based. Had there been more plastics or chemicals, it would've poisoned me much worse than the smoke did.

A month has passed since I woke up to find myself a modern-day Joan of Arc, and a further three days since I was allowed home. Every couple of hours during the day I'm required to breathe into a spirometer, an ugly plastic tube attached to a cylinder that I put to my mouth. It measures my current lung capacity to see if it's improving. Next to it on my bedside table are two packets of blackcurrant-flavoured cough sweets. They're not to tame the constant hacking, but to lubricate my throat. I've also been warned to steer clear of anything that might irritate me, such as cold air, so I've yet to venture outside into the December chill.

The specialist, a stout woman with a mouth so wide she resembled a sock puppet, also advised one of the quickest routes to recovery was plenty of rest and sleep. Normally, I have the latter mastered. But nowadays, it's easier said than done. Sometimes when it's too quiet, I think I can hear the crackling of the flames and feel their heat burning my skin. I can nod off for an hour, perhaps two if I'm lucky, before I wake myself up coughing. And if the night terrors don't leave me screaming or kicking the duvet like a Moulin Rouge can-can dancer, then I'm sitting upright with a tight chest.

Nicu has been by my side every day. *Strictly* producers have given him as much time off as he needs, but I've told him to rejoin in the run-up to the Christmas finale. We need some normality in our lives, if that's possible.

We've communicated more of late than we have in the last five years. I think despite the hurt I've caused him, almost losing me has reminded him that he does still actually love me. I wouldn't say our marriage is back on track, but at least we're now working on it instead of burying our heads in the sand. The next few months are going to be tough, as much for Nicu as for me, but I have a strong feeling this isn't the end for us. I've promised to be honest with him about everything, and I have been.

Almost.

Because sometimes, full disclosure is too much of a burden to place on another person's shoulders. There are things he didn't know that I've been forced to tell him, all thanks to a doctor who made assumptions. And Nicu has handled it surprisingly well.

My connections with Frankie and Tommy have altered beyond all recognition. Both have held my hands as I coughed, thrown away my dirty tissues, steadied cups of cold water as I drink with trembling hands, and rubbed antibacterial creams into my charred skin. They've parented me more than I have ever parented them. It's not even as if we're rebuilding our relationship, because you can't rebuild what didn't exist in the first place. But you can create something new. And I'm enjoying the process much more than I could have ever imagined. We're not exactly the Von Trapps – neither child could carry a tune if I gave them a suitcase to put it in – but I'm enjoying their company. Who knew?

I did a live interview this morning with the TV show *BBC Breakfast News* about my recovery. I might as well capitalise on the goodwill being thrown in my direction by being who they want me to be. So I coughed when I didn't need to and sipped water with the grace of a chapped-beaked hummingbird sucking nectar from a flower. I even told the presenter that I forgave whoever had tried to kill me and that I hoped they would get the help they needed. I tell a better fable than Aesop.

Before letting me go, they asked me to respond to news that the Party Hard Posse had cancelled their forthcoming tour after secret backstage video recordings leaked of three band members mocking disabled fans with foul words and gestures. The band tried to apologise, pointing out the footage was recorded years earlier and that they had since 'grown as people'. But it was too late, social media had cancelled them. I told the presenter it was a pity the band's legacy had been tarnished and that I wished them well with their spiritual growth. And once we were off air, I might have smiled to myself. Negative energy has never felt so positive.

The house is my own until early afternoon, when Nicu brings the kids back from hockey and football matches. So I've invited Anna over for a long overdue tête-à-tête. About twenty-five years in the making, by my reckoning.

At a minute before 11 a.m., there's a knock on the door.

'Hello,' I say as I open it.

She responds with a simple 'Hi', and the ghost of a smile.

I turn my back to her, leaving the door ajar but without inviting her in. It closes behind me as she follows me into the kitchen. She hovers at first, scanning the room and the adjoining lounge as if it's a trap.

'We're alone,' I confirm. 'Tea or coffee?'

She hesitates. 'Tea. Please.'

Even with my back turned, I can feel her eyes drilling holes into me, keen to register what's different. Most of my scars are mental, but physically, there is debris. My hair is a little shorter thanks to a stylist friend of Nicu's who cut away the singed bits. I've filled in the gaps in my eyebrows with a pencil but I can't hide my lack of eyelashes with false ones as the glue will irritate my eyelids. My wrists bear scabs, the remains of burst blisters, and my face and arms are still a crimson colour from the heat. I look like someone from a council estate who's just returned from their first week abroad during a Benidorm heatwave.

I use the hot water tap to fill the teapot, flinching momentarily as the steam passes close to my skin. I wonder if she's noticed. When I sit down at the kitchen table, she finds a spot opposite me.

We lock eyes.

'Well.' I smile firmly. 'Where shall we begin?'

CHAPTER 71

ANNA

The teapot and mugs act as barriers between me and Margot. I clear my throat, trying not to give away how anxious I am. I don't want her thinking she has the advantage in this long-overdue confrontation.

Her text message – a curt *See you at mine at 11 on Sunday* – wasn't an invitation or a request, but an expectation. Drew told me to ignore it and not to go. But I'm done with being controlled by him or anyone else.

'What did Drew tell you before he tried to kill you?' I begin.

'What, no "How are you?" or "I'm sorry for what happened"?' Margot asks with mock offence.

'I think we're beyond pleasantries, don't you?'

'*Your brother,*' she says pointedly, 'told me who you both really were the morning of the bonfire.'

'How? Where were you?'

'We were in his flat.'

'His flat?' I repeat. I think the smoke inhalation must have fogged her brain. 'Drew doesn't have a flat.'

'He rents a bedsit above a Turkish restaurant on the Wellingborough Road. Liv wasn't mistaken a few months back when she thought she'd spotted me leaving the restaurant. If she'd passed me a few seconds later, she'd have seen Drew was behind me.'

This catches me off guard.

'But why would you go to his . . .' The penny drops, along with my jaw. 'My brother was the man you were cheating on Nicu with?' She nods, although there's no pride in her expression. 'But he hates you.'

'I see that now,' she says with a cold laugh. 'Drew was conflicted. I think he hated himself more for falling in love with me.'

I shake my head. 'No, he would never have fallen in love with you.'

'He told me that he had, many, many times. It's why I had to break it off with him.'

Margot recounts how they met on a dating app months earlier.

'After Christmas, Nicu and I were in a dreadful place, and I think I was trying to prove to myself that if he didn't want me, there were others who would,' she explains.

Neither had used full-face profile pictures. She recalls how my brother was flirty and funny and, like Margot, only looking for no-strings-attached fun. After a couple of days of messaging, each realised who the other was. They swiftly blocked one another.

'I'd never once looked at him as anything other than your scruffy, sullen husband,' she adds. 'And then at Frankie's party, we kept catching each other's eye. Our shared secret became a kind of connection. Anyway, Drew must've unblocked me before I unblocked him, because when I did, there was a message waiting for me, asking if I wanted to meet him for a drink. I used a different SIM card for our conversations, as I didn't want to get caught.'

'But you thought he was married to me,' I say. 'Why would you have an affair with your friend's husband?'

Margot raises the remnants of an eyebrow. 'Are you about to lecture me on morality?' she replies, and I back down. 'He told me you two were leading separate lives and had an understanding that you could do whatever you wanted with whomever, as long as you didn't tell the other. Which I suppose wasn't that far from the truth. Anyway, we'd been seeing each other for a few months, once or twice a week when work and family permitted, when one afternoon, out of the blue, he admitted he loved me. I told him that he wasn't allowed to because we could never be anything other than what we were. I suppose I wasn't being entirely truthful with him. You don't spend that much time with a person without feeling something. But I wouldn't give in to it. I wasn't going to trade my life with Nicu, as flawed as it was, to live in a bedsit with a delivery driver.'

'Given all you know now, do you really think he felt that way?' I ask. 'Because you don't try and murder the one you love.'

'Yes, you do,' she says matter-of-factly. 'They've even got a name for it. A Crime of Passion.'

'They're murders committed in the heat of the moment. Yours was pre-planned.'

'Look,' she snaps. 'A lot of men have fallen for me over the years. I know the difference between someone who says it because they mean it and someone who just wants to get me into bed. Your brother definitely meant it. And he took my rejection badly. He bombarded me with messages, begging me to change my mind. But I didn't. I couldn't.'

'When did he tell you who he and I really were?'

'I agreed to meet him one last time on November the fourth,' she recalls. 'A kind of farewell, I suppose. I felt I owed him that. We had a few drinks and one thing led to another and I stayed over at the flat because Nicu and the kids were still living away at that time. In the morning I was woken up with a stinging sensation in my arm. Drew was standing over me, injecting me with a needle. I tried to fight him off but he overpowered me and told me the truth about everything. And that's the last thing I remember before I fell unconscious.'

I'm scared to ask the next question because I don't know how I'm going to respond if the answer is no.

'And did you remember us? What you did?'

For the first time today, Margot breaks eye contact.

'You've been impossible to forget.'

A long breath escapes me. I'm completely aware of how weird it is to admit I'm grateful for this response.

'You had a different surname then, didn't you?' she asks.

'Khan. We changed it to Mason when Mum's sister and her husband legally adopted us.'

'They called you Joanna and Andrew in the newspapers. I followed your story.'

'Why?'

'I wanted to know you were okay. I've searched for you online over the years but never found any trace of either of you. Now I know why. If you'd moved here with those names I'd have recognised you and I'd have put my house on the market the same day.'

A silence passes between us as she allows me to process her recollections.

'The night of the bonfire,' I begin. 'Was what you told me true when you were being carried into the ambulance?'

She nods, almost apologetically. 'Yes.'

'How can I be sure?'

'I have no reason to lie to you, Anna. When your brother told me who he really was, I remembered him being spoken about. Andy, as he'd been known to our gang, was the one who tipped us off about the contents of your parents' safe. If it wasn't for him, we'd never have broken into your flat.'

CHAPTER 72

ANNA

I glare at Margot, trying to read her tells. A twitch here, a break in eye contact there, a quiver of a lip. Anything to suggest she is lying. But there's nothing. She's not that great an actress to pull off a lie as big as this. For my own sanity, I have to believe she is being honest. Because the alternative is unthinkable.

Once again, I recall the aftermath of her rescue from inside the bonfire, and when she was stretchered into the back of the awaiting ambulance.

'I know who you really are,' she half whispered, half gasped into my ear. 'Your brother left the window open for us and told us where the key would be. He owed them money.'

I took a step back and she let go of her grip on my coat. *No, you're wrong*, I thought, *Drew wouldn't have done that. He loved his family too much to put us at risk.*

Before I could ask her anything else, a paramedic forced the oxygen mask back on to her face, then lifted her stretcher into the back of the vehicle. I watched, detached, as it left the village playing fields and disappeared out of view, its blue lights growing ever dimmer.

As I waited inside the community centre to talk to the police, I tried to pick holes in Margot's story. But she knew facts that remained unreported in the press. We'd been burgled in the past, so Dad had become a stickler for security. Later, the police told us a storeroom window had been left unlocked and the alarm hadn't been set. But I knew that every night before bed, Dad made sure to double-check the locks on each door and window before turning the alarm on. The police said he must've forgotten. They were wrong.

Around the same time, Drew had turned fourteen and was pulling away from the family. He was socialising with boys older than him. At six, I was too young to understand the specifics of his rows with Dad, but they upset me nonetheless. I have one vivid memory of standing outside the bathroom, tearfully watching as Dad emptied plastic bag after plastic bag of white tablets down the toilet while Drew scrambled to stop him from flushing them away. He was no match for Dad's strength. I screamed when Dad shoved Drew so hard, he fell and banged his nose against the doorframe. There was blood everywhere.

'You don't know what you've done!' Drew screamed. 'They're going to kill me!'

'Don't be so stupid,' Dad snapped.

Two weeks later and it was our parents who were dead, not their son.

I've waited twenty-five years to learn the truth about that night. Or at least Margot's version of it.

CHAPTER 73

MARGOT

Anna deserves the truth – not *a* version of it, but *the* version of it. So I start at the beginning, painting her a picture of who I was then, my strained relationship with my parents, the gang I wanted to be a part of and how our initiation was to burgle her family's safe.

I explain how things became heated when, once inside, we couldn't locate the key to open it. Then a light was turned on and we were confronted by a man dressed only in striped pyjama bottoms and wielding the base of a bedside lamp.

'My dad,' Anna says quietly, and her gaze falls to the floor.

'He must have thought he could scare us off,' I continue. 'I remember him rushing towards Warren and holding the lamp over his head. Then Warren reached inside his coat, grabbed the gun and fired.'

I hope she never had to see her father as I saw him that night.

'I was numb,' I continue soberly. 'I'd never watched anyone . . . die before. I didn't know what to do.'

Anna grips her mug so tightly, her knuckles are white. 'You could have called for help.'

'It was too late.'

'How do you know that? You're not a doctor.'

'Anna,' I say, 'trust me, it was too late.'

She wipes her eyes with her sleeve. 'And my mum?' she asks. 'She was screaming as she was dragged out of the room. Was that when she saw Dad?'

I nod, silently recalling her panic as she realised her husband's fate. And despite Warren's increasing frustration, she was unable to tell him where the key to the safe was now.

'I truly believe that when Warren killed your dad, it was nothing but a reflex,' I say. 'However, shooting your mum was different. It was deliberate.'

I explain how Zain and Jenny fled down the staircase as the now unhinged Warren unloaded his gun twice more, his bullets fortunately missing them both. But I was too slow to leave. And I was convinced he was going to kill me next until I suggested setting fire to the flat.

'That was your idea?' Anna asks, surprised.

'Yes.'

Her eyes narrow so tightly, her irises are pinpricks. None of this can be easy for her to hear.

'So I'm not misremembering anything,' she says, scowling. 'You tried to murder me and Drew.'

'No, Anna,' I say adamantly. 'I promise you it wasn't like that. Do you remember when we first saw each other?'

'You crouched to pick up a tin of lighter fuel from the bedroom floor.'

'I had no idea either you or Drew was in the flat before that moment. How could I?'

She doesn't respond, so I continue.

'I wasn't that much older than Drew and I was just as frightened as him. I wanted to stay alive. And that's what I wanted for you two as well. I got back to my feet with the intention of telling

Warren we should abandon the plan and leave, but as I reached the door, he already had a blazing firelighter in his hand. And before I could protest, he tossed it to the floor, igniting the room. Then he pulled me downstairs and out into the street.'

Anna hesitates as if she wants to say one thing, but changes her mind before she counters, 'You could have gone back in. You could have tried to help us, but you didn't.'

'You were there,' I say. 'You know I'd never have got back upstairs; you barely escaped yourselves. Drew was in a terrible state when the police pulled him out.'

Her brow furrows. 'How do you know that?' she asks.

'I ran back to the shop after I called 999.'

'You did that?'

'From the phone box opposite. Then I watched as they tried to resuscitate him, praying he'd survive. And I waited until the ambulance arrived and blue-lighted both of you to hospital. Only then did I leave.'

Anna sits back in her chair as I lean towards her.

'To this day,' I add, 'I am convinced that if I'd told Warren I'd found you and your brother hiding under the bed, he'd have shot you as well. And maybe me. By that point, he wasn't in his right mind. I swear to God that I didn't want to leave you there, but at least you stood a chance of surviving the fire. You wouldn't have survived Warren.'

CHAPTER 74

ANNA

Margot wants me to believe her. She wants me to accept that she didn't try to kill me and Drew, and that she actually tried to save us.

She wants me to believe Warren was the only one responsible for the deaths of my parents, and the rest were unwilling participants. However, while they might not have pulled the trigger, they were still there. I doubt Warren would have burgled us alone. They are guilty by association and I feel no remorse for killing them. But I know it's going to take time to unpack what I've learned this morning.

Then there's my brother, the fifth member of this crew, whose participation I knew nothing about until Margot told me on what she thought was her deathbed. The brother who lied to me for most of my life and who is as much to blame as the others. And he knows that I know.

It was in the early hours of the day after Bonfire Night when we came face to face. I was sitting in a darkened kitchen waiting for him to return home when the rear garden security camera was triggered, sending my phone a push notification. The live clip captured a grey figure climbing the fence that separates our garden from the field behind. Then he quietly closed the kitchen door behind him and entered the utility room. When he emerged, the street light outside captured a glint of the metallic shaft of a hammer in his hands. The same hammer he had killed the detective with. I wanted to run.

As Drew headed for the hallway, I rose from my chair and walked barefoot, keeping a safe distance behind him. Suddenly, he turned on his heel and I shrank back into the shadows. He made for the fridge, grabbed a bottle of beer, unscrewed the cap and gulped its contents.

His distraction was my opportunity. Using all my force, I swung a pipe wrench I'd taken earlier from the garage and caught the back of his left knee with a splintering thwack. Drew fell to the floor, screaming, his bottle shattering against the floor tiles. I reached for his hammer before he could grab it and threw it across the room, where it clattered against the radiator. Then I turned on the kitchen cabinet LEDs, which offered just enough low lighting for us to see one another, but without being spotted from outside by early-rising neighbours.

'What the fuck?' he yelled. 'Why did you do that?'

'Why were you carrying a hammer upstairs?' I replied.

He had no answer. Our focus remained pinned on each other as he sat upright and gripped his knee with both hands, his face contorted by pain. I felt both guilty and empowered.

'You've broken my kneecap,' he moaned.

'You've broken my heart.'

'What the hell are you on about?'

I waited for him to play catch-up.

'This is about her, isn't it?' he asked. 'Margot. I don't know what she's told you, but she's messing with your head. You should've let her die.'

'I didn't want her dead.'

'Since when? It was always the plan. You told me that for years.'

313

'I changed my mind.'

'But she deserves it,' he protested. 'You know what she tried to do to us. I only did what you didn't have the guts to do.'

Drew reached for the countertop with shaking hands and tried to pull himself up, yelling in pain but stopping short when I raised the wrench to shoulder height. It weighed several pounds and made my arms shake. But I wasn't letting go of it. And even in that dimly lit room, Drew sensed the balance of power between us had shifted. He knew I'd hurt him again if I had to.

'She's brainwashed you, hasn't she?' he continued.

'It isn't her who's brainwashed me. I know you opened the window in the supermarket storeroom so your friends could break in. And you left the key to the back door for them to find along and turned the burglar alarm off. Mum and Dad are dead because of you.'

His laugh was desperate and staged. I knew when my brother was lying to me.

'Is that what she told you? Because it's all lies, Joanna.' He bit hard on his bottom lip, as if to stifle the ache. 'I almost killed myself trying to save your life. Or have you forgotten that?'

'The life you'd put at risk in the first place by letting them into our home?' I countered. 'Don't worry, I haven't forgotten that. I also remember the fights you had with Dad, how he poured those pills down the toilet, how you yelled at him, telling him someone was going to kill you.'

'It wasn't my fault,' he muttered. 'Dad flushed away ten grand's worth of ecstasy when he found it hidden in my room. Eddie was going to fuck me up big time. Telling him about the money in the safe was my only way out. He promised me they'd be in and out in five minutes. That no one would get hurt.'

'But they did. They're dead because of you. I wish the paramedics hadn't resuscitated you. It should be you in a grave, not them.'

'You don't mean that.'

314

'I mean every word of it. When Margot first became famous and I recognised her, you said you didn't. That was a lie, wasn't it?'

Drew nodded, then let out some sharp puffs of air as if trying to control his breathing. He must have been in a lot of pain. Good.

'Why?'

'I wanted you to forget about it all. Put it behind you and move on, like I had.'

'And how did "moving on" work out for you? Depression, two stints in rehab for coke and amphetamine addiction, and now you're an alcoholic. You couldn't even attack me in my own home without a beer in your hand.'

'Well tell me what I was supposed to have done?' he snapped. 'Told you when you were old enough to understand? "Happy sixteenth birthday, Joanna. By the way, our parents are dead because I got myself in a bit of trouble. Don't forget to blow out the candles on your cake.'"

'You could have found a way. Instead, you said nothing. And I will never forgive you for that.'

A moment of silence passed.

'So what now?' Drew asked eventually. 'How do we move on from this?'

'We don't. You can't be here anymore. In my house, in my life.'

'You're my sister. We're family.'

'Is that what you were thinking a few minutes ago when you were carrying a hammer upstairs? That I'm your *sister*? That we're *family*?'

'Says the woman who's just kneecapped me with a fucking wrench. I am in agony here! Where am I supposed to go?'

'Have I given you any indication I care?'

There was another pause before he removed his phone from his pocket.

'Who are you calling?' I asked.

Then he threw the device at me. And the grin etched across his face will live rent free in my head for the rest of my days.

CHAPTER 75

MARGOT

Anna is both here and far away. She's staring straight ahead, focused on something undefined, but her mind is elsewhere. I say nothing. And when she eventually returns to our conversation, something tells me not to ask where she's been.

'What have you told the police about Bonfire Night?' she asks.

'I said I can't remember anything.'

'Why didn't you tell them the truth?'

'Because it'd prompt too many questions and I'd need to make up too many lies. And the more lies I tell, the more chance there is I'll be caught out. So it's best if I deny all knowledge. But I'm going to need you to keep Drew away from me, Anna.'

'I will.'

'Because if he tries anything again, I won't have any choice but to tell the police what—'

'He won't go near you,' she says.

'I'd like to believe that, but . . .'

She is firmer this time: 'He won't be returning.'

The certainty of Anna's words is reflected in her expression.

'What about Liv?' she says suddenly. 'You were responsible for the hit-and-run, weren't you?'

Her question catches me off guard.

'Drew told me he drove past your parked car on the back road into the village shortly after the accident,' she continues, 'but you told me you'd been sick and hadn't left the house in days. And our doorbell camera caught you cleaning your car bumpers later that night.'

I can't come up with a lie quick enough and she knows it.

'I'll be honest about everything if you are,' she prompts. 'I'm sure there's plenty you want to know.'

There is. So I take a deep breath.

'I was convinced she'd sent Nicu the video of me kissing Brandon,' I begin hesitantly. 'I'd been drinking, and when I saw her running along that road, I got angry really quickly. I wanted to clip her, not kill her. Hand on heart, Anna, I promise you I checked to see if she was okay but there were no signs of life. I honestly thought she was dead. So I left.'

'Twice you've left people to die,' she says. 'Twice is a pattern, if not a habit.'

I can't argue, so I don't.

'And it was Drew who recorded the video and sent it to Nicu,' Anna adds. 'I found it on the phone he used to call you with when you were inside the bonfire.'

'He was at the party?'

'He must've got jealous when he saw you together.'

'Right,' I say and blow out a sharp puff of air.

So I hurt Liv for nothing. I can't offer anything in mitigation, so I take a sip of my tea instead. It's cold.

'Okay,' I say, 'my turn.' Anna nods. 'Why did you move here? To this village. I assume it's not coincidence.'

'No, it's not,' she replies. 'It's the culmination of a decade-and-a-half-long campaign to make your life as miserable as possible.'

CHAPTER 76

ANNA

Where to begin? Do I give her the edited highlights, or allow her to see who I really am?

I recall how I began infiltrating her world soon after I turned seventeen. I'd moved to London to work as a trainee reporter for Zap News Agency. Although, describing what we produced as 'news' is an exaggeration. We paid the public and showbusiness insiders for gossip about celebrities, or we created stories of our own, based on little else but our imaginations. Then we sold them to tabloid newspapers and celebrity magazines. Our words filled pages for an increasingly understaffed print media. Their editors didn't care who our sources were – and often there weren't any. It was morally questionable but perfectly legal unless a celebrity sued, but that was once in a blue moon as libel was difficult to prove and hiring lawyers was expensive.

I tell Margot how I quoted unnamed sources (often me) to invent stories about her. I'd write about how she was desperate to quit the Party Hard Posse and start a solo career, or that she had a furious argument with a bandmate. I'd claim she was spotted worse for wear at a charity function or refused to tip a waitress despite a hefty spend. Ever so slowly, I chipped away at the public's perception of her. The world is all too willing to believe a woman can't be successful without being a bitch.

Margot sits back in her chair. She is fixated on my every word.

'I was also dating one of my colleagues who was Zap's IT man,' I recall. 'Gareth knew much more than I did about social media back then. He was also besotted with me, so he was easy to exploit. I never told him what I knew about you, but I alluded to our paths having crossed in the past. Together, we launched the Facebook campaign group opposing your band's Glastonbury appearance. "Don't Stop the BOP", remember?'

I can see she does. It would be hard to forget. BOP was an acronym for 'Bottles of Piss'. When the band reached the first chorus of 'All Nite, All Nite', it was the cue for hundreds of bottles to be hurled at them by well-armed music lovers who hated manufactured pop.

'That was your idea?' she asks in disbelief.

'Yes, and to be honest, it was even more successful than I hoped. And later that afternoon, I sold the screengrabs to almost every tabloid in the country.'

Margot falls silent. I don't know what's surprising her the most: how matter-of-factly I'm telling her this, how far back my campaign began, or how badly she's misjudged me.

I continue. 'Later, after you were dropped and you launched your solo career, Gareth found a hack that enabled us to give your YouTube music video hundreds of thumbs-down reactions. Apparently that meant the site's algorithms wouldn't actively promote it. We also left negative reviews on iTunes and posted an audio clip on Twitter where we changed the pitch of your singing voice so it was out of tune, then claimed it was a leaked demo. Oh, and sometimes I'd send one of our photographers to wait outside your flat and take pictures of you putting the bins out or carrying bags of shopping, then chose the worst image and write captions suggesting you'd let yourself go or that friends were worried you were suffering from depression.'

'Well you got the latter right, I suppose,' Margot sighs. 'Go on.'

'Are you sure?'

I ask for her sake as much as mine, because I know what's coming next.

'I'm sure.'

I look to our mugs of cold tea. 'Do you have anything stronger?'

She removes a bottle of white wine from the fridge and two glasses from the cupboard. She pours me a generous measure and a fruit juice for herself.

'Meds,' she tells me. 'Another two weeks before I can drink again.'

'Where was I?' I ask rhetorically. 'Well at this point your career should have been over. But then you were given a second chance with *Strictly Come Dancing*. And somehow, you turned it around. You weren't the greatest dancer when you started, but you were the hardest worker. People love an underdog and the tabloids sensed the shift in public perception. They no longer wanted to buy my negative stories.

'Then fate intervened. A call came into the news agency from a cab driver who had footage of you and Nicu all over each other in the back of his taxi. I met him at Waterloo station to see what he'd recorded when he'd turned his dashcam around. I knew it was going to be explosive.

'We deployed a team to follow you and Nicu over the next few days and caught you entering a flat and staying there for hours at a time. I sold the words and images to the *Sun on Sunday* for just over £100,000. I volunteered to break the news to Ioana in person and get her reaction. And as you well know, she was furious. I was able to persuade her she could cash in if she played on her scorned-woman status. She agreed to me acting as her manager, and for months I brokered deals between her and the media.'

'You managed her?' Margot says, scowling.

'As much as you can manage someone like her. But then you legitimised your affair by announcing your plans to marry Nicu. You even sold the coverage to *Yeah!* magazine. But once again, I found a way this could work in my favour. Once I'd discovered the event details, a photographer and I were going to turn up with Ioana and her kids to gatecrash the wedding. Your day would be ruined and we'd make thousands off the back of it. Only, on the eve of the wedding, everything changed.'

'Because Ioana killed herself,' Margot says. 'The ultimate revenge.'

I hesitate. I could just leave it there, allow her to believe what the rest of the world also thinks, and move on.

But then I hear a voice in my head. It takes me by surprise, as all that occupant has done until this moment is listen.

Tell her, they say calmly. *Show her who you really are.*

'I know you were there at the flat the night Ioana died,' I tell Margot. 'I was there to run through the plan for your wedding one last time when you passed me on the street outside.'

Margot is adamant: 'I didn't kill her.'

'I know that. Because I did.'

Her forehead crinkles as she cocks her head to one side. She thinks she has misheard, because I've said it as casually as if I'm recalling what I ate for breakfast. But as my words sink in, she glares at me, wide-eyed, mouth open.

'I asked Ioana what you were doing there and she said you'd turned up to apologise for what you'd done to her and Nicu. She'd told you she was going to make your and Nicu's lives miserable. But she was lying to you.'

I recall how Ioana admitted she'd had enough of working with me. She was too exhausted to play the bitter ex any longer. And she wanted to return to Romania and start afresh with the money she'd made from selling stories about Margot.

'But *after* you gatecrash the wedding tomorrow,' I said to her.

'Are you not listening?' she replied. 'I'm done. As of tonight.'

'But everything is planned,' I protested. 'We have the photographer, the videographer, *The Sun* is holding its front page and a double-page spread inside for this. They are paying us a lot of money. Look, once we get tomorrow out of the way, you can go home and forget all about Nicu and Margot.'

'You are as bad as that witch,' she snapped, then made her way to the balcony. 'All you want is to take things away from me. Well, no more.'

I tell Margot how I moved towards Ioana.

'Come on,' I said. 'You're forgetting who first told you about Nicu's cheating. If it wasn't for me and my contacts, you'd be none the wiser.'

I might as well have pulled a pin from a hand grenade.

'This is all your fucking fault!' she screamed. 'You ruined everything. If you hadn't sold it to your fucking newspapers, then he'd have dumped that bitch and would've come back to me. But you pushed them together. And it's because of you they're getting married. You have destroyed my life. You are no better than her, you parasite.'

I glare at Margot. 'It wasn't planned, it just happened,' I tell her. 'I'd never felt a rage like it. It burned hot inside me. All I could see was that you and Nicu were going to get away with something else. Your marriage was going to redeem you, then you'd bounce back even stronger. Before me or Ioana realised what was happening, I lurched forward, and with all my force, I pushed her so hard that she stumbled towards a coffee table and fell backwards over the balcony.'

Now, as I reflect, I don't remember how much time passed before I regained control over myself from Warren on the balcony and peered over the glass balustrade. Once I adjusted my vision to the darkness, I caught a glimpse of her impaled on the railings below. Zain, Jenny and Warren's deaths had been different to hers. They were all part of the plan. Ioana's wasn't. Yes, I had used her, but then so had Warren. Killing her was his means of escaping me. I don't tell Margot about him or any of the others who I've carried. I don't need anyone telling me how crazy I am.

'I had to erase any trace I'd been in that apartment,' I tell her. 'I briefly considered trying to set you up for her death, as you'd been there only minutes before me. But I didn't have time to think it through. It'd be far easier if the police decided it was suicide. I found her laptop, which was still switched on, slipped on a pair of rubber gloves I found by the sink and typed.'

Margot speaks. '*You made me do this Nicu. You and that bitch.*'

I'm not surprised she remembers it. I also took a photo of the screen and balcony and, later, posted it on all my anonymous social media accounts. It quickly went viral.

I left Ioana's computer open on the coffee table and locked her children's bedroom door to prevent them from going on to the balcony. Finally, I made my way down the fire escape, ensuring there were no CCTV cameras recording me.

Margot dabs at the corners of her eyes with the sleeve of her jumper.

'You got everything you wanted,' she says. 'The world believing Nicu and I had driven a young mum to her death, and the media turning on us again. It torpedoed any chance I had of public forgiveness.'

'It was a thousand times better than the stunt we had planned,' I admit. 'I'll always be grateful to Ioana for that.'

'I need a minute,' Margot says before rising to her feet and disappearing along the corridor and into the bathroom.

I top up my glass of wine and drink it all in one long gulp.

CHAPTER 77

MARGOT

I sit on the lid of the toilet with a hand towel over my mouth, hoping Anna can't hear me cry. Her revelations have floored me. The biggest, of course, is what she did to Ioana. And perhaps I should be sickened. But I kind of understand it. I know how it feels to have been provoked by that woman. Many a time I fantasised about killing her myself in some nasty, drawn-out manner. I guess you don't get much nastier than being impaled on railings after falling fifteen storeys. It scares me to think that it could've just as easily been me who shoved her. You don't know what you're truly capable of unless you're pushed to the edge. Or in Ioana's case, over it.

I can't stay in the bathroom for much longer. This might be my only opportunity for the truth. So I dab my face with a wet wipe, touch up my make-up and return to the kitchen. I refill her empty glass and wish I could join her in having one.

'Why couldn't you have left Nicu and me alone here in Northampton to fade into obscurity?' I ask. 'Why did you have to follow us?'

'Actually I did leave you alone for a while. But when it was announced Nicu was returning to *Strictly* I could predict what was going to happen next. You two would get your lives back together and I couldn't let that happen. You didn't deserve to be happy.'

'Why, because you weren't?' I hit back.

'I talked Drew into moving here to restart the harassment. And when a house came up in the same street as you, we paid our rental deposit and moved in.'

'The packages – severed dolls, photos with my eyes cut out, "murderer" painted along the side of my car. That was you?' Anna nods. 'And the envelope in Liv's bin?'

'You forgot I'd used the bathroom when we arrived. I left it there hoping you'd find it. I was lucky.'

'Was there anything else?'

'I'd alter your Wikipedia page, spread online rumours about you, and I'd move things around your house. I have a key.'

'You have a key?' I repeat incredulously. Is there no limit to her intrusion?

'I got a copy cut so if I knew the house was empty, I could come and go as I pleased. I'd move things around, swap clothes in your wardrobes. I even took your missing Jimmy Choo trainers and dumped them in a Salvation Army clothing bank.'

I want to laugh at the ridiculousness of someone walking around in a pair of trainers worth more than three months of unemployment benefits.

'You never know what you're going to find,' she continues. 'I'd say more, but I wouldn't want to let the cat out of the bag. Or, in your case, the garage.'

'It was you,' I say, my laugh short and humourless.

'She was at death's door when I drove her to the vets' and she took weeks to recover. Fortunately for me, despite it being illegal, they had never got round to microchipping the cat. She only had a metal address tag on her collar that was easy to remove. Meanwhile, I saw your internet search history and read your emails and realised you must've developed a conscience and were trying to replace her. So when the vet released the original one to me, I put her in a cattery for a few days until you picked up a second. Then home she came.'

For all these years, she has always been one step ahead of me.

'I'd use your iPad to report your credit cards stolen or change passwords on websites you regularly access,' Anna explains. 'I also learned the password for your email account so I could access it from home. Most of the time, you weren't sent much of interest, but one day I came across an unread email asking you to rejoin the Party Hard Posse for a tour. I deleted it from the inbox and kept it hidden in the trash can until I'd responded as you, turning them down and telling them how much I disliked every single member. It was only when news broke of the band's reunion that I put both emails back into the right boxes for you to find if you ever searched for them. And Frankie's gender reveal party. I'd like to take the credit for that, but all I did was put the idea into your head, knowing you wouldn't be able to resist making it all about you.'

I don't let it show, but I'm frustrated by how well she knows me.

'What was your endgame?' I ask, unsure if I really want to know the answer.

'To take everything away from you.'

'Again.'

'Yes, again. Until I didn't want to anymore.'

'Why?'

Anna recalls how wrongfooted she felt after I found her bleeding in her bathroom and took care of her.

'You kept checking up on me, making sure I hadn't hurt myself again,' she says. 'There'd been no judgement. And I began to realise that perhaps people can change and that maybe you aren't the same person now you were when you were a teenager.'

'But Drew didn't think the same.'

'He wasn't ready to leave you alone. And it's only today, from what you've said, that I understand he had his own agenda for wanting to hurt you. I think you broke his heart and he hated himself for allowing you to do that. If he could kill you, he'd be able to draw a line under the past for both of us.'

'Did you only target me? What about the others? Jenny, Warren, Zain . . . Did you find them?'

'Oh, I most definitely found them.'

'When?'

She doesn't reply, and just looks at me instead, one eyebrow raised as if waiting for me to understand something unspoken. When finally I do, the enormity of it lands like a punch to the gut. I take a moment to compose myself.

'So Ioana wasn't your first,' I say slowly.

My body wants to fold in on itself. I'm sitting opposite a woman who has killed four people. Like them, I've crossed her. So why is she telling me this? Am I to be her fifth? A gut feeling tells me I'm not. But that same gut feeling also once told me Anna was harmless.

'I think I should feel scared of you, so I don't understand why I'm not,' I admit. 'In some ways I'm even relieved. I've always thought there was a reason why my life hasn't panned out as it was supposed to have. I assumed I was just one of those people who was blighted by bad luck and poor decision-making. But now I realise there's more to it than that. Karma has come calling in the shape of you. I can't help thinking that if you'd left me inside that bonfire, you'd have a conclusion to your story – and I wouldn't be sitting here wondering if I should call the police and tell them everything you've told me.'

'Actually, I'm not wondering about that at all, because you won't be calling anyone,' she replies confidently.

'You seem sure of that.'

'I am. You are famous again because of what my brother did to you. You've been on every front page of every newspaper and celebrity magazine. People love you. I know you're not going to risk losing that or your own freedom by admitting to what you did to me and Drew when we were kids, or confessing to Liv's hit-and-run. We have enough evidence to destroy one another. But what would be the point?'

Anna leans over and refills her glass. I'm tempted to ask for a sip to take the edge off the insanity of this morning. Instead, I move towards the kettle to make another tea. How times have changed. How *I* have changed.

'You can also think of it like this,' Anna continues. 'No matter what happens from here on in, you and I are irrevocably connected. We'll always have someone in our corner if we're ever attacked. If one of us is threatened, we will do whatever is necessary to protect the other.'

I hadn't thought of it like that. She might be right. If I can trust her, could the woman who has made my life hell for so long actually turn out to be my closest ally?

The kettle boils, and for a split second I wonder how much satisfaction I'd get if I poured this scalding hot water over her head. But of course I don't. I have someone else to think of now. I fill the teapot with fresh mint tea leaves instead and return to the table.

'This might be a good time to mention that soon it won't just be the two of us we'll have an obligation to protect,' I say.

'How so?' she asks.

'In about four months' time, there will be three of us. I'm carrying your brother's baby.'

JANUARY

TWO MONTHS AFTER BONFIRE NIGHT

CHAPTER 78

ANNA

The ground is sticky and wet underfoot. The grip on the soles of my wellies isn't thick enough to stop me from sliding across the field's uneven terrain. Drew's laughter at my expense is irritating me. A low settling fog shrouds where we're going, while behind me, I can barely see my house.

I lift the sleeve of my coat to my nose as I walk. It's the first time I've worn it since Bonfire Night, but I swear I can still smell charred wood on it despite it twice being dry-cleaned. Perhaps the smell is like the blood I have on my hands: so deeply ingrained that it'll never come out. I pause when I think I hear someone behind us. I turn, but it's still just the two of us. Given my current state of mind, it's no wonder my imagination is playing tricks on me.

'What about over there?' Drew suggests.

He's referring to a clearing over by the mini-industrial estate that's being built ahead. Roads have been dug, and sewers, water-pipes and cables installed. According to the construction company's website, it's ready for the next stage of development. We make our way towards it and he steers me in the direction of a manhole cover.

'Down there?' I ask. 'You think it'll work?'

'The detective hasn't been found yet, has he?'

When he told me weeks earlier that this was the detective's burial spot, I remember being surprised it was close to home. I'd assumed Drew had driven him miles away. But he's right, I suppose. I've done many bad things, if you want to call them that. But burying a body isn't one of them.

'As you well know, I've never disposed of anyone,' I reply. 'This is a first for me.'

'Likewise,' Drew replies. 'I've never been asked for advice on where to bury myself.'

Again, I can't argue with that either. Because Drew is dead, and has been since the early hours of the morning after Bonfire Night.

I didn't want to kill my brother, but he left me with no choice. He only has himself to blame. He was on the floor of our kitchen, clutching with one hand the kneecap I broke with a pipe wrench. He used the other to throw me his phone.

'Check out the iCloud file called "Ioana",' he said.

Inside was a file that contained two brief video clips. I let out a short sharp gasp when I recognised myself in the first. It was evening, and I was walking along a London pavement and towards a building. The footage was taken from afar but I'd been in that building so many times I knew it on sight. It was where Ioana lived. In the second clip, I was walking in the opposite direction.

'The night you pushed Ioana over the balcony, a supermarket CCTV camera on the opposite side of the road filmed you entering and leaving her apartment block,' Drew explained. 'You'll see it's date- and time-stamped. It proves you were there the night she died. The police don't know it exists because they had no reason to believe her death was suspicious. Feel free to delete it, but I have copies saved elsewhere.'

'How . . . ?'

'All you need to know is that it exists.'

'Then you must have footage of Margot, too, because I passed her on her way out.'

'The camera only captured someone wearing a long coat and a baseball cap pulled down to cover their face. Now press play on that sound file.'

I reluctantly did as I was told and heard my own voice. I sounded different; I was crying as I spoke and my words were hurried. I couldn't place when it had been recorded until I heard myself revealing to Drew how I had killed Zain, Jenny, Warren and Ioana. Then I knew where and when.

'The night you took me to hospital after I cut myself too deeply,' I said. 'You recorded me when I told you everything. When I was at my most vulnerable. Why?'

'Just in case. And if ever there was a just-in-case moment, it's now.'

I replayed the clips, then deliberately dropped his phone to the floor.

'What are you going to do with this?'

'You're a serial murderer,' he replied. 'If I go to the police, you'll be behind bars for the rest of your life.'

'And I'll tell them how you murdered that policeman here in this room in front of me and where you buried him.'

'Which I'll deny. There's more evidence against you for crimes than there is against me. Now call me a fucking ambulance or drive me to A&E or, I swear to God, your life as you know it ends tonight.'

I hesitated, my mind racing through my options. But Drew had only left me with one. And a third person joined our conversation.

'We are parting ways, aren't we?' Ioana asked suddenly. It was the first time I'd heard from her in a while. She sounded as if she had accepted her fate, which offered me reassurance I was about to do the right thing.

'We are,' I replied. 'And for what it's worth, I'm sorry.'

'Sorry for what?' Drew replied, puzzled. I'd never told him about my passengers.

Before he could lift his arm to defend himself, with all the force of two strong women I hit him twice with the pipe wrench, both times across the head. It was the second impact that caved in his skull. The many blows that followed were unnecessary, but not entirely unwarranted.

I've not felt a shred of guilt since his death. It was either Drew or me, and I chose me because I am the only one of us who has a shot at living beyond the past. Even Drew now accepts it was the right thing for me to have done. I sense his presence inside me and sometimes I hear his voice, but it's much less frequent than Ioana's was. And it lacks her malice.

The only fallout from his death has been figuring out a way of successfully dumping his body. For the first few days he remained wrapped inside a tarpaulin I'd paid for in cash at a DIY store and secured around him with parcel tape. It was a fiddly job. Then I stored him in the utility room. Scented candles burned all hours of the day and night. But I couldn't continue indefinitely with him in the house. Burying him in my own garden was asking for trouble. I ruled out shallow graves in wooded areas because dogs and wild animals have a tendency to dig them up. Bodies often float to the surface if they've been dumped in lakes. And I didn't have the stomach to cut him into pieces and dissolve him in chemicals.

So, as a short-term solution, I splurged £200 in cash for a chest freezer I bought from a second-hand electricals shop. Although it took a hell of a lot of effort hoisting my brother up and getting him inside it. Twice, I accidentally tore open the tarpaulin, once exposing his knee and the second time his left hand. I gagged at the paleness of the lion tattoo on the back of it as I scrambled to push him into the freezer. In my haste, his hand caught underneath it and I swear I heard fingers crack and the metallic clink of his ring.

Armed with enzyme solvents to liquify dried blood and hydrogen peroxide Drew had bought to clean up after he killed the detective in the same room, I then scrubbed every inch of the kitchen and even used my cutting blades to scrape contaminated grout from between the kitchen floor tiles before filling them in again.

Then the second stage of my clean-up began. I used Drew's phone to email his boss a resignation letter. It was accepted without question, which suggested Drew wasn't a great loss to the company. I drove to two locations in town, one a bus stop just outside the village and the other the train station close to Liv's studio. At each, I texted from his phone to mine a message announcing he was going away for a while 'to find himself'. If his disappearance is ever questioned, police will discover via mobile phone towers where those messages were sent from. And there won't be any proof that he didn't catch a train to somewhere, because Network Rail's CCTV footage is only kept for thirty-one days before being routinely wiped.

Finally, I packed most of his clothes into bags and left them left on the doorstep of a charity shop in town. The rest I've left in his bedroom, suggesting he might eventually return when he's ready. I won't have to do anything with our shared car, as that's in my name.

But these are likely needless precautions, because no one will come looking for Drew. He has no friends, at least none that I'm aware of, and our aunt and uncle who took us in after our parents' deaths have moved back to Pakistan. I was the only one to stay in touch with them.

I knew that he couldn't stay in my garage forever and I was putting myself at risk each day he remained. Which is why, almost three months after his death, I need to find him a final resting place.

'Well?' Drew asks me, directing me again to the manhole. 'What do you think? I can't see me being found down here.'

'Okay then, if that's what you want,' I reply. 'I'll drive us here and do it tomorrow.'

'Do what tomorrow, Anna?'

I stop in my tracks.

Because that wasn't Drew's voice. It was someone else's, and it's not coming from inside my head.

I'm not here alone.

CHAPTER 79

LIV

'Do what tomorrow, Anna?' I begin.

Anna clamps her hand against the centre of her chest as if she's just been shot by a sniper.

'Jesus, Liv!' she gasps. 'You scared me to death.'

'Sorry,' I reply. 'Who were you talking to?'

Anna hesitates before she answers. 'Nobody, just thinking aloud,' she says. 'I'm thinking about renting a workshop here. I thought I'd take a look around, see what spaces might be available. Get a better work-life balance. Like you have.'

She's being over-complimentary.

'That's a great idea,' I say. 'Start treating it like a career and not a hobby.'

'Yes,' she nods, her face relaxing into her lie. 'And what brings you out here so early?'

'You, actually.'

'Me?' she asks. Now she couldn't look any more skittish if she tried.

'I saw you leaving the house and I followed you here.'

She takes a small, but noticeable, step back.

'Why?'

'Because I never see you anymore. Every time I text you to ask if you're free, you're always busy.'

'I'm sorry, it's been a difficult time lately. I haven't told many people yet, but Drew and I have separated.'

'Oh really? I'm sorry to hear that.'

'It's for the best.' She smiles thinly. 'It's been a long time coming.'

'You should have said something.'

'I didn't want to trouble you.'

'It's no trouble when you're friends.'

'Well, you have a lot on your plate after the accident and with the business and the kids. And I know Brandon's had his hands full looking after you and building the orangery.'

'Actually, the concrete for the floor arrives in a couple of days, so we're going to Cornwall to see Brandon's parents and avoid the chaos. How's Margot, by the way? I haven't seen much of her either. I was beginning to wonder if I'd said something to offend either of you.'

'No, no, not at all,' she protests. 'You know how demanding she can be at the best of times. Especially lately, after what happened to her, as I'm sure you can imagine.'

I nod slowly. 'Yes, I'm very aware of what she's like. And she's one of the reasons why I wanted to talk to you.'

Anna swallows hard. I unlock my phone and show her a clip. Her reaction suggests this is the last thing she expected to see. But if I'm reading her correctly, she is more shocked by the fact the video exists than its content. And I'm gutted by it. She opens her mouth to say something, but the words catch in her throat.

And that tells me exactly what I'm going to do next.

Fuck her.

Fuck them both.

FEBRUARY

THREE MONTHS AFTER BONFIRE NIGHT

CHAPTER 80

MARGOT

I reread the message to check the time we're expected.

Okay girls, it's been aaaages since I last saw you, Liv's text begins. I hate it when people elongate words. *I have the house to myself on Sunday morning. Who's free for brunch? I won't take no for an answer . . . see you at eleven!*

Anna was the first to respond, me a little later. Liv was right, though. As I slip my coat on, I reckon it must be almost two months since we've all been in the same room. Liv has stopped by the house to see how I'm doing, but the kids or Nicu have always been around, so it's never just me and her. But I remember thinking that when I told her I was pregnant, she didn't give the reaction I'd expected. In fact, for a moment, her face became so hard it could have cut granite. She recovered quickly and redressed it with a smile. But I know what I saw. Perhaps I'll find out today what's troubling her.

I've been spending a lot of time with Anna lately, which, depending on your perspective, is either remarkable or plain fucking crazy. There are no hard and fast rules on how to proceed after discovering your sociopathic lover's psychopathic serial-killing sister was responsible for destroying years of your life. But if it wasn't for her, I'd be dead. At least Nicu wouldn't have needed to pay for a cremation. He could have brushed my ashes off the playing fields and straight into an urn.

And while she promises me Drew won't be troubling me again, I feel safer knowing she's around if he decides to return. I don't only have my safety to think about now, but the baby's too. I remain cautious of her, though, I'd be stupid not to. A shark is never going to tell you when it's hungry. It's one of the reasons I've asked her to be the baby's godmother. If she wants to protect her niece or nephew, she is going to have to look out for me too.

Anna was the first person outside the family I told about my pregnancy. And once she overcame her initial surprise, her enthusiasm felt genuine. Although she's fooled me before, so I'm always on the lookout for signs of deceit. She was definitely more animated than I was when I learned I was knocked up at forty-one. It's the understatement of the year to say I was shocked: horrified, if I'm being completely honest. The baby had made its presence known following routine blood tests during my post-bonfire hospital recovery. IUDs are supposed to be ninety-nine per cent effective but I was in the one per cent club. The doctor, assuming Nicu was the father, broke the news to us together. We'd immediately known that unless I'd sleep-fucked him, it wasn't his baby.

I've been pregnant twice before, both of which were swiftly terminated. The first in my early twenties, just as the band was taking off, and the other the same day we learned we had our first number one single. I haven't regretted either for a moment. I'd have made a terrible, selfish mother. But this time is different and I can't explain why. I still have very little faith in my mothering potential, but I know I want this baby. I want to protect it. If it can survive almost being burned alive in utero, maybe it can survive having me as a parent.

But I was convinced it'd be the breaking point for me and Nicu. I admitted to him the man I had an affair with was Drew, that Anna had forgiven me, and that he'd since vanished and was unlikely to return. I didn't mention he and Anna were actually brother and sister, or that he tried to roast me alive. I also told Nicu it was the biggest mistake of my life – which is saying something, considering the back catalogue of fuck-ups to choose from – and that I didn't expect him to understand or forgive me. You can only push a person so far before they up and walk away. He took a few days to process before we discussed it again.

'You helped to raise my kids, now it's my turn to do the same with yours,' he said.

'But I haven't raised your kids,' I protested, as if trying to argue myself out of having him feeling contractually obliged to return a favour. 'They've raised themselves. I've coexisted with them.'

'You could've been better, but I don't think you're aware of the positives you've had on them. They're self-sufficient because of you. They're opinionated because of you. They are headstrong and know their own minds because of you. They are determined because of you.'

'No, they're all of those things *in spite* of me,' I corrected.

'Since the fire, you've been more of a mum to them than you realise. You're already closer than you've ever been. Frankie is thirteen, and it won't be long until Tommy is a teenager too. They'll need you more than they ever have before. Let your family in. If not for our sake, then for the baby's.'

I blame fluctuating hormones for the banshee-like sobs that followed, along with my refusal to be the first to let go when he hugged me.

Almost as unexpected as my pregnancy has been the renewed interest in me from television producers. When *Help! I'm In The House From Hell!* finally aired, it became a ratings hit. The day before Christmas Eve, I signed a contract with a TV production company to start filming a ten-part fly-on-the-wall documentary series. I've been filming three to four times a week since January and the cameras will follow our family for the first few weeks after the baby's arrival. Frankie jokes we're the bargain-basement Kardashians.

I've also been making a two-part documentary for ITV about stalkers. The world still believes it was the person who sent me hate mail that tried to murder me. And I've been helping Frankie film her own documentary for BBC Three about living as a non-binary teen. My manager has also heard rumblings that *Strictly* producers are considering making Nicu and me an offer to return to the show, dancing as a couple. If I'd known all it would take to make me popular again was to hog-roast me, I'd have stuffed an apple in my mouth and jumped on the rotisserie grill years ago.

Anna's been a fusspot, worried about my high blood pressure and urging me to slow things down. But she doesn't understand how fame works. That I need to capitalise on these opportunities while they're being thrown at me. Because I know they can be taken away just as quickly.

All of this work and family time means I haven't had much time for Liv.

I reach the end of my driveway when Anna approaches me.

'Look at you,' she says, eyes fixed on my expanding waistline. 'You're blooming.'

'I'm a blooming water buffalo,' I respond. 'I should be grazing on the Serengeti. I've spent the last twenty-five years fighting to stay a size six to eight, and now if I want to squeeze into a twelve, I need to fast for a week.' I pat the bump as a smile creeps across my face. 'So you'd better be worth it, kid.'

The more time I've spent with Anna, this warts-and-all version, the more I'm learning how to read her. I sense something's on her mind.

'Everything alright?' I ask.

'Yes, fine,' she says.

I'm unconvinced. 'Anna,' I say slowly. 'What are you not telling me?'

'Nothing,' she says and looks towards Liv's door, as if it opening will unleash a new strain of Covid.

'I thought we were going to be honest with each other.'

She deliberates for a moment before speaking. 'There's something I should have told you before . . .'

But Liv's door opens before she can finish.

CHAPTER 81

ANNA

I'm anxious and I don't like it. Liv and I haven't spoken since she followed me to the building site where I was scouting for Drew's burial spot and she showed me what was on her phone. It's been a deliberate lack of communication from my end, and I assume hers too.

I've been tempted to forewarn Margot of what Liv knows, but I'm scared of stressing out her and the baby. She's already being monitored for high blood pressure and she's not helping herself with the number of work commitments she's taken on. She won't listen when I suggest she needs to cut back. She wants to capitalise on this renewed interest in her. But I fear what she's about to hear is going to make things worse. It's up to me to protect that baby.

After all the terrible things two people could have done to one another, she and I have forged an unconventional alliance. Do I think she would sell me down the river if push came to shove? I believe it would need to be a pretty hard shove for that to happen. But we are always going to be wary of each other. Keep your friends close and Margot closer. And while our relationship is more honest than what I had with Drew, I haven't confided in her about my passengers, past and present, or where my brother is now.

He's been pretty vocal lately about how much he disapproves of the understanding Margot and I have. When she and I are together, I can hear him tutting and huffing and cursing under his breath. As much as he still wants her dead, he also knows that while she's pregnant, her welfare is my priority.

'Hi, hi, come in, come in,' Liv enthuses as she opens the door. 'Look at the size of you!' she gasps, and pats Margot's stomach. I can see her try to suppress it, but it's clear how much Margot hates that.

As Liv moves to hug me, I'm sure I see something darker hiding behind those sparkling blue eyes. Or perhaps it's my own reflection.

Behind us, the sound of an engine catches my attention. I turn to see an estate agent's van parking outside my house. They're about to hammer a 'To Let' sign into the front lawn. My offer to buy a turn-key, three-bedroom, end-of-terrace cottage a few streets from here has been accepted by its redeveloper. Unlike Drew, I didn't blow my inheritance on drugs. I also have enough to put towards renting a unit I can use as a studio and take on an apprentice. For the first time in years, there's a future ahead of me that doesn't involve the deaths of others.

'Let me take your coats,' Liv says, and hangs them up by the door before leading us into the kitchen, where we take our seats around the island. In the centre are bowls of croissants, pains au chocolat, fruit and muffins. This is the first place we all sat together, I remember, just over a year ago.

'How are you both?' Liv asks, looking to us both in turn.

'Forty-one, knocked up, and still a little crispy,' says Margot. 'In other words, still living the dream. I'm just unsure whose dream it is.'

'Well you still have your sense of humour,' Liv says.

'Just not my figure,' Margot adds as she unwraps a raspberry and white chocolate muffin.

'You should book some personal-training sessions with Brandon after the baby arrives,' Liv says. 'No one leaves unsatisfied after a one-to-one with my husband.'

Neither Margot nor I are sure if Liv is referring to the last time Margot tried to have one-to-one time with Brandon. And neither of us asks.

'The three of us haven't been together for so long,' continues Liv, 'not since after my accident.'

Margot is too preoccupied by the pastries to notice Liv staring at her.

We make polite chit-chat for a while, Liv asking me about new jewellery designs and Margot discussing her packed filming schedule.

'And the police are no nearer to finding who tried to kill you?' Liv asks.

'No,' Margot says with an actress's aplomb. 'The case is still open.'

'If it was me, I'd be frightened they might come back and try and finish what they started.'

For a fleeting moment, Margot's gaze reaches mine before returning to Liv. 'No,' she says confidently, 'something tells me I'm safe.'

I have wondered if Margot suspects that my brother is dead. If she does, she hasn't asked. She only knows for certain about Ioana and the others.

'How's the studio doing?' I ask, keen to change the subject.

'Not great,' Liv admits. 'These are challenging times.'

Her honesty catches me unawares. 'Sorry to hear that. Why?'

'I was out of action for much longer than I thought I'd be, then we lost a member of staff and we haven't been able to get back to where we were.'

'Things will pick up though, won't they?' says Margot.

'They will with your help,' Liv says, beaming. 'It's why I've asked you over for brunch. You're both going to be my new investors.'

CHAPTER 82

LIV

Margot and Anna laugh as if I'm kidding. I'm not. It's a statement of intent. It's going to happen. They just don't know it yet. My smile remains fixed.

'Oh, you're being serious,' Margot says suddenly.

I nod. 'I am.'

'What do you need the money for?'

'To tide us over for the next few months. Rent, utilities, wages, the cost of living, etcetera. I also need to find two new instructors to take classes, as we're going to start opening earlier and closing later. Also we've had the Land Rover Defender now for two years and the lease agreement is coming to an end, so that needs replacing. And if I'm being honest, I have totally overspent on the orangery.'

I look behind me to the extension we've yet to complete. The glass and brick structure stretches across the back of the house, and it will look incredible once it's done. But there is no money left in the coffers to afford the new windows, plastering and wooden flooring.

'So how much do you need?' asks Anna cautiously.

'About £75,000 from both of you should be enough. Ideally within the next two months.'

'You'd like an investment from both of us to pay for your orangery and a new car?' says Margot, scarcely believing my gall.

'Yes,' I say, nodding. 'As I said, amongst other things.'

'Would you like cash or a cheque, or do you have a card reader to hand?'

I know she's joking, but she's the only one laughing.

Both have lost their appetites and place their unfinished pastries back on their plates. In perfect unison, each shifts awkwardly in her seat, then turns as if trying to read the other's mind.

Earlier, I watched them from behind the lounge window as they walked towards the house, as thick as thieves. I've never really understood the sway Margot has over Anna. I thought that once I confronted Anna about what I know about her friend, she would sever all ties with her. Instead, to my disbelief, they've been closer than ever. I've spotted them skulking to each other's houses. Sometimes they stay for hours, other times it's only for a few minutes.

I no longer think it's Stockholm syndrome that ties Anna to her. I think they have a twisted co-dependency, a circular relationship where one needs the other and the other needs to be needed. Margot feels pointless unless she's wanted by Anna. And Anna is desperate to be of use to someone. Then I came along and, for a time, their circle became a triangle. But Margot couldn't handle that. Because Margot doesn't do diluted friendships, she doesn't share. You are either a fully fledged member of Team Margot or you're not. And she knew that I wasn't. However, I underestimated just how far she would go to reinstate the status quo. Now I know what kind of people they are. They deserve each other. They just don't realise they deserve me, too.

Anna is the first to refuse my request.

'I'm really sorry Liv, but I don't have that kind of money,' she says stiffly. 'Now that Drew's not living with me, money is tight.'

'What about the new house you're buying?'

'And . . . umm . . . as I've mentioned to you before, I'm hoping to rent an industrial unit.'

'There are two spare offices available at the back of my studio. One even has a window. You'll have plenty of space in there. And how much fun will that be, working and hanging out together?'

Margot jumps in.

'It's not something I can afford either right now,' she says with the confidence her friend lacks. 'Nicu is about to go on tour and then he'll be on unpaid paternity leave for a few months.'

'Isn't he part of your reality show?' I ask. 'According to Digital Spy, you'll be earning about £140,000 for ten episodes.'

'Oh you can't believe what you read online.'

'Minus your agent's fee,' I continue, 'which I'm told is likely to be the standard industry fifteen per cent and then tax, it should leave you enough. And that's not including the BBC Three show you're making with Frankie and the stalking documentary for ITV.'

'Someone's done their homework,' Margot fires back.

'And that's not including the magazine deals when the baby arrives, or the sponsorship,' I add. 'I think you'll even have more than enough, should I need a second round of funding.'

Margot pushes her coffee cup to one side. 'We've earmarked that for a nursery and family holiday, which I'm sure you'll agree is just what the doctor ordered after my recent trauma.'

'Of course.'

'I appreciate you thinking of me,' Margot adds firmly, 'but I'm going to have to pass this time.'

'Sorry Liv,' Anna says, blushing, 'but again, I'll also have to decline. But thank you for the offer.'

'That's okay, no problem at all,' I reply breezily. 'I thought it was worth asking my two closest friends first.'

I have never seen anyone in a greater hurry to leave a room faster than these two. They're desperate to pick apart our conversation in private.

'So, what's everyone got planned for the rest of the day?' I ask. 'I'm going on my first run since the accident.'

'Are you fit enough?' Margot asks as if she cares.

'I'll find out soon enough. I've treated myself to new clothes, trainers and a replacement CamMe.'

'What's a CamMe?' Margot says.

'It's a small video camera you wear when you're doing outdoor activities, like cycling, climbing or running. Its wide lens records everything, giving you that added layer of security should anything happen. Like a hit-and-run.'

'It's a shame you weren't wearing one when you had your accident.'

'Oh I was,' I reply.

My words hang there as ice forms across the room. Margo's expression is the first to freeze.

'You were?' she asks, the pitch of her tone noticeably higher.

'Uh-huh. The force of my landing detached it, because I wasn't wearing it when I was discovered. And the police didn't find it because they weren't looking for it.'

'That's a shame,' she replies.

'Luckily I discovered it myself a few weeks later, partly submerged in the ditch water. I tried drying it out in the airing cupboard but it wouldn't work, so I ended up sending it back to the manufacturer in Japan, who got it operational again. I downloaded the images from that day and they're pin sharp and show everything and everyone involved. Honestly, I can't recommend these cameras enough, they're a great investment. Much like my studio.'

CHAPTER 83

MARGOT

Oh shit.

Shit shit shit shit shit.

The blood slowly drains from my face as I realise Liv knows it was me who hit her with my car. That I went to check on her, then walked away without calling for help when I thought she was dead. She has me over a barrel and she knows it. She doesn't want an apology, because she knows my words would be hollow. No, she wants something of worth. Money. Financial retribution.

My brain is like a box of fireworks being lit simultaneously. My thoughts have been ambushed and are firing in every direction and I can't focus on any of them for more than a couple of seconds at a time.

I don't know how to find my way out of this. The only thing I do know is that I want to be sick. I realise my hand is circling my stomach as if protecting my unborn child from a threat I didn't know existed until this very moment.

In desperation, I turn to Anna. But she doesn't look at me. Liv's gaze is fixed on Anna, as if she is expecting more. What else could she know?

CHAPTER 84

LIV

Margot is as white as the ghost of the past that's come calling. She doesn't ask what my camera recorded or what I've seen, because she doesn't need to. She knows. She was there.

Anna is already aware of the clip because I showed it to her the morning I followed her to the industrial estate. I remain convinced she was more surprised by the footage itself than she was of Margot's culpability. She knew.

It was a few weeks after the accident when a strong scent jogged my memory. I caught a whiff of Margot's perfume when she visited me in hospital and again a week or so later, when she picked up the twins to take them to nursery.

'Coco Mademoiselle,' she told me once when I complimented her on it. 'Kind of my signature scent. Expensive, but gorgeous.'

A part of my subconscious brain was linking that smell to the muddied ditch I was left to die in. I assumed it was playing tricks on me until I researched it online.

'Minimally conscious people can react to stimulus such as touch, light or smells,' a psychology website told me. 'Later when they awaken, they are sometimes able to recall little else but that scent.'

My next recollection was much more sudden and stronger but equally as vague. Something about a camera. I had the feeling I might have been wearing one when I was hit. I asked Brandon but he said no, I hadn't, even though he'd been nagging me for ages to buy one. Yet still I wondered. Eventually I checked my Amazon account and there it was in the purchased items folder. A CamMe, delivered a day before my accident. The police hadn't searched the ditch for it because they hadn't known I was wearing one.

So where was it? Unless the culprit had taken it with them after they hit me, it was likely somewhere close to where I was found.

On crutches, it took me an age to reach that part of the road leading out of the village. And after a thirty-minute search, I found it, partially submerged, a good ten metres from where I landed. As I told Margot, I couldn't get it to work so sent it back to the manufacturers. And weeks later, when it was returned, I plugged it into the mains and held my breath as it automatically uploaded all the recorded data to the cloud.

Then I pressed play.

If Margot was to ask this morning what the clip contained, I'd tell her it was footage of her walking from the road to the verge, stopping and standing over my unconscious body with her hands clasped over her mouth. The camera might have landed upside down and at an angle, but a quick editing-software toggle and the re-angled footage was presented in all its crystalline 4HD clarity.

I'd remind her how she searched my wrists for a pulse, my chest for a beating heart, and my mouth for breath. And when she assumed I was as lifeless as I looked, she scurried away like the rat she is.

I don't deny that I cried when I watched it that first time. Had Brandon not tracked me down with the Find My iPhone app, he'd now be raising our children alone.

I thank God for that camera, because without it, I wouldn't know who my friends really are.

I could have told Brandon what I discovered and given my evidence to the police. But I know from experience with my former banking boss Harrison that, sometimes, it's best not to show all your cards at once. Keep some close to your chest in case you need to play them later. In Margot's case, later is today.

But I'm saving the best for last. And Anna doesn't have a clue.

CHAPTER 85

ANNA

Drew's voice is as sudden as it is direct.

'Get out of there,' he warns. 'Remove yourself and Margot from the situation and don't say anything you might regret. Give yourselves time to think it through and come up with an appropriate response.'

It's unusually sage advice from my headstrong brother. Death has granted him some clarity, now that it's of little use to him.

'But Liv said she wants us both to invest,' I remind him. 'So what does she have on me?'

He doesn't answer because he can't. If I don't know, then neither does he. But he's right when he says I need to take charge, because Margot is as good as useless right now.

'It's been great to catch up, Liv,' I say, 'but Margot and I should probably get going. She promised to help me sort through a new delivery of gemstones.'

'Of course,' Liv says. 'It's great that we're all so busy, isn't it?'

She pushes back her chair and rises to her feet. Margot and I do the same.

'Oh, while I remember,' Liv says to me, 'I have something I keep meaning to return.'

She opens a kitchen drawer and pulls out an object wrapped in tissue paper. She keeps it hidden in the palm of her hand before she presses it into mine. I unwrap it and immediately recognise it. And more importantly, I know what it means.

'My wedding ring,' exhales Drew.

It's the one I made myself and that he wore when we pretended to be a married couple. I can't tear my eyes away from it. I can just make out brown speckles on its surface. Dried blood, I assume. The last time I saw it was when I accidentally tore open the bag his body was wrapped in as I hoisted him up into the chest freezer. His fingers caught under the base and I heard a metallic clink, but I assumed it must be the ring hitting the freezer door. I didn't realise it could have slipped off, otherwise I would have looked for it there and then.

'She could only have found it if she'd been inside our garage,' Drew continues. 'A random ring won't mean anything, unless she found something else in there. Me.'

I look to Margot, but she is unaware of its significance.

'I know that, sadly, you and Drew have gone your separate ways,' begins Liv, 'but I thought you might want to give it back if you see him again.'

'She said *if*,' Drew repeats. 'Not when. *If*.'

It's all the assurance I need that she knows Drew is dead.

Liv doesn't offer any explanation as to how it came into her possession, and I don't need to ask. Instead, she leads the way to the front door.

'Let me know if you change your minds about investing in the studio.' She smiles. 'Probably best not to take too long to make a decision. I'd hate to have to involve a third party.'

And with that, Liv closes the door on me, Margot, and both of our plans for the future.

CHAPTER 86

LIV

I stand with my back against the front door, my hand pressed against my breastbone as my heart tries to jackhammer its way out of my chest. I've won a war the enemy had no idea it was fighting. And in doing so, I've protected my business and my family. Margot and Anna might have turned down my offer for now, but they'll come crawling back in a day or two to tell me they've crunched a few numbers and decided investing in my studio is, like I said, a wonderful opportunity. And the most reassuring part of this is that if ever I run into financial difficulties again, I'll have two people who will always come to my aid.

Because they have too much to lose if they don't.

I had no qualms at all about blackmailing Margot because it's her fault my studio is failing. She's learning the hard way that you don't try and seduce my husband, hit me with a car and leave me for dead without there being consequences.

Of course I knew about her clumsy approach towards Brandon. He tells me everything. And it really didn't bother me. Besides, I guessed it was about to happen. On the night of my birthday party, I was in the garden when I saw them together in the dining room, away from everyone else. She had one arm under her tits, pushing them up and out. Brandon could've rested his beer bottle on them. Whatever he'd said amused her because she threw her head back and laughed.

I know my husband is a flirt because I've watched him charm countless women – and men – into signing up to his personal training. But Brandon knows if he ever goes beyond appropriate, he'd be out of the door before he could put his dick back in his pants. I remember wishing Margot luck, because no matter what she might've convinced herself was going to happen, Brandon would always be in my bed, not hers. I didn't see the kiss; he told me after our guests had gone home. And then I screwed him long and hard, a reminder to him that he'll never find better than me.

Blackmailing Anna pricked at my conscience because I'd genuinely liked her. I'd felt protective over her and I thought she'd liked me too. So I decided to give her the benefit of the doubt, convincing myself that I'd misread her reaction to the CamMe footage of Margot standing over my unconscious body midway through her hit-and-run. I went to her house unannounced, but she didn't answer the door. I was about to leave when I spotted the electric garage door was only half unrolled. I attempted to pull it down for her but it wouldn't budge. I ducked under it to go inside because if it was like ours, there would be an override button attached to the wall. I located it near to the floor, and there, half a silver ring poked out from under an empty refuse bag. I picked it up, thinking it resembled the band Anna wore. There were flecked brown marks on it like mud, that wouldn't brush off. I slipped it into my pocket to give to her when I eventually saw her again.

An intermittent beeping caught my attention. I turned my head to the corner of the garage and spotted a huge chest freezer, its bubble wrap packaging still in a pile next to it. I gave it the once-over, and fearing her food might be defrosting, I pushed the lid down more firmly. But the beeping continued. It was the same with my second attempt. Finally I lifted the lid to slam it down.

Inside, it contained only one object. The shape of a human body wrapped in plastic bags.

I let go of the lid as I staggered backwards, losing my balance and falling over a weights bench. I froze, unable to make sense of what I'd seen. Eventually, I mustered up the strength to rise to my feet and look inside again. Poking out from a torn section was an exposed hand with the image of a lion tattooed on the back of it. Drew had the exact same design on his hand. Together with the ring on the floor, I had no doubt as to who this was.

I pulled my phone out to call the police, but after pressing the second nine, something stopped me. My finger hovered above the key as I tried to come up with a reason why someone as considered as Anna would be keeping her dead husband's body in a freezer. She must have killed him. Why? Had I missed the signs she was in an abusive relationship? Or was she the abuser? Or had it been a terrible accident and she'd panicked? Whichever way you looked at it, the right thing for me to do was to call for help.

Yet I didn't.

Instead, I put myself first.

Because I also knew that the right thing to do was to benefit my ailing business and family. So I drew in the deepest of breaths and set about taking photographs of what I had found before leaving as quietly as I'd arrived and telling Brandon nothing on my arrival home.

This morning, Margot, Anna and I have finally met one another for the first time. The killer, the attempted murderer and the blackmailer. We all know where we stand.

My heart is no longer hammering.

I pass the mirror in the hallway and stop, just to check that I still recognise myself. I didn't want to be this person again. I thought that by moving out of London I could be different. I could be my own person, not one reliant on others. But I gave it my best shot and it didn't work. You might want to change, but life and the behaviour of others can so often conspire to stand in your way and fuck around with you until you have no choice but to revert to type. So now, I understand that I am who I ought to be. Who I was and who I am.

And finally, I'm good with that.

CHAPTER 87

MARGOT

I hold on to Anna's arm for dear life as we make our way across the cul-de-sac and back to my house. I fear that if I let go of her, I'll fall down an invisible black hole. My deep breaths are supposed to be calming but they're not working. They're just leaving me more rattled.

'It's like we're in one of those TikTok "Tell Me Without Telling Me" challenges Tommy keeps making me watch,' I tell her. '*Tell me how you're going to blackmail me without telling me.* I'm fucked, aren't I?'

'It would appear that's what Liv wants us to believe,' Anna replies. She's much calmer than me.

'I don't understand what she has over you? What's the significance of Drew's wedding ring?'

'I assume she found it on the floor in my garage.'

'What was it doing there? And why does she have it?'

Anna waits for me to read between the lines. And then my stomach twists when I realise what she's not saying.

'He's . . . ?'

'Yes.'

'Oh.'

It's like the weight of a double-decker bus has been lifted from my shoulders. I know how the death of my unborn child's biological father should make me feel, but I also know how it is making me feel. However, I don't have time to process this now.

'So I was wrong,' I continue. 'It's not just me who's fucked, it's you too.'

'It's not an ideal situation to be in, no.'

We enter my house and I slam the door behind me. Shock mutates into rage.

'Everything I earn from here on in is going to be spent on yoga mats, freshly laundered towels and fucking pan pipe Spotify playlists,' I rant. 'What about you and the house or the workshop? Or the apprentice?'

'I can't do both and pay her what she wants.'

I pick up the nearest thing to me – a crystal-cut vase of flowers – and hurl it at the wall. It shatters on impact, spraying glass like confetti. Anna doesn't react.

'Why aren't you as angry as me at what she's doing to us?' I yell.

'Please don't let this stress you out,' Anna says with a frown. 'Remember your blood pressure.'

'If it shoots off the scale it's because of her,' I reply, jabbing my index finger in the direction of the enemy's bunker. 'For the first time in years I'm finally getting my career and marriage back on track, now she's threatening to take it all away from me. I've already had one person trying to destroy me, I don't need another.'

Anna looks away.

'I'm sorry,' I add. 'I didn't mean that.'

But I kind of did. Anna fills the kettle but I move towards the wine rack and reach for a bottle of Sauvignon Blanc instead. She looks at my swollen stomach and is about to protest, but I beat her to the punch.

'It's medicinal,' I say.

'You shouldn't drink alone,' she replies, and I pour her an equally generous glass.

We make our way into the lounge, where I sink into the sofa. I want to enjoy my drink, but I don't. Either guilt or Liv has given the wine a bitter aftertaste.

'How easy is it for you?' I ask.

'How easy is what?'

It's my turn to expect her to read between the lines.

'Oh, you mean *that*,' she replies and I nod. She considers my question before answering. 'It's only easy when they get what they deserve.'

'And, figuratively speaking, might Liv be someone who deserves it?'

I hold my breath as Anna smiles and takes a long drink from her glass.

'No,' she says and my chest deflates. 'She deserves something altogether different.'

AUGUST

EIGHT MONTHS AFTER BONFIRE NIGHT

CHAPTER 88

ANNA

This modem's connection is painfully slow. We've both forgotten how long it took us to get online before the advent of cable and Wi-Fi. And we'd rather be in the air-conditioned place we now call home than here in this stiflingly hot internet café. But I won't risk going online at the house. You can never be sure who is monitoring you.

I sense Margot looking over my shoulder as a BBC News page loads on the screen. A trial date has been set for Drew's murder, and it's eight months from now. The accused remain on remand in prisons in Derbyshire and Surrey.

'I must admit, I didn't think it would get this far,' Margot begins. 'I assumed the Crown Prosecution Service would've thrown the case out by now.'

'There's still a lot of evidence mounted against them,' I reply.

'There's also a lot of assumptions and holes.'

'That's for the jury to decide.'

'It won't get that far. Trust me, neither of them will make it to trial. Especially now your name has been brought into the equation.'

I don't respond. Instead, we scan the photographs illustrating the story. Every time a news outlet runs an update, they choose an image to suit their house style. And they're spoiled for choice, as there are a lot of them floating about the internet.

Because Liv and Brandon are a very photogenic couple.

BBC News has lifted a flattering shot of husband and wife from the opening night party of Liv's now defunct yoga studio. But *The Sun* and *Daily Star* are using images I took from Margot's phone, clips of Liv and Brandon's OnlyFans dominatrix videos. The day after Drew's body was discovered, I leaked the story, Liv and Brandon's names and the pictures to an old contact on the news desk. 'Cops question kinky couple' was the headline. Once they were charged with his murder, reporting restrictions came into force. But as social media cares little for legalities, it didn't stop the full-length videos from circulating wildly.

I take a moment to stretch my arms and rub my sore eyes. It's not even 11 a.m. and the thermometer on the café wall says it's already thirty-five degrees.

'A Pakistani summer is like no other,' my aunt warned me over breakfast when I mentioned I was going out. It's hard to disagree.

Closing the page, I pat my forehead with a tissue I keep under the sleeve of my kameez, the long tunic I wear paired with my loose-fitting shalwar trousers. I gaze upward at the ceiling fan and the gentle rotation of its blades. They offer about as much relief as a butterfly's wings. I slip several rupees into a vending machine and a bottle of Coke appears in a hatch. I'm about to ask Margot if she wants one but stop myself. I run the ice-cold glass bottle across my face and along the top of my chest before twisting open the top to drink.

I check my phone but neither my uncle nor my aunt have messaged me, so I assume all must be well. Margot is more anxious to return to their place than I am.

'Can we go now?' she asks.

'Not yet,' I say and she tuts.

Returning to the computer, I pay a website $20 from an anonymous balance transfer card to load an image of the cul-de-sac she and I once called home. The dragging modem means it takes an eternity, but I wait patiently until an overhead view of Liv's garden appears. It was taken twenty-four hours ago and it's surprisingly detailed. Rubble sits in a pile outside what's left of her orangery, the remains of police-excavated concrete flooring that once concealed my brother's body.

I buried him there days after Liv first showed me the video footage of Margot looming over her injured body the day of the hit-and-run. It wasn't easy, either physically or mentally. I waited until the family had travelled to Cornwall to visit Brandon's parents before I dug up a section of their orangery floor that had yet to be concreted. Then, as evening fell, I tipped a wheelie bin on its side and, using the strength of two people, pushed my brother's body inside – still wrapped in its tarpaulin – and dragged it through a side gate and into their garden without being seen. I tipped him out and buried him a metre below the surface. I must have been running on pure, double adrenaline because by the time I finished, every muscle in my exhausted body was shredded. Before I left, I made sure there was not a surface stone out of place to rouse the builders' suspicions. Two days later, and with my tendons and tissue still burning and aching, I had a ringside seat from Drew's old bedroom as I watched the mixer pour hundreds of cubic metres of liquid concrete on to the space above him.

It was a risky, yet ultimately fortuitous plan. Because just a few weeks later, Liv believed she was giving Margot and me no choice but to invest in her cash-strapped business to keep ourselves out of trouble. Margot hinted that I could make this problem go away. And I did, just not in the way she was suggesting.

Of course, framing Liv and Brandon for Drew's murder wasn't as simple as leaving his body under their flooring. First, Margot and I approached Liv separately, explaining how it would take time to get the money together that she wanted. Margot blamed a late payment for her television work and I said my delays were down to inheritance investment penalties. Liv proposed a six-week time-frame. And she always spoke around her blackmail as if she feared we were recording her.

'Did you know you can schedule an email to be sent at a certain time and on a certain date?' she mentioned. 'So, hypothetically speaking, if, out of the blue, something happened to me, that email could still arrive in the inbox of somebody important. You can even attach photos and videos. Useful, isn't it?'

I also guessed the reason she insisted we pay her through bank transfers was to establish a paper trail of transactions between us. Should anything happen 'out of the blue', investigators might ask why we'd given her two large sums of money.

But Liv isn't as smart as she thinks. I made an excuse to visit her studio and the space she'd suggested I could use as a workshop. It was wholly unsuitable and she knew it. It would be a power play to have me under her supervision. A constant reminder of her dominance.

I waited for her to teach a yoga class before I placed Drew's bloodied wedding ring and the secret SIM card Margot had used to message him inside an empty changing room locker. I read through every message first to ensure Drew had never used Margot's name, then slipped the key inside Liv's desk drawer. I accessed her laptop and erased the CamMe footage of Margot from Liv's cloud and remotely wiped the device wherever she'd hidden it. I located the incriminating email she'd set up to go to Brandon, the police and the *Guardian* news desk, and deleted all of its contents, leaving it blank. I also located photos she'd taken of Drew's body in the chest freezer in my garage. I deleted them, too, and the following day, cleaned the freezer thoroughly and paid cash for a man with a van to take it away and dump it.

In the meantime, Margot waited until Brandon had left his car unlocked one night to stash in the boot the pipe wrench I'd used to kill my brother. It still contained traces of his blood and hair.

Finally, Margot and I were ready.

An anonymous tip-off to the police suggested a body had been buried somewhere at Liv and Brandon's address. A name was also given, Drew Mason, who I'd registered as missing weeks earlier. Metre by metre, police searched the garden with ground-penetrating radar but found nothing. It was only when one of them spotted new concrete flooring in the incomplete orangery that they switched their search area. Their equipment detected a discrepancy in a void below the ground. Drew's remains were recovered later that night.

Once he was formally identified, I played the shocked, grieving sister. I admitted in my police statement that I'd suspected Drew had been having an affair with Liv, but I hadn't confronted either of them directly. I mentioned the flat he rented above a Turkish restaurant, where Margot and I had purposely left in the wardrobe the clothes she'd won in Liv's eBay auctions.

Once the pipe wrench in Brandon's boot was confirmed as carrying my brother's DNA, he was arrested. Liv's arrest followed a day later when Drew's phone, SIM card and bloodied ring were discovered inside a studio locker. They were both charged with his murder.

According to my police-appointed family liaison officer, detectives believed that after Liv ended her affair with Drew, he bombarded her with messages professing his love, as discovered on the SIM card, which was actually Margot's. But 'Liv' was adamant it was over. The officer went on to explain how they suspected Brandon had discovered the affair, and during a heated confrontation with Drew, he killed my brother. Together, he and Liv tried to cover it up.

Of course, Liv retaliated with her own accusations, claiming Margot and I were setting her up. She alleged Margot tried to run her over, but she had no proof, as I'd erased her evidence. Likewise when she said she had photographs of Drew's body stored inside my chest freezer. No freezer or images were ever discovered.

Many questions remain unanswered, of course. Why had she and Drew never been seen together, not even by the staff who worked in the restaurant below his flat? Why was there no trace of Liv's DNA in his room except on the wardrobe clothes? Plus Liv had alibis for some of the dates she and Drew were supposed to have met. And where were Margot and I?

Because one day, we simply vanished.

Perhaps Margot is right and the case won't even make it to trial. Even if it doesn't, we have done what we set out to do. Ruin somebody who was trying to ruin us.

I know what Margot's about to ask before she says it. 'Have you ever felt guilty for what we did to them?' she begins. 'Brandon didn't do anything wrong. Neither did their kids.'

'I'm surprised you're standing up for him,' I tell her. 'Remember how he led you on and made a fool of you? He's not entirely innocent, is he? In any event, yes, Brandon and the kids are collateral damage. But the kids are safe and living with their grandparents. And as for Liv, it was her or us. We chose us.'

'We did,' Margot says. 'But then *you* chose *you*.'

'You didn't leave us much of a choice.'

'There's that "us" again. This time I assume you're referring to you and Drew?'

'Yes.'

'But what did I do to you that was so awful?'

'We've been through this before, Margot.' I sigh.

'Then tell me again.'

'Before my niece was born, I really believed you'd changed. That you were no longer that self-centred woman I'd spent so much of my life trying to ruin. But from the moment Ellie arrived, you were taking her on TV shows and exploiting her in magazines, all because the fame you already had wasn't enough. You treated her more like an accessory to further your career than a baby. How many times did you ignore Nicu and me when we told you that you were going too far?'

I feel Margot's hackles rise.

'And that's it?' she says.

'You asked me to be her godmother, Margot. And part of that duty is to show her how to make good choices in life and stand against injustices that can cause suffering. Well, she was suffering because the person closest to her kept making terrible decisions about her welfare.'

She laughs long and hard and without any trace of humour.

'You are unbelievable,' she says. 'Is that how you justify murdering me?'

EPILOGUE

MARGOT, THE LAST

Silence descends upon us. And when you don't say anything, it triggers me.

'Don't ignore me when I'm asking you a question,' I snap. 'You really believe that was enough of a reason to kill me and steal my daughter?'

You don't reply because you can't. You know there is no justification for what you did to me.

I still feel sick when I think about the moment I was murdered. Ellie was exactly seven weeks old when I returned with her to an empty home after recording a TV show in London. I was putting her down for a nap in the nursery while you were downstairs letting yourself in with a key I'd forgotten you still had. I had only just become aware of not being alone when a figure suddenly emerged behind me and wrapped a plastic bag tightly over my head. I turned, and through a transparent section, I saw your face. But it wasn't a version of you I recognised. There was a manic expression behind your wide eyes, your nostrils were flared and spit bubbles flew from your mouth. I fought back, God knows; I have never fought for anything as hard in my life.

But I couldn't overpower you. When you finally let go, I slumped to a heap on the floor, drained of life.

Briefly, I felt the presence of another – Drew, I assume – and then it was just you and me.

Now I understand why it felt like you had the strength of two people, because a second person is always living inside you. At least that's what you want to believe. I've tried to convince you otherwise, that you've imagined us all, that you are imagining me right now. You are always trying to deflect the blame from yourself on to others. But you refuse to accept that. So I remain your most recent reluctant passenger.

You acted so swiftly after my death that it had to have been well planned in advance. Quite impressive: tick tick tick, going through your checklist. First, you found Ellie's passport in the unlocked filing cabinet in our office. Then you parked my car in the garage, laid my body in the boot, strapped Ellie into the car seat and drove off. After my spirit's previous container was unceremoniously dumped in a storm drain in the building site behind our houses and my car left in a supermarket car park, you picked up your own vehicle, which you'd left there with your luggage inside, and drove to a long-stay car park outside Heathrow. As you'd expected, the check-in desk staff didn't query why a harassed new mum carrying a stressed, screaming infant had a different surname to her child. By midnight, you and my daughter were on a prebooked flight to Pakistan while the police were searching for Ellie and me.

The orchestration continued, not missing a beat. The aunt and uncle who adopted you and Drew after your parents' deaths had returned to Pakistan years earlier and were expecting your arrival. The taxi they sent to pick up you up from Allama Iqbal International Airport drove you to their sizeable home in the Punjab province. They remembered your teenage accusations against me and how no one had believed you. Now, accompanied by my baby – who you told them was your brother's daughter – they were all ears. You recounted how, even though two others had been charged with Drew's unlawful killing, I was actually the guilty party. Confident in the depth of their gullibility, you laid it on with a trowel: I'd manipulated and seduced a vulnerable man with a history of depression and addiction, and after becoming pregnant, had denied him any potential access to his child after my due date. Then, during a final, fraught confrontation, I'd murdered him and planted evidence to frame our mutual friends.

I listened in disbelief as you admitted to your family how you couldn't bear to see Ellie with me, so for her own protection, you had killed me and kidnapped your niece. Despite their understandable shock – and plenty of unspoken doubts, I assume – they believed that whatever had happened, you had Ellie's best interests at heart. The two of you were the only family they had. And they would do anything to protect you.

I'm only aware of everything else that's happened back home through your research trips to this internet café. Soon after charges were brought against Liv and Brandon, I suddenly went missing with my young daughter. I was dead by then of course, but only you knew that. You told newspapers anonymously that I was being treated for post-natal depression, and Nicu made several desperate public appeals for me to come home. And then, nine days later, my body was discovered around the same time my car was located in the supermarket car park.

I recall how it was our thirteenth day in Pakistan when British police found CCTV of you swapping my car for your own and carrying Ellie. ANPR cameras mapped your route to the airport, and security cameras caught you entering Heathrow and leaving Allama Iqbal. Newspapers have been fascinated by the case, reporting how police have since confirmed you're wanted for questioning in connection with both my and Drew's deaths. And that's why I told you I believe neither Liv nor Brandon will make it to trial, not while you are also a suspect.

According to another report, they've sold everything to hire a top-ranking defence team who will pin everything on you. But I know you *don't care if that happens or not. Because even if you are tracked down by British police, there's no extradition treaty between the UK and Pakistan. So it isn't a given you'll be forced to return home. And in a population of more than 230 million, your family can easily move you to one of the many other homes their business owns. Since our arrival here, they've relocated you four times to different places as a precautionary measure. They also have properties in Saudi Arabia and I know you're considering a move there one day so 'your daughter' can make the most of its highly rated multinational schools.*

Your daughter. Urgh. It sickens me that you think of Ellie as that.

She isn't yours and never will be. She is mine. Only I can't be with her, I can never touch her, comfort her, talk to her, and she can never feel my love. I can only see her through you. I detest that she'll never know who I am, that she'll never have the life I dreamed for her. That she will only ever have you.

'Killing you was in Ellie's best interests,' you say aloud, suddenly but quietly. 'Everyone knew what a terrible mother you were. I did what anyone in their right mind would do.'

'You actually think you're in your right mind?' I laugh. 'You are absolutely crazy, woman! It was your dead brother who convinced you that I wasn't a good mum, whispering in your ear all the time, demeaning me and manipulating you. Not because he believed it, but because he wanted a way out of your head. And the only way he could do that was to talk you into killing someone else. I was an easy target. You're pathetic.'

'Enough!' you say, this time loud enough for other café customers to turn their heads. Aware of the attention, your cheeks flush. But I'm not one to be silenced.

'Just give her back,' I shout. 'Return her to Nicu, Frankie and Tommy where she belongs and allow her to live a normal life.'

'Or what?' you whisper.

'Or I fight fire with fire. I'll intrude into your every thought, day and night, when you're awake and when you're asleep, until I slowly drive you more insane than you already are. You won't know whether you want a shit or a shower. You think what Ioana put you through was bad? By the time I finish with you, you'll be holding that Stanley knife to your neck, begging me to make you slit your fucking throat.'

You take a swig from your Coke bottle.

'I'd strongly advise against it,' you tell me.

'Why? What do I have to lose?'

'My daughter,' you say, matter-of-factly. 'Anything you do to me, you'll be doing to Ellie. Hurt me and you'll hurt her. Torment me and you'll torment her. If I suffer, so does she. She will feel every bit of my pain. I'll make sure of it. And what will that be like, watching it happening but not being able to do anything to stop it? It will be agonising. Never forget, Margot, I am all she has now.'

My hope deflates like a burst tyre because I know you're right. While I'm inside you, Ellie has two people protecting her, not just one. Kill you and I not only kill myself, I kill her too.

A message from your aunt flashes on the phone screen. Ellie is waking up. She needs feeding and you won't let anyone do that but you. You sign out from the computer, and we make our way back to the car.

Once we're back on the road, I reflect on when our paths first crossed, when the burglary at your family home went so wrong so quickly and I found you hiding under that bed.

And how I instinctively knew that if I wanted to save my own skin, I had to set fire to that bedroom to remove all the evidence, living or dead. Warren had spotted you too. Instinctively, and without asking, he suspected what I was about to do. He tried to stop me, but I was too quick for him. I pushed him to one side and threw the cigarette lighter to the floor. The lighter fluid ignited immediately and quickly spread across the carpet and bed above you. There was nothing Warren could do to save you. Although he wanted to.

But I didn't.

You know this for certain because that's what you saw with your own eyes. You edged your way towards us under that bed and your eyes witnessed my hand tossing the lighter. Years later, when you and I laid all our cards on the table, I thought you'd accepted my explanation that Warren was the guilty party, that he'd wanted you dead, not me. It turns out we were each holding back a card. Only now I'm inside you am I aware you know the truth.

'My mum used to believe in cause and effect,' you say as the car starts. 'That all action in the universe creates a reaction that will return to you. That's why you are where you are now.'

If I'd known that back then, I wouldn't have set fire to you. I'd have snatched Warren's gun from his hand and shot you straight between the fucking eyes.

I'd have made certain that I killed you first.

ACKNOWLEDGEMENTS

I don't think I have ever had more fun writing a book than I did with *You Killed Me First*. After the intensity of my last psychological thriller, *The Stranger in Her House*, I wanted to write something shrouded in my typical darkness but with a sliver of light here and there. And that light came in the form of Margot, one of the favourite characters my tiny little brain has mustered up since Christopher in *The One*. She enabled me to unleash my hidden bitch (some may argue it's not actually *that* hidden) and have fun with a character and the situations she finds herself in. I hope you enjoyed her, Liv and Anna too.

First and foremost, I'd like to thank the two most important people in my life. Myself and my accountant. Secondly, my eternal gratitude goes to my husband, John Russell, for his infinite patience and for allowing himself to be used as a sounding board at all times of day and night. Thank you also for adding a little reality to my mad ideas. Thanks to our son Elliot, who thinks Daddy spends his days wandering into random Waterstones bookshops and signing anyone's novels. He's not entirely wrong.

Thanks to the many online book clubs I am a member of. I'm contractually obligated to mention THE Book Club on Facebook and its OG (not OGRE, although both are fitting) Tracy Fenton. Ten years and we're still like Hinge & Bracket. Thank you to

Facebook's Psychological Thriller Readers group and its army of members and mods, all of whom are at risk of regularly passing out from breaths they're constantly being asked to hold. I love every Chapter 39-ing one of you. But please, no more tattoos! Thanks also to Lost In A Good Book, The Fiction Café and BOOK MARK!

I have a loyal group of trusted beta readers I'd like to offer my gratitude to. In no particular order, Freida McFadden (yes, THAT one), Louise Beech (unfortunately, THAT one), Rhian Molloy, Maddy Cordell, Carole Watson, Mary Wallace, Denise Stevenson, Mark Fearn, Kath Middleton, Emma Louise Bunting, Wendy Clarke, Laura Pontin, Fran Stentiford, Ruth Davy, Michelle Gocman, Janice Leibowitz, Elaine Binder and Deborah Dorbin. Apologies to anyone I haven't included. I either secretly hate you or I've forgotten you. Perhaps both.

There are so many people that are involved in the making of a book, from my editors to the cover designers. Thank you to Amazon Publishing and my label Thomas & Mercer, my awesome editor Victoria Haslam for her constant enthusiasm and support, plus David Downing for making me a better writer. Thanks to Sadie Mayne, Rebecca Hills, Liron Gilenberg and Gemma Wain.

Also, thanks to actress and narrator Elizabeth Knowelden, who has been voicing my characters since my very first book, *When You Disappeared*. I adore this woman's voice and how much heart and soul she puts into recording an audiobook.

There are literally too many BookTokers, Bookstagrammers, Goodreads folk, bloggers and vloggers to thank individually – their names could fill a separate book. I'm not going to risk leaving someone out and incurring your wrath, so please accept this cop-out of a virtual collective group hug I'm throwing at you all.

Finally, my gratitude goes to you, the readers, for allowing me to keeping riding this crazy train I've now spent a decade on.

Without you, I'd probably be unemployed. Or worse, working as a showbiz journalist again.

This book is dedicated to every one of you who doesn't fit into a conventional, societal norm, like my character Frankie. I hope you can find the strength to be happy, remain strong and keep fighting to live your authentic lives. And to those who try and hold you back or put you down? Chapter 39 every single one of them.

ABOUT THE AUTHOR

Photo © 2017 Robert Gershinson

John Marrs is an author and former journalist based in Northamptonshire, England. After spending his career interviewing celebrities from the worlds of television, film and music for numerous national newspapers and magazines, he is now a full-time author. This is his thirteenth book. Follow him at www.johnmarrsauthor.com, on X @johnmarrs1, on Instagram @johnmarrs.author and on Facebook at www.facebook.com/johnmarrsauthor.

Follow the Author on Amazon

If you enjoyed this book, follow John Marrs on Amazon to be notified when the author releases a new book!

To do this, please follow these instructions:

Desktop:

1) Search for the author's name on Amazon or in the Amazon App.
2) Click on the author's name to arrive on their Amazon page.
3) Click the 'Follow' button.

Mobile and Tablet:

1) Search for the author's name on Amazon or in the Amazon App.
2) Click on one of the author's books.
3) Click on the author's name to arrive on their Amazon page.
4) Click the 'Follow' button.

Kindle eReader and Kindle App:

If you enjoyed this book on a Kindle eReader or in the Kindle App, you will find the author 'Follow' button after the last page.